# Undercurrents

## Books by Mary Anna Evans

The Faye Longchamp Mysteries
*Artifacts*
*Relics*
*Effigies*
*Findings*
*Floodgates*
*Strangers*
*Plunder*
*Rituals*
*Isolation*
*Burials*
*Undercurrents*

Other Books
*Mathematical Literacy in the Middle and High School Grades: A Modern Approach to Sparking Interest*

*Wounded Earth*

*Jewel Box: Short Works by Mary Anna Evans*

*Your Novel, Day by Day: A Fiction Writer's Companion*

# Undercurrents

A Faye Longchamp Mystery

Mary Anna Evans

Poisoned Pen Press

Copyright © 2018 by Mary Anna Evans

First Edition 2018

10 9 8 7 6 5 4 3 2 1

Library of Congress Control Number: 2017951351

ISBN: 9781464209307    Hardcover
ISBN: 9781464209321    Trade Paperback
ISBN: 9781464209338    Ebook

Poisoned Pen Press
4014 N. Goldwater Blvd., #201
Scottsdale, AZ 85251
www.poisonedpenpress.com
info@poisonedpenpress.com

Printed in the United States of America

*For the children of Memphis and
for children everywhere*

# Acknowledgments

I'd like to thank all the people who helped make *Undercurrents* happen. Tony Ain, Michael Garmon, Rachel Broughten, Amanda Evans, and Robert Connolly read it in manuscript and their comments were incredibly helpful.

The highlight of writing this book was, without question, my research trip. I have enjoyed time in Memphis over the years, especially when I was an Ole Miss student. When I lived in western Kentucky, I was near enough to make impromptu weekend visits, and I did. I enjoyed a memorable week there more recently with my friends Robert and Emma Connolly, teaching creative writing to high school students in the daytime and exploring the revitalized downtown with them at night. In recent years, though, there have long gaps between my visits to the lovely city sitting on its Mississippi River bluffs. As I prepared to write *Undercurrents*, I knew I needed to invest some time if I hoped to give Memphis its due.

Because enjoying blues and jazz screams out for good company, I invited two of my oldest friends, Carla Smith Wynja and Debi Porter Saraswati Lewis, to meet me there. Trust me when I say that we threw ourselves into our task.

We ate barbecue at The Rendezvous, where Debi learned that there are, in fact, vegetarian options on that most carnivorous of menus. We dined at The Peabody, where we met Duckmaster Jimmy Ogle, who is also Shelby County's official historian, among many other things that you can read about at www.jimmyogle.com. Duckmaster Ogle gave us a private tour of the Peabody, regaling us with tales of its storied history. (Did you know that Elvis received his first major record label signing bonus at The Peabody? I've seen the receipt and it's on Peabody stationery. I've also seen the Peabody ducks' condominium.) We toured The C.H. Nash Museum at Chucalissa and learned from its gracious staff. We explored the area around the museum and the adjacent T.O. Fuller State Park, getting a feel for the real neighborhoods that are situated near where I imagine Kali's to be. As would be expected of three former band kids, we grooved to some fabulous blues and jazz on Beale Street. And we went to the river, where we stood at the memorial to Tom Lee and thought of the heroism he displayed in the face of an immense volume of swirling water, armed only with a small boat and, probably, a fervent wish that he knew how to swim.

As always, I am grateful for the people who help me get my work ready to go out into the world, the people who send it out into the world, and the people who help readers find it. Many thanks go to my agent, Anne Hawkins, and to the wonderful people at Poisoned Pen Press who do such a good job for us, their writers. Because I can trust that my editor, Barbara Peters, and the rest of the hardworking Poisoned Pen Press staff will ensure that my work is at its best when it reaches the public, I am free to focus on creating new adventures for Faye. I'm also grateful to the University of Oklahoma for providing the opportunity for me to teach a new generation of authors while continuing to write books of my own.

And, of course, I am always (always!) grateful for you, my readers.

# Chapter One

*He always loved the Madonna-like glow around a mother tending to her child. More than once, this glow had been the thing that called a woman to his attention.*

*He appreciated the way this mother's deep brown skin shone as she bent down close to a little face that was just as beautiful as hers. Her auburn braids cascaded around her face as she leaned in to hear her child's secrets. White teeth gleamed behind full lips that would have glistened even without the frosty pink gloss she wore. Earrings dangled like a hypnotist's shiny watch. Rings adorned every one of her fragile fingers.*

*He had been watching this mother with this child for a long time, longer than he'd ever stalked a woman. His attention had strayed, because certain needs must be met, but he always came back to her.*

*For her, he had broken every one of his rules. They lived mere blocks apart. He knew her name. She knew his. More to the point, the people who would be her survivors knew his name and they knew where he lived. He should have run from her as fast as his feet would take him, but he was transfixed by the graceful tilt of her head as she listened to everything her little girl had to say.*

*As the two of them neared the crosswalk, she held her hand* out in the mother's universal signal of caution. The hand said, "You're too young to cross the street alone." Or perhaps it said, "You're old enough to cross the street alone now, but hold mine, please. I feel safer when you do." Something about the way the child took her mother's hand made him think that the balance was already shifting, years too soon. Perhaps the mother was the one who needed someone steady to look after her.

There was no wedding ring. He always checked for those.

He could have done it, then and there. Nobody could be easier to grab than a woman with a child in tow. Come within an arm's length of the child, flash a knife, grab a wrist, and you were in control. That's where he liked to be, in control.

This woman knew him well. Getting close enough to seize the wrist would be easier than it had ever been, because she knew him. Or she thought she did.

He said her name out loud, again: "Frida."

He liked the taste of it. It vibrated on his lips in the same way that her wrist would pulse against his palm.

Grabbing a woman's wrist was always his first move and, in many ways, it was his favorite moment. There was always a tremble of fear there, playing counterpoint to her rocketing pulse. There was a cold clamminess, too. A hard yank on the wrist could bring her close enough for him to smell her sweat in the very instant that a surge of adrenaline gave the scent a top note of fear. A harder yank could sprain the wrist, dislocate the elbow, sometimes even snap the arm, but he had to wait for that. Until they were alone and no one could hear, he couldn't afford to loose the hungry dog of his desire.

Mother and child crossed the street, hand in hand, and he enjoyed watching them go. The mother had long, slender legs beneath a short skirt that was silky enough to enhance the curves beneath. The daughter's legs were short and sturdy *beneath her athletic shorts, but that would change. She was her mother's image made over. In two years, maybe three, she would be as delectable and he would be waiting. Once he'd broken his rules for her mother, he might as well break them for her too.*

*He let them walk out of sight, but it would be a mistake to say that he let them go. He had decided that they were among the chosen, and this was not a decision that he had ever reversed. The mother was ripe now and the daughter would be soon. They could walk away from him, but they could not escape him.*

*He knew where they lived.*

# Chapter Two

The slow-moving creek carried a thick layer of olive-green algae. Faye Longchamp-Mantooth shuffled along, using her feet to feel her way along a sandy bottom that she couldn't see. Tainted water lapped at sandy banks littered with beer cans, crumpled plastic grocery bags, and an occasional whitewall tire. Anything that had ever been cast aside by anyone in Memphis, or even in most of west Tennessee, could theoretically be hiding under the scum, so she stepped carefully.

She was wearing boots that were water-resistant, but not watertight, and she'd been slogging along this creek for nearly half an hour, so its blood-warm water now saturated her socks. Her shirt clung to her ribs. Even her bra was sweat-soaked. She was mildly miserable, but she couldn't quit now. To quit would be to admit that a little girl was tougher than she was.

She was far behind the girl, just close enough to catch sight of her every five minutes or so. The child couldn't be more than ten, yet she moved in the world like someone who had never been dogged by a protective adult urging her to be careful. There was no question that she knew this creek. Faye had quickly learned to pay attention when her quarry made a random move, stepping deeper into the water than Faye would have expected or crawling up the bank to take a detour that seemed unnecessarily strenuous. When Faye reached the jumping-off points for those odd detours, she inevitably found out the reasons for making them.

Once, a deep hole, hidden by the algae and muck, claimed her leg all the way up to the butt cheek. She'd waited in that hole several minutes, until she was sure the girl was too far away to hear her splash and flail her way out of it. Another time, she'd tripped over a submerged television and barely missed slicing her calf on the exposed shards of an ancient cathode ray tube. Faye had collected ample proof that the girl knew this creek intimately, miles of it. This was despite the fact that, if Faye had been her mother, she would have been years away from receiving permission to leave the back yard alone.

When a culvert came into view, Faye crawled up onto the high bank to get a better look at it. She saw a concrete pipe, maybe four feet across, marking the point where the creek was almost blocked by the bed of a busy road. The pipe throttled the creekwater into a narrower, swifter flow.

Faye hoped that the girl had traveled as far as she intended to go. She didn't want to see her wade into the culvert's fast-moving water, deep enough to splash the hem of her skimpy red shorts. Faye had been following those shorts for nearly a mile, but she'd been keeping her distance. There had been times when the only signs of her quarry were occasional glimpses of their faded crimson through the underbrush.

Why was she doing this, anyway? It had been three days since Faye had first noticed the child hiding in a shady clearing atop the creekbank that loomed over her worksite. Every day since, the little girl had been up there before Faye arrived, ready to roll up her sleeves and do some archaeology. Shortly before noon each day, Faye had seen her creep quietly through the trees lining the bluff, skirting the creek until she believed she was out of Faye's sight. Each day, she returned more than two hours later, closer to three, and waded out of the water at a spot where the creek bluff dipped down to a manageable height. This happened far enough from the spot where Faye worked that the child probably believed that she'd gone unnoticed.

But this had been a tactical error. She'd underestimated Faye, who had also spent her childhood outdoors, albeit in safer places and supervised by an adult. Whenever the girl passed by on the bluff above her, Faye heard the soft footsteps and the rustle of disturbed underbrush. Even the faint splash of small feet stepping into running water was obvious to Faye.

After the girl disappeared downstream on the first day, Faye had listened for the barely audible splashes to fade. Then, certain the child was gone, Faye had climbed up the bluff and checked out her hiding place.

The little girl's stash of treasures was eclectic. Faye found a neat pile of magazines that looked like a sampling of convenience store stock—three issues of *Guns and Ammo*, a real estate circular, two issues of *Car and Driver*, and a dog-eared copy of *People* so old that the cover featured Paris Hilton. She'd also found a cache of pretty-colored stones and a fistful of dried-up yellow water lilies.

There was lots of trash corralled in a plastic bag pinned down by a rock. Faye had admired this act of unchild-like tidiness. Then, because archaeologists are fascinated by trash, Faye had followed her instincts and peeked in the bag.

It was filled with food wrappers, which was no surprise, but Faye hadn't expected the wrappers to lean more toward real food than toward candy and gum. The girl's unkempt hair and too-small clothing had led Faye to assume that she was neglected, but somebody was making sure she ate granola bars, peanuts, and canned fruit. Why wasn't she eating it at home instead of hiding from the July sun in the patchy shade of a copse of water oaks? Was she homeless? Did she live here, outside and alone?

No, that was impossible. There had barely been room in the gap in the trees to sit, much less to lie down and sleep, and there had been no possessions beyond the tattered magazines. This was not the hideout of someone with nowhere else to go.

This line of reasoning made Faye reasonably sure that the child had a home, but was there someone waiting there to take care of her? She studied the girl, far ahead of her in the creek. By her best guess, she was looking at two-days-since-somebody-fixed-it hair, which is a far cry from the hair of a ten-year-old living alone. Some of the braids were starting to fray, but most of the multicolored plastic barrettes still held. A lot of kids' hair looked like that in the summertime.

Where was she going?

• • ● • •

On the first day she laid eyes on the child, Faye had stayed at her work, digging with her trowel in the damp creekside sand and watching the girl trek downstream. Hours later, her spying had been rewarded with the sight of a wet, tired child sneaking back toward her cozy nest. Hours after that, she'd seen her stand and fade into the woods again, this time walking away from the water. Faye had presumed she was going to a home where she had a bed and someone to look after her, but she would have liked to be sure.

The second day had been just like the first day, with the girl spending part of the morning hiding in the woods, leaving for a while, then returning to lurk until late afternoon. The big difference was that Faye hadn't been alone. She'd had a witness to help her watch the child skulk through the underbrush.

She'd wanted to follow her then, but her witness hadn't hesitated to say, "You're nuts."

This was rather bold of him, since she was the one who'd be signing his paychecks. Faye had hired Jeremiah Hamilton as her assistant more for his local knowledge than for his decent-but-not-exceptional archaeological expertise.

Jeremiah was in his late twenties. He held a master's in anthropology, and he was now a third-year doctoral student, but, more importantly, he had grown up in a house that stood less than a mile from their worksite in Sweetgum State Park.

Jeremiah's local knowledge was inarguable. His archaeological knowledge wasn't nearly as extensive, but he thought it was. Jeremiah was one of those people who really liked to explain things to his boss, and he liked to do it carefully and thoroughly. He was probably just trying to impress her, or maybe he just liked to hear himself talk, but it felt like he was doing it just in case she turned out to be stupid.

"Why are you worried about this particular little girl?" he'd asked as the girl in question traipsed out of sight. "Do you know how dangerous this neighborhood can be? And do you know how many little girls live in it? If she's really been sitting up there eating snacks and reading all summer, she might be better off than most of them."

No, Faye didn't know how many little girls lived nearby. She also didn't feel qualified to judge who was better off than whom, and she didn't think Jeremiah was qualified, either. She did know she didn't like Jeremiah's suggestion that she shouldn't worry about one little girl's safety unless she was prepared to make sure all little girls were safe. Since it had been her first day as his boss, she hadn't said, "That's a logical fallacy," out loud. She'd merely shot him an eye roll that said it for her.

Jeremiah might have been an annoying know-it-all, but he'd seen the eye roll and backed down. Nevertheless, Faye had known what he was thinking. It was as clear as if he'd spoken out loud.

*You're an outsider, Dr. Longchamp-Mantooth, and you should mind your own business.*

Jeremiah was going to need recommendation letters for post-docs and faculty positions soon. It would help his case if he learned to be more diplomatic with the people who could write them for him. Faye had held her tongue and changed the subject.

On this, the third day of her new project, Jeremiah had gone to the university to oversee the final day of training for their crew. This was the last day Faye could anticipate working alone for the duration of the project, and she was done with being a passive spy. It was time to find out where the little girl went every day. Making sure a child was safe just seemed like the right thing to do, despite what Jeremiah, the judgmental local expert, had to say.

In the end, Faye's reason for going after the girl was a simple one. She was curious. Curiosity had gotten her into trouble before, but it had also taken her on some adventures.

Being her own boss had its virtues. If she wanted to take a long lunch and spend a couple of unpaid hours slogging down this creek, nobody could stop her. Thus, her curiosity had brought her to this moment, standing in a murky creek and staring at the round dark opening of a culvert.

Crouched behind a stand of cattails, uncomfortable and wet, Faye wondered why she hadn't just called out, "Hey! Little girl! Can I talk to you? Do you mind telling me where you're going?"

Deep down, Faye knew that a direct question would have left her looking at the back of a child who was running away, fast. The child's furtive glances and smooth, silent movements said that she was cautious and that she had good reason to be.

As Faye watched, her quarry walked with purpose toward the culvert, which protruded from its bed at an alarming cant. Stooping her head as she approached it, she didn't slow down.

Dang. She was going in.

Faye watched her wade into deepening water that was opaque with the goop washed off the streets of a major city, not to mention the excess fertilizer applied to the green lawns of Memphis. The water lapped at scrawny brown thighs and faded red shorts as the child strode into the culvert and disappeared.

Cursing herself for her inability to leave a question unanswered, Faye stepped into the sunlight and waded toward the culvert. She could feel the current tugging at her calves, her knees, her thighs. She wished wholeheartedly that she hadn't worn full-length pants with heavy cargo pockets that dragged her down even more than the sodden pants did, but she plunged on.

At five feet nothing, Faye rarely had reason to think, "I'm too tall," but the culvert succeeded in planting that thought in her head. Bending her knees and leaning forward, she was able to enter standing up, though she had to work hard to keep her breasts and belly dry. With both hands holding her phone out of the water, she plunged ahead.

Putting her face so close to the scummy water forced her to acknowledge that it didn't smell very good, but it was too late to turn back. She shuffled her feet through the silt on the concrete bottom of the pipe and made her way slowly, allowing plenty of time for the little girl to stay ahead of her.

The rough concrete undersurface of the culvert dragged against her back, but it kept her oriented in the dark. She knew she wouldn't have to go far in this condition, hunched over and mostly blind, probably just the width of a two-lane road. Still, the light on the other side looked very far away. She headed for it, single-minded in her desire to forget about the smell and the unidentified squishy things under her feet. Soon enough, she stepped into the light...

...and fell into waist-deep water.

She twisted as she fell, because it was imperative that she land butt-first, keeping her phone overhead in both outstretched hands. She'd opted for the waterproof case, but still.

Had she tripped? No. Her foot and shin had definitely struck something solid, but then that something had moved, hooking itself around her leg and throwing her to the creek bottom. Faye shook the water out of her eyes and saw nothing but sunlight glinting off broken green glass.

"Why're you following me?" said the small human

wielding a broken bottle. Her voice sounded thick, rough, choked, with none of the fluty sweetness of childhood.

Faye's foot hurt where the girl had used her own leg to sweep it out from under her. The water in her eyes burned but her phone was still overhead and dry. "I wanted to make sure you were okay."

The girl snorted. "Stand up. But slow. James Roy Curtis tried to take my backpack one time." She brandished the bottle and its fierce shards. "He still drools out the hole in his face."

"Is that true? Did you really cut a little boy's face open?"

Faye was still blinking hard to clear her eyes, so she didn't move fast enough to suit this little person who had just thrown her off her feet.

"It's true enough. Get up! And hold your hands out. Away from your sides."

Faye rose until she was looking down at the white part running through the dark hair on top of her assailant's small head. Dark eyes raked over her body, and a small dark hand reached out to smack the cargo pockets on either side of her pants legs. The girl's wariness faded quickly when she saw that the wet clothes clinging to Faye's slender form hid no weapons.

Faye studied the unsmiling face. Could she really be as young as she looked? Maybe she was under ten and maybe she wasn't, but Faye would have bet money that she was at least a year shy of puberty. Faye had been warned that she'd be working in a dangerous part of a dangerous city, but being face-to-face with a small child who knew how to frisk her for weapons broke her heart.

"Lady, you should go back where you came from. Meth heads don't sleep forever."

The what-are-you-saying? look on Faye's face must have

been hilarious, because the child laughed out loud. Jerking her head toward the creekbanks behind Faye, she said, "They hide up there. To sleep it off."

Faye had always prided herself on her powers of observation, but she'd walked at least a mile without realizing that there was anyone nearby. "What about you? How come it's safe for you to walk through here but not me?"

"I know where I'm going. I know where the bad people stay. I know when they sleep. But you?" She flicked her eyes up and down Faye's body. "You don't know nothing about this place. You should go home."

"How do you know I'm not already home? How do you know I'm not from around here?"

The girl gave another quick, hoarse laugh, but said nothing.

"It's that obvious?" As a woman of color, Faye had thought she'd be able to blend into a city where only a third of the people considered themselves white.

"You look like somebody on TV. Slick. Not even real. Talk like that, too." She leaned her head back and gave Faye's face a hard, cold look. "Rich. I think you're rich, and so will those people sleeping up there. You don't want to be around here when they wake up and try to take what you got."

What did the girl think she had that was worth stealing? She already knew Faye's pockets were empty. Her purse was locked in the trunk of her car. Then she remembered her cell phone and the slim gold band on her left ring finger. People had been killed for less, just not in any neighborhood where Faye had ever lived.

Joe had argued against her taking this job without him, but she'd brushed him off. Frankly, she'd been offended by his insinuation that she wasn't streetwise.

And now she was reacting just as strongly to the suggestion that she was a rich outsider. Faye remembered wearing secondhand school clothes bought with the money her mother made as a nurse's aide, and she remembered the nasty things the other girls had said about those clothes, clean but long out of style. She remembered daily peanut butter sandwiches in her lunch box, because her mother couldn't afford to pay what the cafeteria charged, and she was too proud to apply for free lunches.

Most of all, she remembered the day her mother, giddy with accomplishment, had said, "I got my license! I'm a practical nurse now and I got a new job. I can do better for us now."

Not that this news had stopped the steady flow of peanut butter sandwiches. Oh, no. Faye' mother had been cheap as dirt, and she'd stayed that way till the day she died. Her grandmother, too. Poverty leaves its marks. Faye had more security now, but she would always keep a close grip on her budget.

"I'm not rich," she snapped, then she felt stupid for letting a ten-year-old get under her skin.

The girl's grunt said, "If you say so."

She stood with her eyes on Faye, as if waiting for her to turn tail and run. Faye thought maybe she should do just that, but her stubborn streak was arguing with her, and it was winning. It was asking her what, exactly, she'd be running from. Sleeping drug addicts? Or a bottle-wielding ten-year-old?

"I'm not going back until you tell me where you go every day. And until I know you have a safe place to sleep at night."

Instead of an answer, the girl gave her a small shake of the head, then another. She appeared be thinking hard, but she eventually reached a conclusion, because she tossed the bottle toward the creekbank. It landed in shallow water and sent ripples that brushed Faye's legs while she waited for the girl to speak.

Finally, the child turned and started walking again. "Do what you wanna do. I'm sure the meth heads will be real glad to see you when they wake up."

Faye had seen the undersides of two low-slung bridges since her companion had chucked her beer-bottle weapon into the shallows but she had not, thankfully, had to get herself through another culvert. Slowly, the banks got lower. The creek spread out on both sides until it was hardly more than a linear wet spot.

The girl took this opportunity to walk onto dry land and keep walking without looking back. Faye could see that they were in a wooded park with a playground surrounded by picnic tables.

There were children everywhere. Faye trudged in the child's wake until she was stopped in her tracks by an order to "Wait here."

The idea that the girl had slogged through a mile of water to find a place to play hit Faye in the gut. When she remembered that this happened every day of the week, she felt it in her gut again.

She stopped where she stood, as ordered, and considered what to do. Should she turn around and walk back up the creek, returning to the work that she probably shouldn't have left? Or should she linger while the girl played, so that she could walk her back home?

While she dithered, the girl surprised her again by

walking right past the swings, the slides, the jungle gyms, and the joyful, shouting children. Instead of stopping to play, she headed toward a picnic table loaded with coolers and plastic bags. Faye inched closer to see what was going to happen.

Taking a bag from the table, she turned around without acknowledging the middle-aged man who handed her a juice box. He didn't seem offended. In fact, he reached into the cooler for a second box. This time, the girl gave him a faint smile as she took the second juice box, but she didn't linger. She never even stopped walking. She just got her bag and her juice box, then turned and walked back to the creek.

Within a few steps, she had passed Faye and stepped back into the water. Faye followed her, although she could tell that the child didn't care if she did or if she didn't. She could also tell that the wary girl never stopped keeping track of where Faye was and what she was doing.

Opening the lunch that she'd walked a mile to get, the girl fished out a granola bar and bit off a big hunk. Then she peered into the open bag and considered its contents before reaching in again. Pulling out a bright green apple, she tossed it to Faye.

Truthfully, tossing was a kind word for what she did. She threw it overhand at Faye's left arm, hard enough to leave a bruise. Faye felt a petty joy in plucking it out of the air with her right hand after it bounced off her arm. She was pretty sure that the girl had meant for her to fish it out of the disgusting water.

"You sure you can spare this apple?" Faye asked.

"I got plenty here for today. It's the free lunch people. From the school, you know? In the summertime, they bring the food here every day."

"Weekends, too?"

"Naw. Just during the week. But they bring us whole backpacks full of food on Fridays. It lasts long enough. And I can always go eat with Uncle Laneer, but I don't like to do that. He gives me too much and don't keep enough for himself. He ain't got enough to eat as it is. Anyway, there's always potato chips at home. And popcorn. That's what my mama likes to eat, when she eats. And ice cream. She really likes ice cream."

So she had a home and a family. That was a relief.

Faye bit into the apple, despite the fact that she'd never really liked apples all that well. It would have been rude to turn down a gift of food from someone who'd walked the whole morning to get it. Besides, she was hungry.

It occurred to Faye that she might need to recalibrate her notion of "hungry." She'd been short of money for her whole life, but she'd never lived in a house where her only options for food were to walk for miles or to subsist on potato chips and ice cream.

Her teeth punched through the tough apple skin and released a burst of juice into her dry mouth. Its flesh was crisp and full of tartness, not at all mealy. Faye decided that she might not like most apples, but she liked this one.

"Thank you," she said. "What's your name?"

The girl said something indistinct and Faye said, "Come again?"

Obviously irritated, the girl said, "Kali. K-A-L-I. Not like the dog."

"Oh, like the Hindu goddess? That's a great name. It suits you."

Faye was being honest, because it was a great name and it did suit her. Kali was revered as the Mother of the Whole Universe. Often portrayed with black or blue skin, she was a powerful image for an African-American girl to look up to, even if she did hail from the wrong subcontinent. Faye remembered how hard she'd looked for role models when she'd been a dark-skinned girl on a light-skinned street. She would have been a huge Kali fan.

There was no arguing, though, that Kali the goddess was flat-out fierce. She liked to wear skirts of human arms. Oh, and a garland of skulls, also human. Faye could absolutely see this scowling child growing up to be that awesome.

"A Hindu goddess? Yeah? That's better than a collie. The kids at school say collies ain't nothing but big ugly dogs. Never seen one, myself."

"They're wrong. Collies are beautiful dogs. Truly. Shiny, shaggy fur. Sweet faces. Let me show you a picture." Faye pulled her miraculously undrenched phone from her only-slightly-damp shirt pocket and plucked a picture of Lassie off the Internet.

The dog's happy face made the tiny Mother of the Whole Universe crack a grin, revealing a row of teeth like pearls set in polished iron.

"You went down like a rock when I tripped you. You know that? You sure you can walk and eat that apple at the same time? Not gonna fall again? 'Cause I ain't waiting for you. We gotta get back before the crack heads wake up."

"I thought they were meth heads."

"Don't matter. None of 'em wake up happy."

Faye chewed on a mouthwatering bite of apple. "I can keep up. Just watch."

Kali's grunt sounded doubtful.

"You couldn't lose me if you tried. And Kali? My name is Faye."

# Chapter Three

*He'd hidden his car at the bar down the street, where it blended in with dozens of cars. They were the cars of ordinary people. Unexceptional people. People who were not planning homicide.*

*After locking his car door, he had slipped into the woods behind the parking lot and headed across the creek, eventually stopping at a sheltered spot where he had stood many times before.*

*From this familiar vantage point, he had a clear view of Frida's driveway. If she came or went, he would see. He knew this because he had stood here many times before, watching her live her life.*

*Sometimes, it took her a long time to come home. This only gave him more time to think. He thought about the way she looked and sounded and smelled. He thought of the things he'd done to other women, carefully considering which of those things he'd like to do to Frida.*

*Sometimes, like tonight, she was gone so long that she couldn't possibly be visiting a friend or working late at the restaurant. On those nights, he knew she must be with another man, and the fury rose. Once, it had crossed his mind to take his fury out on the man instead of Frida, but then he'd come to his senses. And he had laughed.*

*No lights had shone in any of Frida's windows since he had been standing there, and it told him that Frida had planned for this late night. The girl was sleeping elsewhere, and this was good. Neither the child nor her keeper were nearby where they might see him.*

*Just as the sun came down, he had seen Kali emerge from the woods, creeping quietly down the street and out of sight, presumably heading for the home of the friend or relative who was watching her now. It wasn't the first time he'd seen her do that, and it made him wonder whether Frida enforced a sundown curfew, even when she wasn't home. The girl's shadow was lithe. It vibrated with youth and energy.*

*In this moment, Frida consumed him. One day, though, he knew he would come back for Kali.*

# Chapter Four

Kali liked ice cream almost as much as her mother did. She just didn't want it all the time. But sometimes, she woke up early and wanted to start the day with a jolt of cold sweetness. And sometimes, when her mother stayed out late, she woke up wanting to be at home instead of at her Uncle Laneer's. On days like this, she liked to slip out his back door at dawn and walk down the creekbank to the back door of her own house.

She was closing the freezer door when she heard the sounds in her front yard. Ice cream sandwich in hand, she peered out the front window first, then out her bedroom window, and then out the window at the top of the back door. She saw nothing in the half-darkness but shapes and motion, but the sounds she heard were horrible.

Her mother's bedroom was empty. Kali tried to connect the dots between the empty bed and the sounds that were rapidly fading into the distance, but she couldn't make her mind work. She couldn't think at all, but she could run.

Slipping out the back door and closing it quietly behind her, she listened for thudding footsteps and the sounds of a struggle, and she followed them.

# Chapter Five

The ground was cold—so cold—and it was hard. Even in July, and even in Memphis, the ground is cold after a long night without the sun, and it is hard when it is rushing up to strike you.

Frida struggled to her feet, knowing that it would get her nothing but another fist in her face. He'd knocked her down, striking her in the jaw with his closed fist. She'd struggled to her feet, only to have him do it again and again.

She was young, only twenty-six, so none of her pliant bones broke when she hit the ground. Frida was no athlete, so she'd never learned to fall. Each time he hit her, she collapsed like a bundle of twigs suddenly untied. She was slender, so she heard the clatter as her uncushioned bones struck the hard ground. Each time, he yanked her back to her feet, holding her in his iron grip while he slapped her and shook her and slapped her some more. And then, again, he doubled up the fist and knocked her to the ground, waiting until she scrabbled to her knees to reach his big hand out to grab the fabric of her dress and yank her upright.

It had only been minutes since she'd stood in her own driveway, suffused in the warm glow of a first date that had gone very well. She'd been on too many first dates to take this warm glow seriously, but she'd lived too many hard days not to appreciate a good one when it came. She had wondered at herself for shedding her customary wariness, born of a lot of hard years, for this man. An all-night first date was out of the ordinary for her, but he was no stranger and tonight had been a long time in coming. Hope for the future had been a long time in coming, too, but she owned it, if only for a night.

The black sky, the dark prickles of starshine, the pink haze of dawn in the east, all of it had made her happy to be alive. She'd stood for more than a minute on the broken cement of her front sidewalk, taking it in. Then she'd bowed her head over her purse and foraged for her keys, one for the doorknob and one for the stout deadbolt that had cost her more money than she'd wanted to spare. She'd learned the hard way that a door without a deadbolt was an open invitation, scraping together the money for this one when her unbolted door was broken by someone who wanted to take what little she had.

Disaster had happened in the last moments of the sun's battle with the streetlights, when it was light enough to see but not light enough to see well. Her attacker had come from behind, so she couldn't see his face, but she could tell that he was twice her size. This was no real identifier. Everybody was twice her size. She had a bird-like body that wasn't of much use beyond catching the attention of men.

If he'd grabbed her an instant later, she might have had the keys in her hand. She thought she might have been able to rake them across his eyes and get away, but maybe not. Her shoes' heels were too high for an escape quick enough to save her. Their straps were barely wide enough to bind them to her feet. The odds that she could have shaken off his grip and outrun him were achingly low, but if she'd had her keys to use for weapons, she could have tried.

He had easily lifted her off those teetering heels and wrapped a long arm around her middle. Before she could draw in a breath to use for screaming, he'd stunned her with a hard slap and carried her, running behind her house and through her back yard, taking a hard turn when he reached the creek.

His grip had slipped, but not enough to let her escape him. Her feet had dragged through briars that whipped around her legs, digging their thorns into her bare ankles. At some point, one of them snagged a sandal strap and yanked her shoe right off her foot.

The arm encircling her chest had been a python crushing the breath out of her. When she'd struggled, he had squeezed tighter. Still, she'd clung to hope. There had been nothing else steady in the world but hope and the arm dragging her deeper into the darkness.

When it was over, she had thought, she would take her chance. When his rage was spent, and his lust, she would run. If her body held together, she would be able to run.

Her half-shod feet had dangled in the water as he hauled her across the creek and onto the far shore, where the ground was so, so cold. Now, where no one could possibly hear, he battered her with punches and slaps, knocking her to the ground and yanking her to her feet again and again.

When she'd been sure that he'd never stop, his meaty hand had closed around the fabric of her dress one last time, and he had yanked her uphill, away from the shallow creek crossing and up onto a high bluff where a thick copse of trees made a terrible darkness. The dawning sun's light was growing, but it was still pale and sickly. It didn't penetrate the trees' shadows at all. She didn't want to go into those shadows.

She let herself go fully limp, which didn't stop him from dragging her toward the darkness. Perhaps her feet, still dragging on the ground, slowed their progress by a second or two. Eventually, even her knees dragged, but he knew where he wanted to go, and he was intent on taking her there.

As they reached the shadows, she felt the ground grow softer under her knees. It was looser, as if someone had been at work with a hoe or shovel, preparing to plant a season's seeds. For a moment, her knee balanced on the soft earthen edge of a great hole, then it slid down into the hole and took her with it.

He loomed above her, holding a shovel. Now she knew two truths.

First, this was the tool he had used to dig her grave, so there was now no question that he planned to kill her.

And second, she knew this man. The men in Frida's life had, by and large, done her no favors, but knowing that this particular man planned to kill her made her want to die.

But she couldn't die, not when Kali needed her. She had to get away, but she had so little left inside her. No strength, no heart, no hope.

Still she lunged at the rim of her grave and tried to throw herself out, again and again, but it was no use. Her attacker was armed. He wasn't armed with a gun or a knife, only the shovel he'd used to dig her grave, but the shovel was enough.

# Chapter Six

It wasn't even seven o'clock yet, but the sun was coming up fast. Even the parking lot that served this part of Sweetgum State Park was lovely. It was a vast park to be located within a short drive of a large city's downtown district. It encompassed a popular campground, a golf course, soccer fields, tennis courts, and more, but Faye would be working in a section that was still pretty wild for an urban park. Bordered by the creek she'd waded with little Kali, this part of the park was undeveloped other than a few walking trails.

The state of Tennessee wanted to build another campground near the creek, and they had hired Faye's cultural resources firm as part of the preliminary work. Her job as an archaeologist was to make sure that workers didn't destroy any irreplaceable traces of the past while they were building their new campground.

Faye sat in a parking lot surrounded by leafy trees and underbrush in a million shades of green. Hers was the only car there. She could have sat there for an hour, enjoying the greenery, but she had a job to do.

Closing her car door, she headed for the trail leading from the parking lot straight down to the creek. She, and sometimes Jeremiah, had been doing preliminary work here most of the week—except for the time she'd spent splashing through the creek with Kali—but her full crew was on its way. She had arrived early because there were still some things she wanted to check out before they arrived.

To get from the parking lot to her site on the far side of the creek, she had to get her boots a little wet. Maybe damp was the right word. The trail crossed the creek at a spot where the water was just an inch or two deep, with stepping stones to help people with a real water phobia get across. She could have parked in other lots that wouldn't have required her to wade the creek to get to work, but she would have had to haul her equipment further. Besides, this was the quietest and the prettiest place to park, so she was happy to get her water-resistant boots a little wet at the beginning of the day and again at the end.

Carrying a heavy load of equipment made the creek crossing harder than usual. Her feet slid off a wet rock in midstream, taking her into the shallow water with a splash and a reflexive curse, but the stumble didn't slow Faye down. She was enjoying her usual early morning good humor, which was precisely why she had started early in the first place. It only made sense to make efficient use of her favorite time of the day.

As it turned out, taking the wet route to work might not have been the best use of her morning efficiency, because splashing across the creek reminded her of Kali, which caused her pace to flag. Faye tried to shake off the memory of the little girl's daily hikes for food. She needed to be focusing on her work, not on a kid who had a mother to look out for her. Granted, the mother didn't seem like an outstanding specimen, but Kali was taking care of herself pretty well. And maybe her mother was just perfect, other than her dubious nutritional choices. Faye and her daily candy bars were not innocent in that regard.

As Faye stood on the creek's low bank, unpacking the bag holding her tools and field notebook, she was focused on the bluff above her. Kali must be a morning person, too, because Faye was pretty sure the girl was already up there. She had heard leaves rustling above her the whole time she was approaching the bluff. As the quiet footsteps had pattered along, Faye had expected them to bring a little face to gaze down at her, half-fierce and half-friendly. She had been wrong.

It was embarrassing to admit it, even to herself, but she was hurt that Kali had chosen not to climb down to the waterline and say hello. Faye had thoroughly enjoyed the mile-long conversation between Kali's free lunch pickup and this spot, but Kali apparently hadn't enjoyed it as much as she did. If she had, she wouldn't be up there hiding from Faye.

Two people can learn about a lot about each other while taking a long walk. Kali might not have known who Lassie was when they set off walking—and how many ten-year-olds did?—but she'd known the entire discography of Isaac Hayes. How many ten-year-olds could say that?

"My Uncle Laneer worked with Isaac Hayes at the meat-packing plant back in the day," Kali had said. "Played bass in his band for a while, till the boss put him on the third shift and he had to quit. Third shift pays better, but you can't play the clubs when you're working midnights."

Faye had agreed that was true, then started singing the guitar intro to "Shaft," complete with wah-wah effects. Her funky "Bomp-bugga-bomp-a-bomp" must have been good, because Kali had laughed until she splashed butt-first into the water. Faye considered this one of her finest musical moments.

Knowing that her fellow funk-lover was keeping her distance this morning hurt Faye more than it should have, but she shook it off. The only sensible thing to do was to leave the child alone and get to work.

This spot at the edge of Sweetgum Creek would have been pretty minus the green scum on the surface. The scummy water burbled over a pebble-studded sandy bottom, cutting through a small ravine it had carved for itself. Some of the trees lining the creekbed were the sweetgums that had given the creek its name. When a breeze rustled through all those leaves, Faye understood why Kali chose to be outside in the July heat. This was a peaceful place. And a fascinating one for an archaeologist.

Sweetgum Creek had clawed its groove all the way across Memphis, exposing some fascinating strata. Millennia ago, a primeval version of the Mississippi, far larger than the current river, had flowed over the area, covering it with thick layers of silt. Those layers of sediment had entombed ancient tree trunks which were now petrified, mineralized into gleaming, colorful rock. In other parts of Memphis, Sweetgum Creek had exposed those old trunks and much more.

More pertinent to Faye's expertise were the traces of Paleolithic humans that had been uncovered by this flowing water. They had left little behind but their magnificent spear points of fluted stone and, sometimes, the fossilized skeletons of the wooly mammoths brought down by those spears. Across town, Sweetgum Creek had uncovered one of those woolly mammoths, and a handful of Paleolithic tools, too. Faye burned to find a woolly mammoth.

When she looked at a map showing such spectacular

finds upstream from where she stood, she asked herself the question that had kept her going for her entire career: "Why not here?"

Then she gave herself the same answer she always did: "You won't know unless you look."

Faye was in Memphis because the state of Tennessee had a problem. They wanted to expand a campground that brought in good income for this park, and their problem had taken the form of a longtime resident of the surrounding neighborhood showing up with a sheaf of old photographs. Those photos showed that a campground along this creek would be nothing new.

When the park had been developed in the 1930s, the Civilian Conservation Corps had done the work of clearing trails and building bridges and structures out of rough-hewn brown stone. It had taken months to do this, maybe years. The CCC had built a huge camp to house their crew, and they had done it right here along Sweetgum Creek.

The thing Faye found most interesting about this camp was that every last one of the workers had been African-American because the CCC program had been segregated. Even the New Deal hadn't managed to treat everybody the same way. It had been the same old deal.

Those people were part of the park's history now, and they had a story to tell. The state was going to have to cool its heels until Faye did a cultural resources survey to find any traces the CCC workers had left behind. The time she'd spent poking around at the foot of this bluff had been above and beyond her scope of work, but Faye had been willing to do it, because, well…mammoths! If she was going to be this close to the possibility of a mammoth, she was damn sure going to try to find one.

Never mind that she wasn't a paleontologist. Some things were bigger than trivia, like whether a lot of self-guided study and a raging sense of curiosity qualified her to do paleontology.

As Faye noted the date in her field notebook, she heard another sound from above, and it wasn't footsteps. It was a human voice, but the soft, muffled sounds were not words. Was it Kali?

If the little girl was hiding, why would she be making these noises? More concerning to Faye was the pain in the sounds she was hearing. Somebody was in trouble.

Faye laid her trowel down and didn't waste time by running downstream to the place where the ravine's walls sloped down to her level. She used both hands and both feet to scale the bluff's face at its tallest point. As her head cleared the top, she looked around for her young friend.

She saw no one, but she did see a large area of disturbed soil, soft and damp. It hadn't been there the last time she had stood in that spot, when she was looking for Kali's hiding place. Her skin prickled. This didn't look good.

Pressing her hands hard into the top of the bluff, she reached up a knee to rest on its lip. With one shove, she was on level ground and moving fast. Something was very wrong with the way this soil had been dug out and replaced, then carelessly covered with dry leaves and pine needles.

Faye didn't like the size of the filled-in hole, six feet long and two feet wide. It was the shape of a bed. Or of a grave.

She liked it even less when the soil shook and moved, disturbed by something beneath. The roiling dirt looked like something out of a cheap horror movie, but it was real. Something underground was alive.

Dropping to her knees, she stared at the unnatural shivering of the earth. The leaves strewn over its surface stirred and rustled, even though there was no wind to move them.

Then a hand rose through the dirt and leaves like a plant sprouting from seed. Its fingers were bloody, with broken fingernails, and they grasped at the empty air inches from Faye's face. She lurched back and screamed. In answer, a raspy voice sounded from underground.

She needed to call 911, but she couldn't spare the time to talk to a dispatcher while someone was smothering to death in front of her. Her Solomon-like solution was to dial the numbers, then toss the phone on the ground and hope that the dispatcher could use the signal to home in on her location.

The hand clenched into a fist and shuddered, then a second hand pushed through the dirt. The wordless groaning that had brought Faye to this place came again and it made the skin between her shoulder blades crawl. She wished for her trowel, but there was no time to climb back down and fetch it. The person buried here—this woman buried here—was suffocating before her eyes. For these were a woman's hands, small, slender, with tapered fingers. There were eight rings on each of her hands, one for each finger, including the thumb, with an extra three stacked on each index finger.

Faye allowed herself an instant to think, "Thank God. It isn't Kali," then she got to work.

Faye used one forearm to rake the leaves off the makeshift grave, then began clawing at the dirt with her bare hands. Her own fingers were instantly bloody, like the hands of this woman trying to dig herself out of her own grave. Judging that the 911 dispatcher would have picked up, she yelled, "I've got a woman buried alive here. Send help while I dig her up. Sweetgum State Park, south side, near the creek." Then she forgot about any help that might or might not come, and concentrated on digging.

Checking the location of the woman's hands, she made a guess as to where her face was and started scraping at the dirt. It was hard-packed, as if the person doing the burying had stomped on it, but Faye made headway out of sheer persistence. Her frenzied digging forced dirt deep under her splintering fingernails, but there would be time later to think about how much it hurt.

When a single one of Faye's fingertips made contact with something quivering and alive, she worked her hand through the dirt to palpate it. The flesh vibrated with the buried woman's voice, and this told Faye that she had misjudged when she aimed her digging for the groaning sounds. She'd imagined that this would take her straight to the woman's mouth and nose. Instead, her hand was on a throat gasping for air. Grateful that she'd dug gently enough to avoid crushing the woman's windpipe, she shifted her efforts further away from the struggling hands.

A chin emerged from the soil, then a mouth, relentlessly opening and closing. Faye used her dirty finger to clear it of dirt, hoping that this was enough to open her airway, then she kept working upward.

A nose emerged and Faye did her best to clear that, too, of the dirt blocking the air that might save this woman's life. It was bleeding, broken, perhaps by the feet stomping the dirt into a hard layer above her face and body. She did her best to bring the bleeding nose to light without hurting the woman even more.

Again, she yelled in the general direction of the phone, "She's breathing now, but she's hurt. Get somebody here quick."

Gently, she cleared the buried eyes and forehead of their burden. The woman's eyes didn't open and the writhing of her arms didn't slow, but her face was in open air and she was breathing, so Faye finally felt safe to stop digging and pick up her phone.

The dispatcher was saying, "Ma'am? "Ma'am? Are you there? I can barely hear you."

"I've got a woman in distress, apparently the victim of an attempted murder who was buried alive. She's hurt bad. I'm just inside the southern boundary of Sweetgum State Park."

The 911 operator made a choking sound. Faye figured that terrible stories were a daily part of this guy's job, but that this one shocked even him. He took a long snort of air like it was a bump of cocaine that might give him the jolt he needed to get through this.

It must have helped, because he rallied and said, "Buried alive, you say? Okay. Okay, I'm sending somebody right now. That's a big park. Can you give me some details about where you're at?"

"I'm about five hundred feet upstream from the south parking lot, across the creek and on top of the bluff. They'll need to cross the creek right there at the parking lot, where the banks are low on both sides. The water's shallow there, so they won't have any trouble getting across. Once they get to this side, the woods here are pretty open. They can get a stretcher through, easy."

"There's no place closer that they can park?"

"They'd have to haul the stretcher down a long trail and through some thick underbrush. This is easier. Trust me."

"Give me a second to get them that info."

The woman moved, arms and legs spasming again and again. A splash of red at the base of her throat was visible even through smears of dirt.

Faye tried to clear the dirt from the open wound, but the effort was futile. She gave up and put both hands on it, pressing gently but firmly in hopes of stopping the bleeding. If it helped, she couldn't tell. It was possible that the pressure of the earth had stanched the bleeding and saved this woman's life. For now. She couldn't wait long for help to come. Later, it would be time to worry about sanitation and infection.

"Okay, I've got paramedics on their way to you. What can you tell me about the patient's condition?"

"She's injured, but I can't tell how it happened. Maybe she was shot. Maybe she was knifed. I don't know, but she's bleeding from her upper chest. A lot. I'm guessing the person who buried her thought she was dead. Or didn't care."

"Any idea how long she was there?"

"No. I mean, I was in this very spot a couple of days ago and she couldn't have been there then. There was no sign of digging." She stopped, shaking her head to clear it. "What am I blathering about? This blood is fresh. We're not talking about days. We're not even talking about hours. She had to have been here when I got here this morning, because I would have heard digging. And I—" She stopped short and glanced around her.

"Ma'am? Are you okay?"

"I'm sorry. I was thinking. I'll stand by what I just said. I would have heard somebody digging a hole big enough to dump a body in, and I didn't. But I did hear footsteps. Maybe I got here just in time to hear the person who did this leave."

"How's the patient now?"

"Still breathing, but not well. Ragged." Faye reached for her wrist. "Pulse is okay, I think. It's really fast, but it's there."

"Do you know CPR? Just in case."

"I do."

Faye couldn't stop thinking about the footsteps. Had she heard this woman's attacker? Or had she heard Kali?

Praying that the little girl hadn't seen any of this, she looked toward Kali's hiding place, but couldn't see through the leafy undergrowth. She would have loved to hurry over there and look, but the person in front of her was struggling more for every breath. Faye was right where she needed to be.

How had this woman lived more than a few minutes underground? An air pocket was the only explanation. There must have been an air pocket near her nose or mouth, with the overlying soil being just porous enough to keep her alive.

Or to ensure that she died slowly, depending on how you looked at it.

Faye stomped on those thoughts, refusing to imagine what it must have been like for the woman to see the hole waiting, to feel the impact as she was thrown into it, to lie in the iron-cold grave and watch the soil fall on her own body.

Did she fight back? Maybe. Her hands were free. More likely, she'd been unconscious or too injured to move when she was dumped here. It would have been impossible to cover a struggling body so completely.

"Ma'am?" the 911 operator said, and from his tone, Faye realized that he was repeating himself. "Are you still okay? How's the patient?"

"I'm fine. She's about the same. I'm going to dig some more of the dirt away from her torso. Maybe it will help her breathe."

"That sounds like a good idea. But only enough to get her stable, until the police arrive. Evidence."

*Yes. Evidence. Wouldn't want to mess that up, but I cannot sit here without trying to make this poor woman more comfortable.*

Faye began gently pulling soil away from the woman's chest, careful not to disturb the wound that was spilling more blood by the second. As she worked, she scanned the shallow grave and the area around it, hoping that the butcher who did this had left clues behind. She saw nothing.

She rocked back on her heels to survey her work. There was no more dirt on the woman's chest or abdomen to restrict her breathing. She was still buried from her pubic bone down, but Faye couldn't justify disturbing the crime scene any further.

Faye was no doctor, but she'd had extensive first aid training to prepare her for leading field teams on projects that were often remote and in dangerous terrain. One of the first things every first aid instructor said was always, "Look at your patient."

So Faye looked. She saw dark skin, ashen with shock. She saw eyes rolled back under eyelids, their sclera red, raw, and caked with dirt. The woman's lips, too, were covered with dirt and the inside of her mouth was still caked with it, impairing her breathing.

Faye kept a rag in her pocket when she worked. An archaeologist never knew when she might need to wipe dirt off something, but this was the first time she'd ever used it to clean soil out of a human mouth.

The mouth moved. Air and a sound passed out, and Faye half-believed that the sound was "Thank you." The rational half of her believed that this person was too far from consciousness to frame even that reflexive phrase. That rational half also heard the disturbing rattle in the woman's breathing and hoped the paramedics got there before she had to decide what to do about it.

The sun was rising higher. Faye noticed that she was finally getting warm. She'd been too distracted to notice the chill morning air. The warming rays of the sun reminded her, again, to look at her patient.

The ground where the woman was buried was cold and damp. Faye always wore a long-sleeved, button-front shirt to work, because it protected against sun, bug bites, and briars. In recent years, she'd begun wearing a thin white undershirt under it, for those times when she just couldn't take the heat. She peeled off her outer shirt and laid it over the woman's exposed torso, wondering how much longer it would take the paramedics to come.

Even as she tucked the shirt's fabric around the wounded chest, bright blood began to soak through it. Flashing lights, just as red, appeared through the trees that separated her from the parking lot. A siren screamed. And the rattling breaths of the woman in front of her stopped coming.

Faye grabbed a cool wrist with one hand. With the other, she used the other hand to grasp the injured woman under the neck and upper back, hoping to open her airway while she searched for a pulse that simply wasn't there.

Crying out, "Here! We're over here," she put the heel of her hand on the woman's breastbone and laid her other hand atop it. As she began counting compressions, she shouted, "She's crashing. Come quick!" but she doubted they were close enough to understand her words over the burbling of the flowing stream between them.

The sound of slamming ambulance doors was sharp enough to pierce the background noise of creek and birdsong. A moment later, she heard the voices of people who were splashing across the creek to bring her help, but it seemed like the faraway sounds were coming from another country.

Using the weight of her upper body, she pressed on the limp woman's chest a hundred-and-twenty times a minute, wondering if help would arrive before she needed to switch to mouth-to-mouth resuscitation. No help came.

She clasped the back of the woman's neck with one hand and put the other on her forehead, looking for an airway angle that would work a miracle. None was forthcoming, so she used the cloth to wipe the inert woman's mouth, then leaned down and gave a rescue breath. She was relieved to see the wounded chest rise, so the patient's airway was open.

She gave another rescue breath. No response.

The crackling of feet on breaking twigs and fallen leaves approached, but help still hadn't reached them. If she remembered her training right, it was time to do more chest compressions. Faye was in the middle of her third set of compressions, kneeling on the hard ground with both hands pressing into a limp woman's bloody chest, when a paramedic grasped her shoulders, gently moved her aside, and took over the job.

"Do you know her?" he said, dropping to his knees beside his patient.

"No, I just found her here."

He didn't answer. He simply threw her some alcohol wipes to clean herself up, then went to work trying to save a life.

Faye scuttled backward on hands and knees, trying to get out of the way of the professionals who didn't seem to be having any more luck than she'd had. She knelt on the ground, compulsively using the wipes, one after another, to clean her face, her mouth, her hands.

As the rescue team worked, she focused on the face of unconscious woman. The victim looked young, probably not even thirty, and she was very thin. Traces of makeup still showed on her face. Grains of sand and dirt clung to red lipstick and thickly applied mascara. Her hairstyle was a mass of tiny auburn braids that must have taken hours to plait. She had several golden hoops in the ear Faye could see, and there was also a bloody tear in her earlobe where yet another hoop must have been.

She looked like a woman who had a lot of living yet to do, but none of the paramedics' efforts had brought her back and Faye didn't think they ever would.

# Chapter Seven

*He had been robbed of something dear.*

*He had waited so long for his time alone with Frida. An hour would have been enough. Two hours would have been an explosive joy. He wasn't a demanding man, but the few minutes he'd been given to vent his love and rage simply had not been enough. He deserved more.*

*The splashing of feet in the creek, a stumble, and a soft curse had alerted him to the intruder. He'd had no choice but to dump Frida into the ground without ceremony, tossing a few shovelfuls of dirt over her before he fled.*

*And now he was left with no outlet for his hunger.*

*Worse, he was left with the question of whether the interloper had seen him. He had been hunting and harvesting women for a long time, but he was smart and the rest of the world was dumb. He had never come so close to being caught.*

*Perhaps he shouldn't have run. Perhaps he should have stood his ground and laid two women in this grave. She was no taller than Frida, although she was more muscular and she moved with more authority. She took up more space in her world than Frida, but he could have swatted her to the ground with one hand. If he'd been clear-headed, instead of besotted with the fragile Frida, he would have killed her as* soon as her head cleared the bluff, instead of giving her time to dial 911. The 911 call changed everything.

What if she fought back, even a little, and the emergency personnel arrived before he could finish the job? What if she saw his face and he didn't have time to silence her? He was a cautious man and this was why he was not sitting on Death Row. It was also why this woman had not been swatted out of existence with a shovel.

His caution had kept him from silencing her on sight, but now he was left with the fear that she'd seen him. Even if she hadn't seen his face, perhaps she had seen something else, a piece of evidence that would eventually surface from her subconscious and lead the police to him.

He memorized her face, because he would need to find her again. She had deep brown eyes with the intelligence and intensity of a deer sniffing human scent. He memorized her tears trembling on her lower lids because she was too busy digging to wipe them away. He memorized brown hands that were both strong and delicate as they worked to free Frida from a grave where he'd intended for her to stay. The set of her jaw had said that she would not be deterred from this task or any other. He needed to know her name, where she lived, what she did every day.

This woman moved him as much as Frida had, and this was a good thing. He was going to need to silence her. He might as well enjoy it.

# Chapter Eight

Nobody was looking at Faye. Quietly, she backed away from the paramedics, working hard to save a woman who needed them badly. She needed to know that Kali was not watching this.

Stepping between the bushes and tree trunks that hid the little girl's hiding place, Faye entered the small clearing where Kali whiled away her days. She expelled a relieved sigh when she saw that no one was there.

The magazines were right where Faye had seen them, still wrapped in plastic that was now beaded with dew. Kali's bag of trash hadn't moved, either. Only one thing was different. Trash was scattered across the small patch of grass where the little girl sat. Faye knew this was where she sat, because there was no room for her to sit anywhere else.

The trash bothered Faye for two reasons. First, throwing garbage around seemed uncharacteristic for a child who cared enough about her space to keep a trash bag handy. And second, it made no sense for there to be trash in the only open spot large enough for sitting unless Kali had dropped it as she left, probably in a hurry. Otherwise, she would have been sitting on an ice cream wrapper.

Looking more closely at the ice cream wrapper, Faye's

heart sank. It held a half-eaten ice cream sandwich, and the chocolate mass cradled between flat chocolate cookies was only partially melted. She knew Kali's mother kept ice cream around the house. All evidence pointed to Kali sitting right here, and so recently that she must have seen terrible things. She'd almost certainly seen Faye find the buried woman. Worse, it was entirely possible that she'd seen her be buried. She might even have seen her stabbed or shot.

A lightly worn path led from Kali's hiding place and Faye followed it. The path paralleled the creek, and the water sounds got louder with every step as it descended to another shallow crossing like the one near Faye's parked car. Once across, it took a hard right away from the creek and put Faye within sight of the back doorstep of a modest home.

The house's white vinyl siding was cracked and mildewed. Dark windows watched Faye like fathomless eyes. A metal swingset that looked as old as Faye stood rusting in the yard with no swings at the end of its chains. It wasn't a beautiful home, but the roof was solid and the yard was neatly kept. Maybe Jeremiah had been right when he'd said that there were a lot of children who were worse off than Kali.

Faye heard more voices behind her saying, "You say there's a witness? Where is she?" so she turned away from Kali's house. The police had come and she needed to go help them find a monster.

The detective was not impressed with Faye's ice cream clue, or he said he wasn't. She showed him the wrapper, hidden in a circle of trees, and he was only marginally interested until she told him that the ice cream in it was still frozen.

Upon hearing that news, he yelled at her for disturbing evidence. She wanted to say, "Which exactly is bothering you? Are you annoyed that I showed you a worthless piece of trash, or are you annoyed that I disturbed something worthwhile? That's ironic, since you would have ignored it if I hadn't been here. Besides, how was I to know that the ice cream wasn't melted unless I checked? If I had waited for you, we would never have known that it was still frozen when I got here."

But she said nothing, because the detective did not seem like someone who really wanted to hear what people thought.

Instead, she asked the question that never left her mind. "How is she?"

The man had introduced himself as Detective McDaniel. He didn't answer her question about the victim's condition, but Faye could see the paramedics starting an IV and dead people didn't get IVs. The woman was still limp and unresponsive, but maybe there was hope.

"Can you tell me who she is?" he asked.

"No, I don't know who she is," she said. "I wish I did." She wasn't sure he believed her. Why else would he ask, again, "Are you sure?"

She answered him with "I've never seen her before in my life," despite feeling insulted that he had asked her to tell him, yet again, that the injured woman was a stranger.

His "Hmm," was loaded down with doubt. "Ma'am, I need you to explain to me how you came to find this poor woman."

"I heard some noises up above me—"

He interrupted her to ask, "What kind of noises?"

"Footsteps. A voice—"

He interrupted her again. "The killer's voice?"

"No. I didn't hear any words that I could understand. Once I got up there, I realized that I didn't hear any words because there weren't any words to hear. I was hearing her groan. She—"

"You didn't answer my question about how you found her in the first place. I need you to back up and tell me what you were doing alone in these woods at the crack of dawn."

Faye, who considered herself even-tempered in the extreme, wasn't quite able to keep the edge from her voice as she said, "I could answer your questions if you stopped interrupting me."

This was his cue to apologize. He did not. He gestured at the parkland around them—trees, creek, wildflowers, tall grass. "Why were you out here before sunup?"

"I'm doing a cultural resources survey. For the state."

He looked at her blankly, so she tried again.

"I'm an archaeologist with a state contract."

Faye looked around her and realized that she had nothing to prove she was who she said she was. No identification, because her purse was locked in the trunk of her car. No proof that she was a respected professional who was currently in the employ of Tennessee's state government. No piece of paper stating that she held a doctorate. No tools to support her statement that she had arrived early to prepare for her crew's arrival. Nothing, not even the trowel she'd left at the bottom of the bluff when she heard the moaning of a woman buried alive.

When she realized that she had nothing but the clothes on her back and her brown skin, she stopped being irritated and began being afraid. It became imperative that she convince this man that she was no threat to him or to anybody else.

"I have the state contract in my car that will explain everything. It's got contact information for their archaeologist. Ordinarily, he'd be on-site, but we're just getting started. He'll be here Monday."

And then, despite him saying, more than once, "This isn't necessary," she led him down to the creek. On its bank, she bent down to retrieve her trowel, then she pointed out the first load of equipment that she'd brought with her from the car, intending to go back and fetch the rest.

He tried to tell her that he was satisfied with her story, but he ended up saying it to her back, because she wasn't finished. Trowel in hand, she strode across the creek. He followed.

When they reached her car, she reached deep into her right pants pocket to retrieve her car keys. A small object, hard and metal, brushed her hand and it scared her. The object was nothing new. She'd owned it since her teens, when her grandmother gave it to her. And it wasn't particularly scary, despite its sharp blade. It was just a pocket-knife that she carried because it was handy to have while working in the field. When faced with a law officer who seemed to dislike her for no reason, she felt the urge to shove the knife down further in her pocket, where he could never see it, so she did just that.

Easing her keys out of pocket, she left the hidden pocketknife right where it was, and she unlocked her trunk. In it were an array of digging tools that supported her claim to be an archaeologist. Unfortunately, they also would have been useful to anyone needing to bury an assault victim, so they scared her as much as the pocketknife did.

Reaching past them into the far right corner of the trunk, she pulled out a bankers' box full of files. "See? Here's my contract for a cultural resources survey to be done in this part of the park. And here's my correspondence with the state's contracting agent, including the project schedule."

He wasn't looking at the contract, so she took it out of its folder and thrust it under his nose. There were still traces of crusted dirt and blood on the hand holding the folder, and her forearms weren't any better. The alcohol wipes the paramedics had given her hadn't done much more than spread the filth around. She did think she'd gotten her face pretty clean, because she'd spent a lot of time scrubbing it. God bless the man who had reached in the ambulance's glove compartment and pulled out an undershirt, still in its package, which she guessed he kept there for occasions like this. It didn't fit well, but it allowed her to shed her own dirty shirt, so she was grateful.

She knew there was still wet dirt in her short, straight black hair. Her fingertips were abraded and raw, and there was more mud under them. The too-big undershirt gapped at the armholes, so she instinctively held both arms crossed across her breasts in protection. Faye knew that her body was covered decently, although just barely, but Detective McDaniel stirred up every defense she had. His smooth, bland face gave her no sense that he felt any compassion for her, a witness who was literally smeared with bloody horror.

She was so rattled that she'd begun babbling. "Look here," she pointed to the project calendar. "My crew is due to arrive at nine. Doesn't it make sense that I might want to get here early this morning, so that I can be ready for them?"

"It's what I would do."

There was a shred of grace to his "It's what I would do." It broke a barrier between them. It suggested that they were conscientious people who thought alike. It made her bold enough to ask the question that fully occupied her mind.

"Am I a suspect?" A warm breeze stroked her shoulder, and she crossed her arms tighter.

"There is no reason to suspect you at this juncture. Killers around these parts don't generally bury people alive, then dig them up and call 911. And then do CPR. I won't say that's never ever happened anywhere, but our killings in south Memphis aren't usually that complicated. Besides, you showed me your work truck full of tools and your file box full of contracts saying that the state hired you to be here. You're no suspect. I thank you for doing what you could for the victim."

For the first time, the man's mouth stretched into something resembling a smile. It was not convincing.

If he had ever once smiled before that, Faye wouldn't have been nervous enough to trot out her contracts and tools to prove she had a right to be where she was. She'd lived her entire life as a person of color, but this was the first time she'd ever worried about being considered guilty-while-black.

"I need to get back to the scene. You're an important witness. I have more questions, so I'd like you to come with me."

So she'd followed him back across the creek to the place where medical personnel were pulling the still-unconscious victim from the ground, preparing to transport her to a hospital. Faye wanted to go brush the hair off the woman's dirt-crusted forehead and smooth the wrinkles out of the pale yellow dress that was emerging from the ground as the rescuers dug more dirt from the woman's body and worked to free her legs.

Even from a distance of fifteen feet, Faye noticed a series of dark blotches on the top of a foot still shod in a silvery sandal.

"What's that?" she asked, moving close enough to make out the tattoos. The unfriendly detective followed her closely, as if he were afraid she might do something stupid or dangerous.

Tears came to her eyes as she got a good look at the four little marks on the wounded woman's foot. The tattoo consisted of four letters and they spelled K-A-L-I.

"I know who she is," Faye said, wiping her eyes on the back of a hand that was shaking. "I know who she is," she said again, and her knees went so weak that she had no choice but to sit down on the ground, hard.

Faye was the kind of person who never faltered in a crisis. It was her way to cry after the fact, when her child's fever broke or when a friend's funeral was done. She dealt with things as they came, as cool as if she had ice water in her veins, but everybody has limits. Eventually, the time came when adrenaline failed and she crashed. Today, this was her limit: seeing a little girl's name tattooed on the foot of a woman who could only be her grievously injured mother.

Deep down, she had already known. While clawing dirt away from the beautifully plaited hair, while wiping the full soft lips clean of caked dirt, while doing her level best to press life back into the bleeding chest, Faye had known that this was a little girl's mother. Knowing that there was no way to protect Kali from hearing this news, she sat on the ground and cried.

McDaniel bent over her and this time there was softness in his voice, maybe even kindness. There might also have been respect, but he had already raised Faye's hackles too much for her to be sure.

"Ma'am. You say you know who she is. Can you tell me her name?"

Between sobs, she said, "I don't know her name, but I know her little girl. They live right there," and she raised her arm to point down a path worn through the woods by little feet.

At the end of the path, Kali waited for the news that Faye didn't want her to hear. Worse than that, if she was the one who had abandoned a half-eaten ice cream sandwich, she already knew the news that Detective McDaniel would soon be bringing to her door. It was possible that the little girl had just seen something that nobody should ever have to see. She led the detective across the creek and along the path that would take them to Kali.

# Chapter Nine

Detective McDaniel knocked again, hard. Nobody came to the dead-bolted front door.

He looked at Faye. "Ma'am, does anybody else live here but the victim and her little girl?"

"I don't know. I couldn't swear that either of them live here, but I've seen the girl walk down the path we just walked. She said she lived with her mother, and she didn't mention anybody else living with them. That's really all I know."

The curtainless windows on either side of the front door revealed nothing. No lights were on and the television was dark. McDaniel stared at the blank façade. He had to be worried that he would soon be adding a missing child to his report of the morning's crime. The detective looked like he was wishing as hard as Faye was that Kali would miraculously appear.

Nothing of the sort happened inside the house, but a deep voice behind them saying, "Officer, can I help you?" made both Faye and the detective jump.

Faye turned, hoping that Kali was beside the owner of that deep voice. Instead, she saw an elderly man and a middle-aged woman coming up the front walk toward them. Faye was wondering how they had known to come, when the woman answered her unspoken question. She had a voice like an organ, deep, reedy, and rich.

"When the police come knocking before breakfast, that can't mean nothing good. You people looking for Frida?"

The policeman spoke up. "Woman in her twenties, African-American? Long braided hair, tattoo on her foot?"

The woman nodded, and said, "That's Frida," but the old man just stood there quietly, like someone who'd gotten bad news before.

"I'm Detective Harold McDaniel. Do you know her?"

"She's my late sister's granddaughter," the old man said. "Is something wrong?"

"I'm sorry, but she's been attacked."

Both the woman and the man bowed their heads and stood silent for a moment. Finally, the old man spoke. "Is it bad?"

Faye was trying to let McDaniel do the talking, but she couldn't help herself. She nodded. The man held her gaze. "How bad?"

Faye looked down at the blood and dirt stains on her pants and boots, and his eyes followed hers. She could see tears welling in his eyes. Still, she let the officer do the talking.

"The paramedics have taken her to the hospital. Dr. Longchamp-Mantooth administered first aid and CPR, or they might have gotten here too late."

The old man's eyes returned to hers and there was gratitude in them, but his companion was still doing the talking. She took one look at the too-big sleeveless shirt that was barely covering Faye's body and took action. Shrugging her big shoulders out of a heavy black cardigan, she held it out. Faye took it, grateful for the chance to cover herself.

"I know Frida won't mind if we go in and get you a pair of her pants, at least until you can get to your own clean clothes," she said. "Did he say 'Doctor'? Thank the Lord you were there!"

"I'm not that kind of doctor. My doctorate is in archaeology."

The woman hesitated. Faye figured she was thinking, "What kind of good does that do us? What kind of good does it do anybody?" because she frankly was thinking the same thing.

"But what happened?" The woman was wearing a black-checked apron with deep pockets and Faye could see her hands in those pockets, opening and clenching shut.

"All I can tell you at this time is that she was attacked," McDaniel said, stating something terrible as a simple fact.

"It was that damn boyfriend," the old man said.

"Which one?" said the woman in the apron. "The new one? The old one? The other old one?"

"She was dressed for a date," McDaniel said. "Do either of you know who she might have been with? Where they went? What time they went out? When she came home? Whether she came home? Anything at all would be a help."

"I told that woman that she should give up the men," the woman said, jamming her hands into her apron pockets. "And that she shouldn't be wearing the kind of clothes that get their attention. To tell you the truth, Frida is so pretty that she really oughta stop wearing makeup. She needs to hide from all the men that keep coming after her."

"Ain't no crime to be pretty. Ever since she was a little thing, Frida was the prettiest, sweetest child." And now the old man finally broke down, bringing a big, long-fingered hand to his eyes.

Faye pictured the hand grasping the neck of a bass

guitar and violated her resolution to let McDaniel do all the talking.

"Sir, is your name Laneer?"

"It is. Actually, my name is Lucius Laneer Billings, but people call me Laneer and you saved my Frida, so you can, too. How did you know my name?"

"I met Kali yesterday, and she mentioned her Uncle Laneer. I'm Faye." She reached out and shook his hand. "I'm very worried about her. Do you know where she is?"

McDaniel, eager to regain control of the conversation, shot Faye a look that said, "Would you please shut up and let me do my job?"

Laneer paused before answering her question about Kali's whereabouts. He looked at the police officer out of the corner of his eye, then skipped the answer altogether. Instead, he pointed to his companion and said, "This is Sylvia Cochran, Kali's candy lady."

The woman said, "You can call me Sylvia."

McDaniel had noticed Laneer's side eye, so he pressed the question. "Do you know where Frida's daughter is?"

Laneer looked like he wanted to claim he didn't know but he knew that lying to the police wouldn't go well for him. "Kali is at my house, asleep," Laneer said. "Been there all night."

McDaniel said, "That's not possible. We found ice cream in a place where Dr. Longchamp-Mantooth says that the little girl likes to play. It hadn't even melted. She had to have been there just a little while ago, and she may have seen something important."

Laneer was long-legged and raw-boned. He stooped a bit, but it wasn't an old man's stoop. It was the stance of a tall man who had spent sixty or seventy years trying not to look threatening, yet refusing to look subservient.

He paused a moment before speaking. Perhaps it was to gather his thoughts, but perhaps it was to let McDaniel know that he didn't have full control of the conversation, just because he was an officer of the law. Finally, he said, "I don't know nothing about any ice cream, but I know what I know. Kali's at my house and she's been at my house. She ain't got nothing to say to the police."

"Somebody left that ice cream there and I've got good reason to think it was your great-niece."

Ever the persnickety genealogist, Faye said, "Great-great-niece."

McDaniel didn't say, "Would you keep your pointless comments to yourself?" but his sharp blue eyes said it for him. This made Faye want to complicate his life, so she did.

"Kali said that her mother loved ice cream," she said, "Maybe Frida dropped the ice cream sandwich when she was attacked."

This would have required Frida to be in Kali's hidden space in the trees or for her attacker to randomly throw the melting ice cream into just the right spot. Faye didn't necessarily think that these possibilities were plausible. She was just having a moment of seriously disliking McDaniel. And she also didn't mind taking some of the detective's focus off Kali, but it would have to return there eventually. Faye did honestly agree with him that the girl might have been watching when her mother was attacked and buried alive.

"Where's your house?" McDaniel asked to Laneer. "I want to talk to the girl."

Laneer turned and the others followed him. Faye expected at any minute McDaniel would tell her to go away and let him investigate this crime in peace, but she was resolved to tag along until he did.

Laneer's house was on the same side of the street as Frida's, several houses down. The street hugged the curve of the creek, so Frida's house was invisible from his, hidden by a row of their neighbors' houses. It was noticeably older than hers, but its siding had a fresh coat of emerald green paint and the window frames were bright blue. The colorful house was a fitting backdrop for the vegetable garden that took up most of his front yard. Big red tomatoes and small yellow ones hung on head-high plants with feathery green leaves. Underneath, bulbous purple eggplants peeked from their own broad leaves. Behind them, yellow okra flowers stared at them with black eyes.

They all followed Laneer onto his porch and waited for him to unlock his shiny red front door. Key in hand, he turned to them and said, "Shhh. She's asleep."

Laneer pushed open the door to reveal a small living room. It was stuffed with furniture yet still managed to look orderly. There was color everywhere—yellow walls, 1960s turquoise furniture, and pale green curtains—and little Kali lay nestled inside all those brilliant hues, asleep on the couch. She was covered with a patchwork quilt that brought all of Laneer's love of color together in a single yellow, turquoise, green, red, and purple object.

"I told you she was here all night," Laneer whispered. "She don't know nothing. I'm gonna have to tell her what happened to her mama when she wakes up. Can you let her sleep till then? Please?"

McDaniel surprised Faye by whispering, too. "I'll call you sometime after noon and I'll be back right after that. Make sure she's here."

Faye took a step to follow him, but he put up a hand. "I'm going back to the crime scene. No unauthorized personnel are allowed until we're done with the forensics. I'll let you know when I release it so you can start your dig. A couple of days should do it, I'd think."

As McDaniel walked away without so much as a good-bye, Faye paused on Laneer's porch, surrounded by the happy colors of his vegetables and his paint. She wasn't sure how she was supposed to get back to her car. It was a only few minutes' walk away, if she could walk down the creekside path that McDaniel was blocking with his crime scene, but she couldn't. She had no idea how to get there any other way. And also, Joe would kill her for walking alone in an area that suffered under the crime rate this one did.

It occurred to her that the attack on Frida was not going to help Joe's attitude at all.

She reached out a hand to shake Laneer's, planning to say both "Good-bye," and "Can you help me figure out where I need to go?"

Before she could speak, Kali rolled over and opened her eyes. Just one word came out of her mouth, and it was "Faye."

Simultaneously, Sylvia and Laneer said, "Come in and shut the door."

# Chapter Ten

Kali pushed back the quilt and sat up. She was still wearing her clothes from the day before, red knit shorts and a sleeveless black top. When Faye, Laneer, and Sylvia entered the room, she bolted.

The girl crawled over the back of the couch and tumbled to the floor, her legs snarled in the quilt. If Faye had been trapped like that on the floor, with three pursuers just steps away, she would have been just as panicked.

Panicked or not, Kali was quick and she was strong. She grabbed the back of the couch, pulled herself upright, and just ran. The quilt clung to her bare legs for several steps, hobbling her retreat, but it fell away as she reached the closed door.

The door must have been out of square or covered with many coats of sticky paint, because it didn't open right away. The little girl yanked hard on the cut-glass doorknob as three adults advanced on her. When the door opened suddenly, with a creak, she was thrown off balance, but she was still able to dart through it before they reached her. She slammed the door shut behind her, and it closed with the grinding screech of a slab of painted wood that didn't quite fit in its frame.

Faye looked from Sylvia to Laneer for guidance on what she could do for this child that, quite frankly, she barely knew.

Sylvia said, "Leave her be."

Laneer said, "Can't do that. She'll go out the window if we leave her alone in that room."

"Not if we're standing out in the back yard passing the time of day." Sylvia moved fast for a woman carrying a few extra pounds around the middle. She was out the side door before Faye or Laneer had time to say, "That sounds like a good idea."

Laneer's back yard was too shady for vegetables that made large fruit, like tomatoes and eggplant, but leafy vegetables don't need much help from the sun to grow. His back porch was lined with green plants growing in flower pots in all shapes and colors. The pots overspilled with herbs, lettuce, and cooking greens.

Faye immediately saw that Kali was at the window, trying to force the latch open. It, too, was probably glued in place by years of paint. When she saw the three of them standing guard outside, her little face fell, then she turned quickly away.

"She's going to try the front door now, so I believe I'll go sit on the porch. That'll stop her," said Sylvia as she headed to the front of the house. Her steps were light and quick for a woman who had to be well along in her fifties. A cell phone had emerged from one of her apron pockets and she was tapping on it as she spoke. If McDaniel had wanted the details of Frida's attack to be kept secret, he should probably have made this plain to Sylvia.

Laneer shook his head and gave Faye a gentle smile. "That child ain't going nowhere today that Sylvia don't let her go."

"You called her Kali's candy lady. What's that?"

Laneer gave her the same appraising glance she'd been getting all week, first from Jeremiah, then from Kali and Sylvia. Even Detective McDaniel had given her that look. It said, "Can't quite figure you out. You ain't white, but you ain't poor, and anybody can tell that you ain't from around here."

Laneer gestured toward his house and, presumably, toward the woman sitting on its front porch. "That apron Sylvia's wearing? Them pockets are full of candy. Sylvia makes her money selling it."

"You can make a living selling candy?" Faye was quick-thinking enough not to insult his home by following that question with a disbelieving "Here?", but Laneer knew what she meant.

"She gets a check from the Social Security since her husband died, but the candy money don't hurt. And people do for her when they can, 'cause everybody's kids need a candy lady."

"To look after them when their parents aren't around."

"Sure. Can't nobody be all the places all the time."

Faye's children were a thousand miles away with Joe, so she knew that.

"Besides, kids tell their candy lady stuff that they wouldn't ever tell their folks." Laneer leaned down to pluck a bug off a lettuce leaf. There was a ladybug next to it and he left it alone. "I found Kali on my front doorstep this morning, not an hour before we heard the sirens."

"You told McDaniel she was here all night."

"She was. Frida sends her down here when she's gonna be out late. I don't know what Kali was doing out of my house at daybreak. She won't say. Won't say anything at all. When she said your name just now, it was the first time she talked at all since I found her on the doorstep."

"McDaniel needs to know this."

The old man stared at her silently. He didn't have to say, "You would trust the police? With the well-being of a child?" His face said it for him.

Figuring there were other things Laneer hadn't told McDaniel and might never tell him, she asked the obvious question. "Do you know of anybody who might have wanted to hurt Frida?"

Laneer then launched into a list of truly terrifying people. "There's her ex-husband, Linton. He comes to mind first. She kicked him out when he slapped her, couple years back, and more power to her for finally getting smart. I never thought much of that man. I saw him standing in front of her house last week, so he's either back with Frida or trying to get back with her. Me, I think he was just hoping she'd get weak and take him back, but Frida's too smart to get hit twice."

Laneer heard what he'd just said and his eyes slid shut. Faye remembered Frida's broken nose and the blood spreading over her chest. Maybe Frida was as smart as Laneer said, but it hadn't kept her from getting hit again.

"Is there anybody else besides Linton who you think might want to hurt Frida?"

"Never liked the looks of her boss at the restaurant. He was always trying to turn her head but she wasn't having none of it. Don't actually know why. Never heard anything bad about him," Laneer said.

"She works at a restaurant?"

"Yeah, downtown where the tourists go."

"She works waiting tables? Cooking? Hostessing?"

"She cleans the place in the evenings, after everybody goes home. Kali's here most nights until it's time for her to go to bed. I go with her to Frida's and sit with her until her mama comes home."

"Her boss. What's his name?"

"Armand's Rib Palace is the name of the place where she works, and Armand's her boss."

"Okay, so we add her boss to the list. Anybody else?"

"I most especially never liked Mayfield, down at the store." Laneer waved his hand down the street.

"You mean the convenience store at the end of the block? Has he worked there long?"

Laneer made another vague gesture with his hand. "He works there for now. Night shift. Linton works days."

"Frida's ex-husband?"

"Yep. Linton's a piece of work, for true, but Mayfield is the one I can't stand the sight of. He don't think much of nobody but Mayfield. He's all the time asking Frida to go out with him, and he's all the time putting little extra things in her bag. Candy bar. Bag of chips. Pack of gum. Let me tell you something 'bout guys like that, trying to kiss up to pretty ladies by stealing from the stores where they get their paychecks. They ain't never any good. You're a pretty lady, too, so you know how it works."

Faye gave him an "Aw, shucks," shrug.

"Yeah." Laneer said. "Mayfield had a crush on Frida back in high school and it ain't never gone away. Linton's still kinda new in town—been here six years, maybe seven—but Mayfield goes way back. Born here, I think."

"Linton's only been here six or seven years? So he's not Kali's father?"

Laneer shook his head. "Frida never would tell a soul who Kali's daddy was. She knew. I know she knew, because she wasn't never one to run around with a lot of men. She just wants one man that wants her back and keeps wanting her. And treats her right. Good Lord, she has had a devil of a time finding one of those and I couldn't tell you

why. Anyway, it wasn't Linton that was Kali's daddy, that's
for sure, since he didn't even live here then."

"Do you know their last names?"

"Linton's last name is Stone, same as Frida's. Mayfield?
Not sure. Everybody just calls him 'Mayfield.' Maybe that
is his last name."

Faye needed to call McDaniel as soon as she left Kali and
her family. He needed to know that one simple question
to Laneer—"Who might want to harm Frida?"—had
resulted in three names in as many breaths: Armand the
restaurant owner, Linton the ex-husband, and the single-
named Mayfield. One of those names might belong to
a man who wanted to hurt Frida, or wanted to put her
in her place, but it was entirely possible that Laneer and
Sylvia would never trust a policeman enough to share that
information.

The top of a small head appeared at the bottom of the
window they were guarding. Faye watched it rise slowly
until a pair of eyes peered over the sill. After a few seconds spent scanning the back yard and glaring at Faye and
Laneer, the little head dropped out of sight again.

"Somebody wishes we would go away and let her make
an escape," she said.

"She likes you, Faye. Anybody can see that. Do you
think maybe you can get her to tell us what's wrong?"

Faye wanted to say, "We all know what's wrong. She
just saw her mother buried alive," but the words wouldn't
help Kali and saying them would be like punching Laneer
in the gut. Instead she said, "I'll do my best."

"Don't you want to tell the police about these people
who might have hurt Frida?" she asked. "Armand?
Mayfield? Linton?"

"You tell 'em. But also, you tell 'em to keep theirselves
and their badges and their guns away from that little girl."

Faye wasn't exactly sure how she was supposed to do that. As soon as she told McDaniel that Kali had been outdoors at the time of Frida's attack, he'd put that information together with the half-melted ice cream sandwich. Then he would immediately be on Laneer's front doorstep, and he would be wearing his badge and carrying his gun. She wanted to say, "The police are here to help us. We need to let them do their job," but she knew how naïve that would sound to Laneer.

Two little eyes rose again above a bright blue windowsill. McDaniel was busy gathering evidence and he'd said that he wouldn't be gone long. Faye decided that she was willing to give Laneer a few hours, just until McDaniel came back that afternoon, to get the little girl to talk to him instead of to the police. But no more.

# Chapter Eleven

*He was falling, just as he always did, falling from the dizzy heights of a kill. A rush so powerful could not last forever.*

*One moment, adrenaline was pushing him along, adrenaline and all the other seductive brain chemicals. Dopamine, serotonin, endorphins—after a kill, he had no doubt that they were all pumping from every gland he had. They made everything fun, even the tedium of hiding his tracks. Even the fear. When the biochemical magic flagged, taking their rosy glow from his world, he remembered to be afraid.*

*It ate him up inside to imagine being caught. How would he explain himself to a policeman while standing beside a car's open trunk, when the trunk held pieces of a shovel that had once been very bloody?*

*As he came crashing down, the paranoia settled on him like a black velvet cloak. Everywhere he looked, he saw people who surely must know that he had done terrible things. And beside them stood people who might not know, but they could guess.*

*What did the woman who found Frida know? Who was she, and what was she doing in Sweetgum State Park at the crack of dawn? She had no right to be there, not when he had been so careful to choose a place where he and Frida could be alone.*

*If she could have seen his face, and known it, then a detective would have come knocking on his door by now. But had she seen his body? Had she seen the way that he moved as he ran, the way his left elbow hung just slightly closer to his body than his right, just as it had since the last time his father beat him? The woman had to go. There was no doubt about that. He just had to find out who she was.*

*The idea thrummed inside him, an electric spark that was fresh and new. He had never committed a killing so close on the heels of another, but this felt right. The thought of killing this woman brought the lovely brain chemicals back.*

*He had no doubt that his victims left his hands and went directly to heaven. He chose them for their air of innocence, and surely paradise welcomed their purity. Perhaps this unnamed woman was as pure or, at least, perhaps she was pure enough. Paradise was probably waiting for her with arms outstretched.*

# Chapter Twelve

Faye's phone rang. It was McDaniel, wanting to know if Kali was up.

"Not yet," she sort of lied, thinking that a child who had been crouching beneath a bedroom window for hours was not technically "up."

Since McDaniel left, there had been time for Faye to clean herself up in Laneer's shower and change into a pair of pants Frida kept in his guest room. There had even been time for her to call Jeremiah and tell him that they needed to delay the start of their project.

When she emerged from the house after her shower, Laneer and Sylvia were right where she left them, and Kali was still lurking by the window. The four of them—Faye, Laneer, Sylvia, and Kali—had spent the entire morning like this. At noon, Laneer had gone inside to make some sandwiches, and the adults had eaten them while waiting for the child to get hungry enough to come out of her room. The detective had said that he'd leave them alone till after noon, and he seemed to be a man of his word, because here he was on the phone.

Faye wanted some privacy for her talk with McDaniel, so she walked around the side of the house.

"I can't put you through to Kali, but I do have some information for you," she said. "You'll find two men who knew Frida down the street at the convenience store. Mayfield works nights. Linton works days. Laneer seems to hate Mayfield even more than Linton, despite the fact that Linton is Frida's wife-beating ex-husband. Not sure if that's relevant, but I thought you might want to know."

Then she said a quick good-bye and hung up without telling him what he really wanted to know, which was that Kali was awake. The child just wasn't talking to anybody.

As she pocketed her phone, she heard voices in the front yard. The top of Kali's head was still visible, so Faye knew that she hadn't strolled outside for a chat with Sylvia. Somebody else had arrived.

Laneer was still in the back yard, crouching next to a barrel-sized ceramic pot full of mustard greens. He was plucking weeds, so Faye squatted down and helped him. Keeping an eye on Kali, he told her, "I hear somebody talking to Sylvia. You go check that out. I'll stay here and watch for a bit."

In the front yard, Faye found a man about her own age, early forties. He was chatting amiably with Sylvia, who looked to be standing straighter and smiling bigger. One capable hand was smoothing the apron down over her hips, and the other one was offering the newcomer a handful of candy.

Faye could see why. It wasn't that this man was so very handsome, although he was tall, heavily muscled, and flat-bellied, and he stood with confidence. His eyes were a little too deep-sunk for beauty's sake and his teeth were a little crooked, but he had an open smile that would have shone all the way to the back of a Broadway hall.

"Faye, this is Mr. Walker—" Sylvia began.

"Call me Walt," he said. His deep voice was as arresting as his smile. He looked at Faye just long enough to say, "Sylvia just calls me 'Mr.' because I teach school," then he turned his expansive charm back to Sylvia, leaving Faye in the cold. "I came to check on Kali. I missed her at the playground today."

Faye shoved away the feeling of being snubbed. Kali's well-being was more important than her feelings, so she needed to know more about who this man was. Giving him a closer look, she said, "I remember you. You gave Kali an extra juice box yesterday, didn't you?"

"Yep. That was me. She's a sweet kid and I don't want her to get thirsty. Besides, a little extra Vitamin C never hurt anybody." And again, he returned his face to Sylvia.

"So true," Sylvia said. "Laneer does his best with this garden, and he does grow the sweetest tomatoes I ever had, but we're all grateful for the calories you sneak into that girl. Lord knows she needs some calories. Which I don't. And vitamins. She needs them, too."

"That's why I'm here. Kali would never miss picking up her lunch on Friday unless something was bad wrong, so I came straight over here when we finished giving out the food. Today's the day we hand out backpacks for the weekend. You know that, Sylvia. Kali counts on that backpack so she's got what she needs to eat till Monday. Food's not high on Frida's priority list. Anybody can tell that by how skinny she is. You and Laneer can only do so much."

"Poor Frida," Sylvia said.

Walt's face went still. "What are you saying? What's wrong?"

"Somebody hurt her last night. Hurt her bad. She's at the hospital."

Walt looked at Faye. "Is that why you're here? Are you some kind of social worker? I wondered what you were doing following Kali around yesterday."

"No. I just got worried about where a little girl was going every day by herself, so I followed her."

"You go around saving little girls all the time? Is that how you get your jollies? Nobody in your neighborhood needs help, and you've got to come to ours to be a do-gooder?"

Faye had to force herself not to take a step back from his hostility. Her own adopted daughter, Amande, had been a young girl who needed a home and Faye had given it to her. The decision to make Amande part of her family had given her more joy than she could explain to this man. He didn't know what he was talking about, but she wasn't about to bring the decision to adopt her daughter into this conversation. Faye would be damned if she'd give this man a chance to taint it.

"I don't like the sound of 'do-gooder,' not the way you say it, but my mother and grandmother taught me to look for the right thing to do, then do it."

"Did they do it the ladies' club way? Sell each other tickets to a fundraiser luncheon, then write some charity a check? That way, they could forget about all those people who need help when they sat down at their luncheon and filled themselves full of iced tea and cucumber sandwiches?"

Faye looked down at her borrowed clothes and wondered how it was possible that she seemed so rich to this man. Was it the way she talked? And also...cucumber sandwiches? Was this guy for real?

Did Laneer, Sylvia, and Kali see her that way? Her mother had taught her never to argue with a fool, but when Walt Walker insulted the memory of the women who had raised her, he'd earned a few moments with the rough side of Faye's tongue.

"My mother was a licensed practical nurse who worked the night shift. My grandmother was a secretary for a man who never paid her any more than he could get away with. And my father died before I was two. Mama and Grandma didn't have time nor money for ladies' club lunches, but they always found a way to help people. The checks they wrote for charity and to their church weren't very big, but they did write them."

Walt said nothing. To his credit, he looked taken aback, but Faye wasn't through with him.

"You didn't know my mother and my grandmother. It's not okay for you to insult them when you don't like me because…I don't know. Why don't you like me? Because of the way I look? The way I sound? Do I smell bad?"

"No, no, no. I didn't mean to be a jerk. I'm really sorry." This time the expansive charm was focused on Faye. "I get too involved with my children. My students. And their families. About twice a year, some people come in here and convince these people that they have all the answers. They talk big about their jobs programs and their after-school programs and their charter schools and their legal aid programs. Then they fade away and nothing has changed."

Faye decided it was time for her to be the one asking the questions.

"Is that why you work at the summer lunch program?"

"Yes. Well, I volunteer when they need me, which is a lot these days. It's work that actually does something for people. I'm happy to give them some of my time."

"And that's why you teach? Because you like to help people? You seem like a capable man. I feel sure you could get a job that pays better."

Walt's face softened. "Yeah. I teach because I want to help people, and I do it here because this is where I live. I want to help my neighbors' kids."

"Well, I'm here to do a job that I need quite a lot, and I hired five young people to help me who really need the jobs. I'm working through a local man, Jeremiah Hamilton."

"I know Jeremiah."

"Then maybe you know that he's associated with a nonprofit that helps disadvantaged young people from…"

"From places like this?" Walt asked.

Faye realized that she'd just firmly slapped Walt's home with the label "disadvantaged." Not good. At least she hadn't called it "the inner city." Her misstep embarrassed her, but it hardly mattered. Walt seemed to have hated her on sight, anyway. She might as well plunge ahead.

"Yes, I guess I do mean 'places like this.' Jeremiah finds jobs for his kids. He teaches them to do job interviews and helps them find the right clothes for work. He knows all the local college admissions people. He hires at the community college, then he helps his workers with their applications for a four-year degree. He gets their application fees waived or he finds the money to cover them. I'm here because of him and I brought jobs with me. When he heard I'd gotten the Sweetgum State Park job, he wrote me, out of the blue, and told me he had a proposition."

"A proposition? Ain't nobody ever told you not to listen to fast-talking men?" Sylvia jammed her hands in her pockets and rocked back on her heels "I know Jeremiah, too. He says a lot of things. You believe him when he talks?"

"A proposition for my firm, not for me. He knew I'd need technicians for this job and he wanted me to subcontract that work through his nonprofit. I interviewed Jeremiah pretty hard before I signed a contract with him to provide me with labor for this job. He convinced me that I could get my work done while doing something good for somebody else. Does any of this bother you, Mr. Walker? Am I such a do-gooder that you want me to close down my project and go home? Do you want me to go back to Florida and hand those jobs over to somebody who won't want to waste energy helping kids?"

Laneer appeared at the corner of the house, but Walt didn't see him. He was too busy venting his frustrations at the expense of a woman he'd just met.

"No, stay," he said, his mouth curled into a sneer. "By all means, stay. I'm sure you can single-handedly save those kids. I can sure see that you think you can save Kali. But why stop there? If Kali needs you so much, then what about every kid on the street? What makes her special? Take them home. Take them all home. Adopt them. Maybe that will make the guilt go away."

"What guilt?"

"You know what I'm talking about."

Maybe Faye did. She reflexively glanced up and down the street, revealing herself to Walt as she took in peeling paint, iron-barred windows, and signs announcing that people should keep the hell out. She'd never felt rich and she'd sometimes felt poor, but she'd never lived in a place like this.

Walt saw her and his smile turned triumphant, but Laneer interrupted him before he could use the troubled expression in Faye's eyes against her.

Laneer's face said, "Would you people pay attention?" but his voice said only, "We've got company."

Little Kali stood on the front porch. "I'm going home. I've gotta find my mama."

• • ● • •

The child was fast, but Faye already knew that. She'd already spent a morning chasing her down a creek, struggling to keep up with short legs that were all muscle and no fat.

Laneer was a bit too old to be that fast, and Sylvia was a bit too heavy. Walt had long legs and he moved like a man who ran for fun, so he was going to beat them all to the little girl. Something inside Faye hated that, so she put on some more speed.

She wasn't keeping up with Walt and she certainly wasn't catching up with Kali, but she was holding her own until her phone rang. She tugged it out of her pocket, planning to just glance at the phone but let it roll over to voice mail, unless the name on its screen made her think the call was important.

Caller ID said that Detective McDaniel was trying to get hold of her, so Faye reluctantly shifted down to a walk and put the phone to her ear.

"Is the little girl up yet? I'm coming to talk to her."

"Oh, she's up. And running, but I'm right behind her. She's going back to her house, looking for her mother. Somebody's going to have to tell her what happened, just as soon as we catch up with her, so come quick."

"Oh, I'm not just coming. I'm already there."

As Faye rounded a curve in the road, she looked past the running child and found the white house she was running toward. McDaniel was standing on Frida's doorstep and there was another man beside him. McDaniel was still wearing the polo shirt and khakis Faye had seen on him earlier. The second man was in a suit.

Clad in black from head to toe, the stranger stood with his head slightly bowed, his chin just a few degrees below horizontal and his eyes on the ground a few feet in front of him. In his hand, he carried a black book. Faye was still too far away to see the book, but she knew what it was. She knew that it was probably leather with its pages printed on fine vellum, and its cover was probably ornamented with gold leaf. Perhaps some of its most venerated words were printed in red ink.

Everything about the man who had come with McDaniel to talk to Kali said that he was a minister. The presence of a man of God when police came to give bad news was a bit of grace intended to bring comfort in times of pain, but Faye didn't think it was going to help today. Kali was too little, too young, too innocent to be told that her mother had gone to a better place. Even if the minister was right that Frida was in a better place, Kali needed her mother here with her.

Now McDaniel and the man in black were walking toward them. The sight of the approaching law officer and minister hit all the adults chasing Kali, and it hit them hard. Walt's full-out speed slackened and halted. Sylvia stumbled for a step, then tried to get moving again.

Laneer, who had been walking more than running and yet was still breathing hard, stopped dead-still. When he spoke, his words gushed out in a single breath, like a prayer.

"Oh, Lord God, don't do this, don't take this baby's mama away from her."

Ahead of them, Kali skipped the steps and jumped flat-footed onto the porch. Pulling a key out of her pocket, she used it to burst through the front door of the home where she had lived with her mother until today. If she saw McDaniel and the strange man in black, she didn't let on. She just disappeared into the dark house and let the door slam behind her.

# Chapter Thirteen

Six adults hovered on the doorstep of Frida's house. Faye supposed it was now Kali's house, if Frida had owned it. If she had not, and Faye couldn't imagine that the salary of a restaurant cleaner would pay a mortgage note, then thirty days or less stood between Kali and eviction. Homelessness. Not that a ten-year-old had any business living alone, even if the house was hers, by purchase or by lease.

Laneer was her great-great-uncle. Sylvia was her candy lady, whatever that was, but it didn't seem to mean she was blood family. Unless Kali had closer kin, Faye presumed that the girl would sleep at Laneer's house that night and every night for the foreseeable future. She looked at Laneer, standing bent over with his hands resting on his thighs, breathing deeply, and she wondered how long the old man would be able to take care of his great-great-niece.

Maybe there were other relatives to step in, if need be. Faye had only just met Kali and Laneer, so she had no idea. She found the situation inexpressibly sad.

The adults stood uncertainly in the front yard of Frida's—Kali's?—house. Laneer had caught his breath enough to speak, so he stood up straight and addressed the stranger in black.

Exuding the dignity of a patriarch doing what his family needed him to do, he spoke. "Reverend Atkinson, are you here to tell us something about Frida?"

Faye was close enough to see the small, shield-shaped pin on Reverend Atkinson's lapel, adorned with a cross and an anvil. She remembered her friend Douglass wearing a pin like that when he was making deacon's visits to the people in his congregation. This connection with her cherished father figure made her feel a little warmer toward the somber-faced man.

Reverend Atkinson looked at McDaniel, who nodded, so he cleared his throat to speak. "Ms. Stone breathed her last about an hour ago. She has gone to be with the angels."

Tears washed down Laneer's cheeks. "She was an angel her own self. Always was. Just the sweetest child. Her little voice was like music. Like bells ringing. And that pretty face of hers."

Sylvia's hands were clenched in her apron, wadding its black gingham fabric in both fists. "If it wasn't for that pretty face, she'd be here right now. Wouldn't have been raising that little girl on her own since she was a teenager, neither. Frida had the kind of face that brought the man-rats scurrying her way."

"I give her credit," Laneer said. "She was smart enough to run 'em off whenever she figured out she'd done it again. When she saw she'd let another rat into her life, she told him to get out. The thing is that there was always more where they come from."

Sylvia gave a firm nod. "You said it. And now one of her rats has gone and killed her."

McDaniel looked like he wanted to ask Laneer and Sylvia to give him a full accounting of Frida's man-rats, but he knew that this wasn't the time. "We have to let the little girl know about her mother."

"Did Frida wake up at the end?" Laneer asked. "Did she have any last words for Kali? Something that would let her know that her mama was thinking about her and loved her?"

The minister shook his head. "I was with her when she passed. No, she didn't speak. Couldn't speak. Couldn't breathe, not really, not after what that monster did to her." He looked at Faye. "You're the one that found her, right? You saw what bad shape she was in."

Faye, trying not to think about what she'd seen, let out a few feeble words. "Yes. It was me."

"I've watched lots of people die, so I could see she was going soon," the minister said. "Frida hasn't been so much for church since the baby came along, but I remembered about the little girl. I said I'd see to it that she was looked after, and she squeezed my hand. That's worth something, don't you think, for the little girl to know that her mama wanted her safe and happy?"

Laneer was sobbing again, so he just nodded his head as he walked toward the front door of the house where Kali had lived with her mother. When he drew near, he reached out a hand to touch the doorknob, just in time to hear the deadbolt thunk into place.

The adults looked at each other. Now what?

Faye hoped to goodness that McDaniel didn't do something stupid like yell, "Open up! It's the law!" She also hoped that Reverend Atkinson did not try to invoke the will of God to get Kali to let them in, because she didn't think the bereaved child would pay him much attention.

Did Kali know she was bereaved? She had to suspect it. How often did her mother disappear, replaced by a herd of grown-ups like this one, some of them weeping? It must be obvious to her that something was terribly wrong.

If, as Faye feared, Kali had seen the attack on Frida and had watched her being put into the ground, she had probably thought her mother was dead from the moment she ran to Laneer's house. But knowing it and hearing somebody say it were two different things. If Faye were Kali, she wasn't sure what it would have taken to get her to open that door.

There were windows on either side of the front door with venetian blinds hanging down nearly to the windowsill, leaving a wide crack at the bottom where light could get in. McDaniel and the minister hunkered down to peer into one window. Laneer and Sylvia did the same at the other one.

Faye and Walt, who both had no real reason for being there beyond circumstance, stared awkwardly at each other. They had been in the wrong place at the wrong time, and neither was sure what was expected of them. His confrontational air was gone.

Leaning toward Faye, he murmured, "You were there? You found her?"

She nodded.

"I heard…" His voice trailed off, presumably because nobody really likes saying the words, "I heard she was buried alive." He swallowed and found the guts to say them.

"You heard right. But how did you hear?"

He gave a soft laugh. "Sylvia's been texting. She's good at that. Cell phones have made children's lives a lot harder, now that their candy lady can tell their mama when they've done wrong. Nowadays, she can do it before they can run home and tell a lie big enough to save themselves."

"So yeah," Faye said. "Buried alive. I'm guessing the bastard thought she was dead. Or maybe it's worse than that. Maybe he's getting his jollies right now, wondering whether she's dead yet and wondering how long it took her to go."

Walt shuddered. "Where did you find her? People usually try to hide it when they've done something like that. You must have been way off the beaten path."

"I'm an archaeologist. A lot of my work happens off the beaten path. That's why I'm here in Memphis. I'm doing an excavation in the park for the state of Tennessee, mostly along the creek and on the bluff above it. That's where I found Frida."

"You picked a fine time and place to start a job in Memphis."

"No kidding," she said. "I can't believe I'm saying this, but this isn't the first time I've found a murder victim. I guess it's an occupational hazard for an archaeologist. Every time we put a trowel in the ground, there's some chance that it'll uncover a dead body. But this is absolutely the first time I've ever dug up somebody who wasn't dead yet. I'll remember the look in her eyes for as long as I live."

Walt didn't speak. There was horror on his face and Faye was sorry she'd put it there.

"I've said too much," she said. "I'm sorry. We should focus on Kali."

"I'm sorry I was hard on you."

"I wouldn't like someone who thought my people were charity cases, but I'm not like that."

"I can see that now."

He looked away, maybe to avoid meeting her eyes or maybe to watch McDaniel, Laneer, and Sylvia, standing at the front door and trying to coax a frightened little girl out of her lonely house.

"There are a lot of people out here who want to help

you, Kali," McDaniel was saying in a surprisingly gentle tone.

Sylvia reached into an apron pocket and pulled out a handful of candy wrapped in colorful waxed paper. She held it up to the window, and said, "Come see. I have your favorite."

The blinds stirred, but no face appeared. The door stayed locked.

Laneer reached past Sylvia and tapped on the windowpane. "Kali, honey. You need to let us in. I know how much food you ain't got in that house. You can't lock yourself up in there forever without starving. Come out and I'll make you a tomato sandwich just the way you like it. Nice soft white bread and lots of mayonnaise."

Maybe it was the promise of candy, but Faye really believed it was the thought of Laneer's tomato sandwich that did the trick. This was a child who liked real food well enough to hike miles for it, when she could have been eating ice cream sandwiches at home.

At long last, Faye heard the deadbolt slide open and the screech of yet another overpainted and out-of-square door. Kali stood in the open doorway, but she didn't step out and she didn't speak.

The minister got down on a knee next to her and said, "Kali, sweetheart, I came to tell you about your mama. She…well, she went to be with God this morning. I was with her, and her last thought was for you."

"Somebody killed her, right?" The girl's voice was rough-edged, but there were no tears in it, not yet. "She didn't just *go*."

The minister blinked at her like a deer that had stepped into the headlights of a Mack truck.

"And also, I don't think God took my mama to be with

him and left me here all by myself. Why would you say that?"

Her eyes darted from face to face, quickly leaving Laneer's and Sylvia's, as if their pain was more than she could take. They rested no more than a second on McDaniel's and then the minister's. Why should they? She didn't know them at all.

They lingered on Walt's face for more than a moment, and Faye though maybe this was the person Kali would choose to trust. After all, he was her schoolteacher, the person who had been her day-to-day parent for an entire school year. He was also the man who made sure she got two juice boxes when she wanted them, plus a weekend backpack full of food, so that she wouldn't go hungry or thirsty. But still Kali didn't speak. After Kali finished studying Walt, her eyes traveled on until they stopped on Faye's face.

Reaching out a hand to grab Faye's wrist, Kali said, "I wanna know exactly what happened to my mama. You're the one that can tell me."

Laneer and Sylvia took a step toward the girl and the front door where she stood, apparently presuming that they would be sitting down together with Kali and Faye to discuss Frida's death, but Kali shook her head.

She pointed to Faye. "Just you. I don't wanna talk to nobody else."

Faye sat on an old brown couch, next to the window. At her left elbow, there was a single end table holding a brass lamp, its plating pitted and corroded. The carpet under her feet was rental-house tan. The walls were painted rental-house beige. The only color in the room came from a few toys lying in the corner and a few movie magazines stacked on the floor beside the couch.

She knew Laneer was standing on the other side of the window glass, straining to hear. They were all out there, behind the venetian blinds. If she pushed aside those blinds, or leaned down to look beneath them, she would see all five of the people on the porch peering in at her. But she didn't really need to look. She knew they were there, and so did Kali.

"What happened to my mama?"

"Kali, why are you asking me? There's a policeman out there who's working really hard to find out what happened to your mother. He doesn't know it all, but he's trying to find out. He's the one who can help you."

Kali said nothing, but Faye could read between the lines. There was one excellent reason the child might think Faye knew the truth about her mother's death. She would think that, if she had seen Faye find her.

"I've told Detective McDaniel all I know, Kali. Do you have anything to tell him?"

"Only stupid people talk to the police."

Faye wondered who had convinced the little girl of this. In Kali's world, it could have been anybody. And in Kali's world, the notion that only stupid people talk to the police might even have been true.

"You still ain't told me what happened. I ain't got all day, Faye. That policeman won't leave us by ourselves forever."

Kali was right. Still, Faye stalled. How much should she say? The girl deserved to know something, but there was no way a ten-year-old should hear the unvarnished truth: "Your mother was beaten and buried alive. She must have felt a lot of pain and she must have been terrified. I don't know how long she suffered, but it was too long."

Instead of unloading all that truth, Faye kept stalling. "I don't know everything that happened."

The stern little face offered no mercy. "Didn't say you did. You can still tell me what you know."

Faye caved, a little. "She was beaten up pretty bad. Whoever did it buried her and left her for dead. I found her and I called the police. That's the story as I know it."

Kali was looking at her with a face that said, "I know there's more to it." And, again, Faye believed that this meant that Kali had been there, so she decided to go on the offensive, but just a little. How aggressively should a bereaved child be questioned?

Faye's answer was "Not aggressively at all," but she wasn't sure what Detective McDaniel's answer would be. She really wanted to get Kali to tell what she knew without suffering through an official interrogation that might be too harsh for a bereaved child. She decided to push her a little, gently.

"I found the ice cream you left behind and I know you were there. What did you see?"

She got no answer but silence. Silence, a steely pair of black eyes, and two lips, firmly pressed together.

"Did you see somebody hurt your mother?"

Silence.

"Did you see somebody bury your mother?"

Silence again, but there was no "No."

"Did you see who it was? Do you know who did it?"

First silence, but then a tiny shake of the head and four words. "No. It was dark."

"Are you saying that you were there, but you didn't see the person who attacked your mother? Or that you did see, but didn't know who it was?"

Try as Faye might, she couldn't get the little girl to speak another word.

● ● ● ● ●

After a time spent sitting with the girl, face-to-face and silent, Faye heard a firm double-knock. McDaniel's voice came through the door. "Dr. Longchamp-Mantooth, it's me. We've got a social worker here. She wants to talk to Kali."

Faye reached out to brush a loose curl back from the child's brow. "This social worker is somebody who knows more than I do about how to help you. I'm going to step out so she can talk to you in private."

Kali was shaking her head at Faye's suggestion that being alone with the social worker might help in any way, but Faye backed out the door and closed it behind her. The arrival of the social worker brought with it the looming shadow of the foster care system, and Faye was having flashbacks. Her daughter Amande had come so close to being swallowed up by that bureaucracy. Faye was still stunned sometimes to realize that the state of Louisiana had let Amande go, releasing her to Faye and Joe, who were not relatives and who lived two states away.

Perhaps she wasn't being fair to state child welfare systems. Louisiana had been wise enough to give Amande to her. She could only hope that Tennessee would be wise enough to do the right thing for Kali, although Faye couldn't swear that a scenario that was right for Kali even existed. The best thing for everybody was for Faye to stick to archaeology and let the social worker do what she'd been trained to do.

Thinking about the dark days when she and Joe weren't

sure Amande would ever be theirs, Faye needed very much to talk to her husband. Actually, she needed to see him, and thank God, there was a device in her pocket that would have been futuristic not so very many years before. She pulled out her phone and put in a video call to Joe.

Joe looked like he'd just gotten out of the shower, with his long hair, almost black, hanging around his strong-jawed Muscogee Creek face in wet tangles. He was saying, "Are you out of your mind?" Actually, he was kind of yelling it. Almost.

Joe's voice hurt her ear, and that said something about how upset he was. He never raised his voice. His next words underscored her husband's troubled state of mind.

"Get in your car and drive it home. I mean it, Faye."

Joe never told her what to do. Well, not too often. To be fair, he knew exactly how well it usually went for him when he tried it, but he also was not dictatorial by nature. Not even close. He was the gentlest soul Faye knew.

"Our company has a contract to fulfill," she reminded him. "With the state of Tennessee? Remember it? Do you want me to renege on that contract? If I do, we'll never work for the state of Tennessee again. And maybe not for any other government agencies. Those people talk to each other, Joe. You know that. Every time we compete for a job, they make us list our previous government contracts, on pain of perjury, so they can check our references. I can't just walk away."

"There won't be any more jobs if you get yourself killed. If all the government agencies in the world decide they won't work with us because you quit a job that was too damn dangerous, then that's the way it is. There was a murder, Faye."

"And it had nothing to do with this job."

Faye knew she was tiptoeing out on a flimsy limb with that statement, argumentatively speaking, because the dying woman had been found on the very land she'd been hired to study. Still, the job had nothing to do with Frida, and Frida had nothing to do with the job.

"I'm not stupid, Faye. You went to work this morning. First week on the job, I might add. You found a bleeding, dying woman, buried alive. Don't tell me it didn't have nothing to do with this job." Joe still wasn't quite yelling, but she could tell he wanted to.

"Fair enough. But remember that this morning was the last time for me to be here working alone. Jeremiah is bringing his crew of student workers. When McDaniel opens up the job site, hopefully soon, I'll be surrounded by young, strong people. Truly, Joe. I'll be okay."

"In the daytime, you'll be surrounded by people. What about at night?"

Faye was really not looking forward to spending her first night after finding Frida alone in her cabin. Joe knew exactly which of her buttons to push, but she pretended that he was wrong.

"Why should I be afraid? I'll still be surrounded by all those young, strong, enthusiastic young people. That's the best part of this job, remember? The client is putting us up in a block of state park cabins, for free. Fully furnished. Full kitchens. Jeremiah's planning nightly campfires. I've been in my beautiful cabin all week and it's like being on vacation."

"You live on an island with a beach and three boats. I build you nightly campfires. How is this better?"

"Um, it's not? But I'm bringing in a paycheck. And you know we need that check."

"It scares me to think of you being alone there."

"Everybody I've met has been very nice." *They've also been scared to death of all the men the poor dead woman ever dated or married, but never mind that.*

"You haven't met everybody. And also, did you forget that I can see you? And where you are?"

Faye turned around and looked behind her. The two houses that were serving as the backdrop for her video chat both sported heavy bars on every window. The tall man walking in front of them wore a tank top exposing arms that were fully inked. His tattoos had the simple, brutalistic look of ink gotten in prison. His tall mohawk swayed in the wind. She didn't believe in judging people by the way they looked, but she was pretty sure this guy would still be scary if he were tattooless, mohawk-less, and dressed for Sunday School.

"Does your cabin have bars like that on the windows?"

"It has a deadbolt, just like any hotel room, and I use it. I'll be careful, Joe. I promise."

She hung up the phone and went looking for McDaniel. She hated to betray Kali's trust, but it was time to tell him everything the little girl had said. The detective needed all the help he could get to find the killer who took her mother away from her.

# Chapter Fourteen

"So you're telling me that Kali was a witness. To the killing? To the burial? Both? Was she there when you found her mother?"

Walt Walker and Reverend Atkinson had left. Faye and McDaniel were standing in the street in front of Laneer's house, giving the bereaved family a little time to regroup, but McDaniel was making good use of the time by grilling Faye. She could tell that the hot afternoon sun was bothering him.

McDaniel had the sandy-haired, florid look of a man who had spent too much time at a golf course. Or on the back of a tractor. Or at a bar. It was hard to tell.

"I want to be clear about this," Faye said. "She didn't tell me anything that would give me the answers to your questions. I don't even know for sure that she was there. All she did was ask me to tell her what happened to her mother. I think it's significant that she picked me, that's all. Why would she do that unless she knew I was the one who found Frida, and how could she know that unless she was there? And also, don't forget the ice cream sandwich."

The sweater she'd borrowed from Sylvia was scratchy, and Frida's pants were tight. Faye wanted nothing more than to go back to her cabin, douse herself with shower water, and put on clothes that belonged to her.

McDaniel rubbed at the pink skin on his face and made it pinker. "None of that means anything, not really, especially not the damn ice cream sandwich that could've been left by the killer, for all we know. A half-decent defense attorney would pick everything you just said to shreds. Maybe she picked you because she thought you were a pushover who'd be more likely to answer her questions without asking any of your own. Maybe she picked you because she doesn't trust police, and she thinks Laneer and Sylvia are too old to be of much use. Maybe she just likes you. Did you think of that? Maybe she feels like she can trust you."

He stared at Faye just long enough to make her uncomfortable. Finally, she said, "And?"

"And nothing. I was just thinking that you're the kind of person that people trust at first sight. Steady eyes. Quiet voice. And you ask the right questions."

This was a far cry from the borderline suspicion that McDaniel had directed her way just hours before. She may have made a bad first impression on him, but his second impression must have been amazing. Her first impression of him had not changed. He seemed competent and hardworking, but she didn't trust him as far as she could throw him.

"She can't possibly mistrust Laneer," she said. "Nor Sylvia. They obviously love that child and she knows it."

"Sure, but imagine yourself growing up surrounded by people whose whole lives have been hard times. Maybe they'll be able to pay this month's bills, easy. Or maybe the car will bust a belt, and fixing it won't leave enough money to pay the light bill. The car takes your mom to work, so the money goes to fix it and the lights get cut off. Even while you all sat together in the dark, you'd know they loved you, but—" He spread his hands, palms up.

"But everything in your life would feel insecure." Faye tried to imagine her childhood without the rock-solid stability of her mother and grandmother, not to mention their ability to always find a way to pay the bills. She couldn't.

"Exactly. The whole world is an insecure place for a child who's dependent on somebody like Frida—sweet, but maybe not real savvy about the way the world works. Now, just look at yourself. You've never once had your phone cut off for nonpayment, have you?"

Faye had spent some time living off the grid, but for all the years she'd had bills to pay, she'd been able to pay them, so she gave him a truthful answer. "No."

"And it shows."

"How can my credit rating possibly show?"

He spread his hands again. "I can't explain how, but it does. I agree with you. It's significant that Kali chose you to ask about her mother. Still, I don't want to read too much into it." He ran a hand through the stubble of his buzz cut hair. "It may just be that Kali saw a woman of color, full of the kind of confidence that she doesn't see a whole lot, and she instinctively reached out to you for help."

Faye felt suddenly guilty for having always been able to cover her phone bill. This guilt made no sense at all.

"Is there anything else I need to know, Dr. Longchamp-Mantooth?"

Faye knew that Laneer wanted her to keep the next bit of information to herself, but she just couldn't do it. McDaniel needed to know. "I understand that Kali left Laneer's house this morning about daybreak."

"You understand this? Are you saying it that way so that you don't have to tell me who's keeping important evidence quiet?"

Faye shrugged. "In conjunction with the ice cream sandwich, I think it means that Kali might have seen something, so I thought you should know. I don't think she'll talk to you, though."

McDaniel's face was so flushed that it had passed pink and gone straight to red.

"Detective, I think she told me all that she's willing to tell anybody. If you try to lean on her, it'll only make things worse."

"You don't think I know how to talk to little girls? I have nieces."

"That's beside the point. I just think that this little girl has said all she's going to say. And maybe she's said all she knows. If you push her too hard, you'll never get her to open up."

"We'll see," he said, but she noticed that he changed the subject. "Did Laneer and Sylvia say anything else that I should know?"

"Make sure they give you a full list of Frida's terrifying boyfriends. Seriously. They told me about them, and I'm still shaking in my boots. While you're doing that, I'm going to go to my cabin and lock the door until you find the one who did this."

"That's sensible. Unless you'd prefer to run for home. That would also be sensible."

Faye shook her head. "I'll be fine, as long as I don't spook myself tonight, sitting alone in my fancy cabin."

"Those are nice cabins where the state's putting you and your crew up. Brand-new and ready to rent. After you all leave, people are going to pay good money to stay there."

"They'll be building more soon. That's why I'm here. They want me to check out the building site and make sure they won't be destroying anything historically interesting when they break ground. That's presuming I ever get a chance to start this job."

He stuck out a hand and shook hers. "Give me and my forensic people till Monday with the crime scene to look for evidence, then you're free to start excavating, okay? Unless we find something that changes things, obviously. Will that cramp your style too much?"

"I've got some things for them to do at the museum and the library. Keeping my crew busy will be a trick, but I'll manage." She turned to go, but he stopped her with a word.

"Faye." He started to speak, then caught himself short. Clearing his throat to cover the awkwardness, he said, "I mean Dr. Longchamp-Mantooth."

"You can call me Faye."

"Thanks, Faye. I'd say you should call me Harold, but nobody does. They just say McDaniel, which I like better because it doesn't sound like somebody's grandfather."

"McDaniel works for me."

"Look, do you even know how to get back to your car?"

She laughed. "Actually, no."

"Let me take you."

As she settled herself in his passenger seat, McDaniel cranked the engine, eyes straight ahead. He kept them straight ahead as he steered it slowly down a city street pocked with potholes and lined with a network of cracks. The people who owned the houses on either side of this street paid taxes like everybody else, and Faye got more pissed off on their behalf every time the car's suspension screamed in pain.

McDaniel drove for a while without speaking. When he did speak, it was slowly, as if he was choosing his words carefully. "If you think of anything else, or if Kali tells you anything else, you'll tell me? I'm willing to give the two of you some space, because I know she'll say things to you that she'd never say to me. So will Laneer and Sylvia. They all will."

"Because you're a cop and I'm not?"

"That's part of it."

"And the other part?"

Silence settled over a man who didn't want to say out loud what he was thinking.

She spoke for him. "Is it because you're white and I'm not?"

"You said it. I didn't. But anybody with eyes can see that I'm in the minority here. On any given workday, I might not cross paths with a solitary soul who looks like me. I don't blame them for mistrusting me. Honest. I don't. But it keeps me from doing my job, and my job is to help people."

Faye wanted to say that starting from a presumption of innocence might help, but she didn't want to remind him about his harsh treatment of her that morning. They seemed to be getting along better and she didn't want to spoil it. She wanted to be on good terms with the person who was trying to get justice for Frida. And for Kali.

"Do you want something from me?" she asked. "It sure sounds like it."

He took his own sweet time to answer her. They were nearing the parking lot where she'd left her car, and he stayed silent until he'd steered his own car into the slot beside it. Then he was silent for another moment. Faye used the time to look around at the beautiful trees. It had been early morning when she'd last seen them and it was only afternoon now, but they had lost their hazy beauty. She knew that they were no different than they'd been when she last saw them, leafy and green, but she was a different person now. She'd done her best to save someone who needed her, and she'd failed.

"I'm not asking you to do anything dishonest or unethical, Faye. I don't want you to do anything out of the ordinary. I'm just telling you that this is a case where doing your duty as a citizen is pretty damn important. That child, for whatever reason, is willing to talk to you. My guess is that her community will be a lot more willing to talk to you than to me. And, yes, it's because of the color of your skin. So shoot me for saying so."

Faye started to interrupt him, but he held up his hand, asking her wordlessly to hear him out.

"I can't emphasize this enough. Don't go playing detective like someone who's watched too much TV. Don't run around questioning suspects and, for God's sake, don't poke around in the business of dangerous people. But I get the sense that you're not going to walk away from Kali, or even Laneer and Sylvia. If one of them tells you something that might help me crack this case, remember that I am asking you personally to help me do that. Bring me the information and then get out of the way, because there are dangerous people around us."

Faye remembered Frida's injuries and said, "No kidding."

"Get me any information you can, but beyond that? Stay safe. Please."

Faye noticed as McDaniel backed out that he was angling his car so that he had a good view of her car door as she unlocked it. Then he lingered while she tucked her purse under the passenger seat, started the car, put it in gear, and backed out.

• • ● • •

Faye's nutritional choices weren't always the best, and today she was feeling downright self-destructive. It was mid-afternoon, she'd had a hellish day, and she was hungry. She wanted a greasy piece of pizza and she wanted a Hershey bar and she wanted a frosty can of Coca-Cola, and she wanted them immediately.

She'd seen a convenience store at the corner where Kali's street met a bustling, four-lane thoroughfare, and she knew it was where Frida's exes, Mayfield and Linton, worked. The place hadn't looked like much, but it would sell her everything she needed, and she could drive there in minutes.

Kali's neighborhood wasn't so far from the urban center of Memphis, but each house was on a small lot with a grassy lawn and trees, and the creek snaking through those lots added a bit of natural beauty. The downside of having enough room for grass and trees was that the houses and business were more widely spaced than they would have been in the center of a city. Faye pictured trying to live in this neighborhood without a car, then she tried to remember if there had been a car in front of Frida's house. Faye judged that it might take an hour to get downtown on a bus and another to get back. If Frida, a single mother of a small child, had done that every day, then her life was one notch harder than Faye had been imagining.

She saw the convenience store on her left, just as she remembered, and pulled into the parking lot. No other cars were parked there, so no one would witness her suicidal food choices but the person who sold them to her. Good. Now she was inspired to make her pizza a Meat-Lover's Special.

She put her car in park and stepped out onto broken, oil-stained pavement. The air smelled like diesel and old garbage, so she hurried to get inside.

The battered door was located between two plate glass windows covered by bars. When she opened it, a bell sounded, and the clerk magically appeared at a cash register where no one had been before. She passed a magazine rack as she made her way to the register, which made her wonder whether this was where Kali got her inappropriate reading material. She didn't like to think of the little girl being in the same room as the silent clerk, who was completely creeping Faye out. He watched her, wordless, as she gathered the candy and soda she wanted. His nametag said that his name was Linton.

Actually, "watched" wasn't really the word for what he did. He was eyeballing her. His eyes rolled over her face and down her body, and they took way too long to do it.

Customer service didn't seem to be high on his priority list, so there would be no "Good morning!" or "How can I help you?" coming from this guy. Faye had never before wished for a long line at the check-out counter, but she wanted one today to ensure that she was not alone with this man. She broke the silence with a chipper "Here you go!" as she laid her purchases on a counter covered with taped-on lottery ads.

The man's muscles bulged under his work uniform and his head was shaved slick-bald. When she ordered her Meat-Lover's Special, he reached without looking into a display case full of pizza waiting under a heating element. Head still down but eyes on her, he dragged the soda can toward him. It left a damp trail of condensation on the countertop. He scanned the soda's bar code, then dragged the candy bar through the can's damp trail. During the entire transaction, he only spoke once, and that was to ask for her payment.

She handed him a credit card. Somehow, she wasn't surprised when he violated the retail worker's cardinal boundary by touching her bare hand with his. His close-clipped fingernails tracked the length of her first two fingers as he withdrew his hand too slowly.

Faye quickly pulled her own hand back, forcing him to lay her card on the counter when he returned it. When the transaction was done, she collected her money and fled, wishing that Joe were beside her. She hated herself for that wish, not because she wasn't missing her husband's company, but because she had always resisted anything that impinged on her independence and she always would.

Today's argument wasn't the first one she'd had with Joe about this job. The contracted amount wasn't big enough to support both their salaries, so having him join her had never been on the table. Still, she'd been unprepared for him to insist that he didn't want her to go without him. Joe had never once wavered in treating his wife like an equal, so she hadn't known how to respond when this demand came from out of the blue.

"You're telling me what to do? How Victorian," she'd said, but he hadn't backed down.

"Memphis is one of the most dangerous cities in America. I looked it up."

"Sometimes I wish I hadn't taught you to use the Internet."

She had regretted that comment immediately. Faye had always been better than Joe at things like books and school, but this had never been an issue in their marriage. He had knowledge and skills that she didn't, and she was truly happy that she'd been able to help him overcome the learning disabilities that had come between him and a formal education. She had never lorded her PhD over Joe and she didn't intend to start now, so she had immediately blurted out, "I didn't mean that." Then she had pressed her lips together to squelch the other unkind comments bumping around inside her.

"Well, the cat's out of Pandora's box," he'd said, mixing his metaphors but succeeding in his goal of reminding her that he did now have an education that included Greek mythology. "I've gotten real good at the Internet and I looked up the part of Memphis where this job is. Don't go. We don't need the money that bad."

She'd said, "We need it bad enough," which was true. She hadn't said, "I've been independent too long to let you tell me what to do, so you've forced my hand. Now I have to go."

But she'd thought it, and it was true. And now here she was, alone in a convenience store parking lot in one of the most dangerous parts of one of America's most dangerous cities.

By the time Faye unlocked her car door, she was no longer the only person around. Someone was walking up the street. He walked closer to her than she liked as she opened her car door, but he didn't look her way as she got in. She quickly locked the door, chagrined to think that he was hearing the loud thunk of her automatic locks, but not chagrined enough to sit unprotected so near a man with such an angry face.

He wore a nametag like the one pinned to the shirt of the man who had just groped her hand while selling her a slice of pizza. It said that his name was Mayfield.

She'd seen Mayfield before, walking down Kali's street. She recognized the tattoos and the towering mohawk. Like Linton, the handsy convenience store clerk, he didn't bother to speak to her. But he looked, and he kept looking until she drove away.

# Chapter Fifteen

As Faye neared the campground where she would be staying with her crew, she noticed a nondescript gray-blue car driving behind her that she was virtually certain was McDaniel's. Had his route coincidentally overlapped with hers? How likely was that? Or had he maybe been following her ever since she got out of his car, waiting down the street while she bought an awful slice of pizza?

She'd never know for sure whether she'd had an unofficial bodyguard escorting her back to her cabin, but she was comforted by the thought, nonetheless. And also, it would make Joe happy to know there was a policeman looking out for her.

No, it wouldn't. It would completely freak him out to know that a detective, who would absolutely have a feel for how much danger she was in, had thought she *needed* to be protected.

She did know one thing for sure. Nothing on Earth could coerce her into telling Joe about her conversation with McDaniel or about the straightforward bluntness an experienced detective had used to describe the danger surrounding her.

Jeremiah and his crew were already at the campground, moving in. He met her at the car, saying, "We set up the clotheslines and the camp stoves close to your cabin, but kept the campfire far enough away so the noise won't disturb you."

Jeremiah was a big guy, with big hands, big feet, big ears standing out straight beneath his close-cropped black hair, and a big mouth. He grabbed her duffel bag and jerked his head in the direction of her cabin. Faye didn't stop him, but she also didn't really need help carrying her gear. Years in the field had taught her to travel light. The heaviest thing she carried was her bargain-sized jug of sunscreen.

"I've hired you some great kids, Dr. Longchamp-Mantooth. Smart, enthusiastic, strong, funny. You'll like them. And energy? We've been staying in the university dorms for a week while they did their training, and I learned on Day One that I had to make plans for the evening or they'd do it for me. I didn't spend all the training budget you gave me, because I wrote my own teaching materials instead of buying books, so I used what I saved to take them to movies in the evenings. I hope that was okay?"

Jeremiah really should have asked permission for that kind of budget-juggling. Faye would have said yes, but still. She held her tongue, though, because she admired his initiative, even while she wished he was a bit more respectful of the chain of command. She was also a little dizzied by the force of Jeremiah's personality and the amount of information he was dumping on her.

"We grocery-shopped on the way here. Hot dogs were on sale, so I had enough left in the food budget for marshmallows, chocolate, and graham crackers. That'll keep 'em busy in the evenings."

This was a bit of budget-juggling that Faye could totally

get behind. "I was wondering why you were planning to build campfires in this heat."

"Is it ever too hot for s'mores?"

The answer to that question, in Faye's mind, was a resounding, "Are you out of your mind? No!" and she said so.

She took her duffel bag from Jeremiah and said, "I need to shower. Badly. And I need to get my work clothes organized. You've told them where the laundromat is? After a week, they probably need to do some washing. I sure do."

Faye clutched Sylvia's cardigan shut to hide her ill-fitting clothes. She couldn't bring herself to talk about the reason she needed to shower and do laundry.

Jeremiah nodded that, yes, he'd shown his employees where the washers were, and Faye wasn't surprised. Anyone with Jeremiah's over-the-top level of organization had surely given them a thorough tour of the campground as soon as he parked the ancient sedan he used to carry them around. Faye was spoiled, because she usually had the unobtrusively efficient Joe as an assistant, but Jeremiah seemed more than up to the task.

It had made sense for Joe to stay home and tend the children and the garden. He might even get the porch painted before she got home. She didn't like being forced by finances to do this job without him, but it looked like Jeremiah and his contract employees had been a good choice for hired help who could get this job done.

Faye had rather enjoyed watching Jeremiah herd his young charges through dinner, barking orders and cracking jokes with every breath. He had pooh-poohed the camp stove, insisting that they roast their hot dogs on sharp sticks over the campfire while he pulled ketchup, mustard, relish, and mayonnaise out of his cabin's refrigerator.

She'd laughed out loud when he had handed a rangy twenty-something named Richard an onion and a paring knife and told him to chop. Richard, who wore his long hair natural and who also wore a perpetual smile, had set the onion on a picnic table, then stood studying it with his knife pointed at its papery, golden-brown skin.

His friends were enjoying the fact that Richard had no kitchen skills.

"You gotta peel the thing."

"Seriously. Just pick it up and start cutting."

"Dude. It won't bite you."

Faye had a hand reached out to help him when Jeremiah swooped in with a cutting board, spouting instructions at a million words per minute.

"Y'all, Richard's going to cry. He just is. That's what onions make you do. Nobody look. He'll be okay."

A few minutes later, Richard was setting a platter of chopped onions beside the relish, and Jeremiah was chatting up a woman about Richard's age. Her head was crowned with spiraling braids that made Faye catch her breath at the thought of Frida.

"Stephanie," Jeremiah said, "don't you laugh at Richard and his onions. We're having burgers tomorrow and we'll need onions again. You're next!"

Jeremiah's nonprofit hired young people with challenges and helped them develop marketable skills. For this job, he'd brought community college students, ages eighteen through twenty-two. Ordinarily, Faye would be muttering about the wisdom of training anyone to be an archaeology field tech with some misguided notion that it would be a path out of poverty. The job didn't pay so very well, to put it mildly, not when you considered the wear-and-tear on the body. In this case, she wasn't as crotchety about the effectiveness of this program, and the reason was Jeremiah.

She'd seen the curriculum for the training session he'd just put her new hires through, and she approved. He'd taught them how to handle the tools of her trade, but he'd also taught them basic workplace skills. She remembered one line from his syllabus clearly: "Show up on time. Don't yell at anybody, especially your boss."

Before she'd started her own business, she wouldn't have thought anybody needed to be told that. She would have been wrong. Faye had fired a lot of people whose background would never have been labeled "disadvantaged," just because they couldn't manage those simple things. If Richard, Stephanie, and the others listened to Jeremiah, they'd be ending their summer with a glowing recommendation letter from Faye. And so would Jeremiah.

Jeremiah had even taken them to a bank and helped them open bank accounts where their paychecks would be deposited. He'd done a budgeting lesson that had taught them how the money for their project flowed, but Faye had been able to read between the lines. Jeremiah was also teaching them to handle their own money.

In every interaction the man had with these young people, there was only one message: "Succeed and prosper!" Faye liked that approach very much.

When it came time for marshmallow-toasting, Jeremiah's charges grew quiet, focused on bringing their marshmallows to the perfect shade of brown, then sandwiching them between graham crackers and chocolate for optimum gooeyness.

"You're gonna get 'em sugared up. They're younger than we are. I'm not sure we can keep up with them," Faye said.

"We can't. No doubt about it. But I worked them hard today," Jeremiah said, raking a string of dried marshmallow off his cheek. "They'll sleep."

She pointed at each of the techs in turn. "I see Richard. And there's Stephanie. You can't miss her with that gorgeous hair. What about the woman talking to her, the one with the red buzz cut? Is that Ayesha?"

"You got it."

She pointed at the woman next to Ayesha. "The tall woman with the amazing green eyes is Yvonna, right?"

"Yep."

"And the young man with the muscles and the tattoo on his hand that looks like a knot? Remind me of his name? I remember that it's almost like David, but not quite."

"You have a good memory. His name is Davion. He says the tattoo is a west African symbol for wisdom."

"Nice choice! If I were ever going to get a tattoo, I might get that. To be honest, though? I've been moving dirt for so long that my shoulders are wrecked and my neck isn't much better. Tattoos hurt and I hurt enough already. I'm probably going to stay ink-less."

Faye bit into the s'more and the world took on a rosy glow. She could have sworn she felt the pain in her neck ebb a little. Maybe marshmallows should be a controlled substance, but she sure hoped the FDA never figured that out.

"Take a look at these people. They're gonna do good work for you," said Jeremiah, holding his arms outstretched at his sides like a minister blessing his flock. "I promise. And when they're happy, well-adjusted, educated adults, you'll have the pleasure of knowing that you gave them their first job."

"Me and the state of Tennessee."

He raised his no-name brand root beer, purchased cheap so the food budget would allow for the marshmallows that Faye and her aching neck were loving so devoutly. "To the state of Tennessee!"

She raised her own root beer and drank deeply. It had been a long, hard day, and it had taken her an inordinately long time to scrub the memory of Frida's blood off her body. She was ready to sleep.

Tomorrow was Saturday, and even though it was the weekend, she had planned to spend at least a half-day both days orienting her new crew and getting the project started—and also keeping them busy and burning off their youthful energy. But Detective McDaniel had told her that it would be at least two days before he would release the crime scene, so now she had a problem. How was she going to keep these people busy and productive until then?

The museum director had helped Faye and Jeremiah put together a museum tour that should be fun. It would get them prepared for hands-on archaeology, and they'd get the ego boost that comes with seeing things that mere tourists don't get to see. That would take care of Saturday, or most of it.

On Sunday, she guessed she could take them to the university library to pore over several piles of books and documents detailing what was already known about the site.

Would these things hold the attention of five energetic young people who were itching to put their hands in the dirt? Faye was doubtful.

As she racked her brain for more options, Jeremiah's phone sounded. Giving her an apologetic glance, he walked away to take the call.

Faye sat in silence, watching the young people set their marshmallows aflame, then run around with them held high like torches. They were having so much fun doing something so simple, but none of them had ever done it before. Nevertheless, once Jeremiah had shown them how to strip a green stick of leaves and stick a marshmallow on the end, they were instant marshmallow-toasting experts. When Faye thought of all the other simple pleasures they'd probably missed, she wanted to cry, but she figured her energy was better spent making a grocery list that said, "Buy more marshmallows."

Quick footsteps sounded behind her and she turned around. It was Jeremiah, and he was crying.

"Why didn't you tell me?"

Jeremiah had shape-shifted into a different man. The cheerful, almost goofy, big kid was gone. In its place was a towering man who was both grief-stricken and angry.

"What? Tell you what?"

"Why didn't you tell me about Frida? Why didn't you tell me that she was the dead woman you found?"

"Wait. You know Frida?" She corrected herself, awkward and miserable. "You knew Frida? Memphis is a big town. It didn't occur to me that you would know her."

"Know her? I loved her. I—" He closed his eyes, shook his head, kept shaking it.

"You loved her? Oh, Jeremiah."

"That was a silly thing for me to say. It was middle school. We were just kids. Children. But—oh, God, when I think about what happened to her…"

He bowed his head and wept. Their five young charges noticed and the loud shenanigans stopped dead.

Faye answered the question in their eyes. "He just found out that someone close to him passed away."

Richard lowered the long, graceful hand that held up his flaming marshmallow, blowing it out. "Frida?"

"You knew Frida, too?" Faye said. "I didn't know any of you were from Memphis." It didn't make sense to her that people who lived just a few miles away would be sleeping here at the campground instead of in their own beds. "If I'd realized any of you might have known her, I wouldn't have been so quiet about her death. I just…I guess I wanted us to get to know each other without that shadow hanging over us. We can talk about it, if you all want to."

Richard spoke up. "You weren't wrong. We're not from around here. Davion's from Kingsport. Ayesha's from Chattanooga. The rest of us are from Nashville or thereabouts. But my family's from Memphis and we came here every summer when I was a kid. Frida was older, but all my cousins were friends with her, so I knew her pretty well. She just lived one street over from my grandma, on the same side of the creek."

Jeremiah wiped the tears off his cheeks and said, "It's a big neighborhood, but not that big. People know each other and they care."

Richard nodded. "Yeah. They do."

Jeremiah turned his head away to wipe his cheeks again. He kept his face turned away as he talked, as if that would somehow hide the fact that he was crying and everybody knew it. "That's why I run this program the way I do. The kids get work skills that they can take to a job back home, wherever home is. They may want to move away from Nashville or Chattanooga or Kingsport, or they may not, but I don't want them to have to move. Not if they don't want to go. I didn't. I still live two blocks from my parents, but I've got this job that I made for myself. It pays the bills, it lets me live where I want to live, and I only have to leave if I want to. Everybody should have that choice."

Jeremiah gave up trying to hide the tears. He turned toward the others and let them flow. "Frida should've had that choice," he said his voice rising until it cracked. "She tried. She really did, but life kept throwing boulders at her."

He hurried away, disappearing into his cabin. The others moved away in a clump, muttering among themselves.

Faye's snack was cold. The gelid marshmallows had mingled with the soft, cool chocolate, and the graham crackers were getting soft. Thinking of children who would never toast a marshmallow in their lives, Faye threw away the sticky mess and went to bed.

# Chapter Sixteen

As the dark night pressed in through windows so big that they let in all the outdoors, Faye looked around her cabin from the comfort of her freshly made bed. She wished Kali had such a nice place to live. The cabin was brand-new and immaculate, with pine floors and pine-paneled walls. It was built for a vacationing family, a big one. It had a full kitchen with a full-sized refrigerator, not to mention two bedrooms that she wasn't even using. The bedrooms were furnished with bunk beds, and the sofa in the living area had a pull-out couch.

Too bad she was going to have to leave it. She was going to have to take Jeremiah and his crew of happy young people away from the campfire and the s'mores and the fresh air, because they weren't safe here.

The day stretched out behind her forever, from her futile attempts to save Frida's life to this moment. It was only now that Faye had enough silence to focus. It was only now that she could see the truth.

It made absolutely no sense for her to keep her crew in this lovely—not to mention free—place, not when an unsolved murder of exceptional violence had just happened a few miles away, on the far side of this self-same park. She had to take these people someplace safer.

Like anyone who hadn't grown up with a lot of money, Faye was a cheapskate at heart. When she added that natural cheapness to her natural talent for crawling the Internet, she was capable of googling up some screaming deals. Already, her computer sat on her lap, open to a travel website offering a seriously screaming deal. She'd found a hotel so desperate to rent its rooms that she could afford to house herself, Jeremiah, and all five of their field techs for the duration of the project.

Given the circumstances, the state of Tennessee might be willing to pony up the added expense, but she could manage it if they didn't. Her profit margin would be wafer-thin, but that was a small price to pay for the safety of the people in her care.

Her budget allowed for three rooms, and the fairest way to divide them seemed to Faye to be two women in the first room, two in the second, and all three men in the third. Stephanie, Yvonna, and Ayesha would be flipping a coin to see who got the unpleasant assignment of sharing a room with the boss. The other two women would share the second room, and Jeremiah, Davion, and Richard would flip another coin to see who slept on the roll-out bed in the third room. Nobody would be comfortable, and Faye's inner introvert was screaming at the loss of privacy, but this was what she could afford. If she were a killer, she'd go looking for someone vulnerable and alone, so she was actually doing everyone a favor by cramming them into such tight spaces. Her employees would survive the loss of these beautiful cabins, and so would Faye. She made the reservation and fowarded the details to Joe.

Faye, in particular, had no excuse for complaining.

When the project was done, she'd go back to occupying an entire island with her family of four. She could certainly stand living in a crowd until then. She just wasn't sure she could stand the stress of this one night, knowing that Frida's killer was out there somewhere, perhaps close by.

Without thinking, she picked up her phone and dialed McDaniel's number. When he answered, it took her a moment to clear her overstressed mind and realize why she'd called.

"I forgot to tell you something that Kali said. When I asked her if she saw who killed her mother, she said, 'It was dark.' That got me to thinking. I don't know how tightly you've been able to establish a time for the attack, but it was just getting to be daylight when I found Frida. Unless the killer was working with a flashlight, there had to be a little light during the attack, so it had to happen between the first few minutes of sunup and the half-light when I found her. Maybe you've got astronomers or meteorologists or something who can tell you what time that was. I was too busy to look at my watch, so it's not like I can give you the time to the minute."

"I've got the time of your 911 call."

"Back up from that call a few minutes and you'll know when I heard the footsteps. The attack had to have happened after dawn and before that time. Maybe that will give you something to go on."

"I'll do that. I appreciate the thought you're putting put into this."

Faye didn't answer right away. Then she let the silence hang longer than she'd intended.

"Faye? Is there something else?"

"I've found a hotel for my crew over near Beale Street. It's far enough away from where Frida died that I can pretend that we're safe. Tonight, though…" She drew a deep breath. "Tonight, we're too close to the place where it happened and that scares me. Would you have somebody drive past our cabins now and then? Just to check things out?"

She didn't say, "Since I think you followed me here to make sure I was safe, maybe you won't mind doing me one more favor." If he did indeed follow her, he knew it.

"There will be officers out all night, looking for the person who did this to Frida," McDaniel said. "It will be no trouble at all for them to swing through the campground from time to time. Maybe get out of the car while they're there. Walk around and check things out. That would make anybody lurking in the bushes think again, don't you think? You okay?"

"Yeah, I'm okay. Well, I'm okay when I'm not thinking of Frida. Or Kali. Or of Laneer and Sylvia and Jeremiah. Or of the person who did those terrible things. Which is to say, never."

"Only a sociopath could rest easy after seeing what you saw this morning. But you should close your eyes and try to rest anyway. First, though, draw your drapes. There are going to be a lot of officers of the law driving around outside your window. I'll make sure of it. I wouldn't want their headlights to keep you up."

• ● ● ● •

By two a.m., Faye was not missing her privacy. She was thinking that maybe she never wanted to be alone again. She was wishing for the company of two or three lively young women. Stephanie, Ayesha, and Yvonna could have hopped on her bed to eat crackers and talk about their love lives for hours, and she would have been perfectly okay with that.

Heck. Why limit the companions at her imaginary slumber party to the women on her crew? At this time of a dark, scary night, Faye would have been happy for Richard, Davion, and Jeremiah to crowd in with them while they all ate crackers and talked about boyfriends and girlfriends and whatever else young adults talked about these days. Cell phone plans, maybe?

Faye would have been happy to see them all. A cabin that is delightfully isolated at noon can be a lonely place when the clock ticks past midnight.

With every hour that passed, the shadows in the corners of Faye's bedroom grew darker and the rustlings outside her window grew louder. Her hand kept reaching for the phone, aching to tap Joe's number, but she couldn't let herself admit to him that she was scared. It had been less that twenty-four hours since she had rejected his request (demand?) for her to come home, which he had made because he was scared. If she made that call and heard his quiet, comforting voice, she would cave. Before breakfast, she would be on a highway going south.

Nope. Crime statistics were clear, and she knew them because she had looked them up. Something like two-thirds of murdered women in America are killed by an intimate partner, and the statistics are even worse for black women like Frida. What is more, only ten percent of murdered American women are killed by strangers. It was overwhelmingly likely that Frida was killed by someone she knew, and it was overwhelmingly likely that her killer had no interest in killing someone he didn't know. Specifically, he had no interest in killing Faye, since she knew almost none of the people in the woman's life.

Nevertheless, Faye had gotten out of bed twice in an hour, once to jam a chair under the cabin's front doorknob and again to jam a second chair beneath the knob of her bedroom door. Now she was eyeing her bedroom window, the entry point for the rustles and grunts made by every nocturnal animal in Memphis. Should she move her bed in front of the window, letting the headboard block most of the opening? Or would that cut off her escape if somebody homicidal made it past both of her inexpertly blocked doors?

As much as she tried to herd her wandering mind onto safer paths, she found herself reliving the moment she had laid eyes on Frida's face. The memory took her back to the moments afterward that she had spent freeing a living woman from the earth, feeling flesh under her hands and cold dirt under her knees.

The wordless groaning of a mortally injured woman crawled back into her ears. It had never left her ears, not really. Every time Faye laid her head on her pillow, she heard Frida's suffering voice.

# Chapter Seventeen

*It had been almost a full day, and still the police hadn't shown up at his door.*

*He'd been doing this for years without getting caught. By now, it was reasonable to assume that he never would, because he was that good at what he did.*

*His cool façade covered a careful attention to detail. Rubber gardening gloves contained his fingerprints, and they kept his skin oils and DNA off the women's bodies. If rape had interested him, he would have had more trouble keeping his DNA to himself, but no. Physical intimacy could never compare to the rush of locking eyes with a woman who knew to her soul that he was preparing to take every single minute she had left.*

*He was obsessive about containing their hands, so he had a perfect record of staying out of reach of his victims' razor-sharp nails. The trick was to incapacitate the woman fast, leaving her alive but unable to do a damn thing to save herself from the grave already waiting.*

*A rain jacket with tight-drawn hood kept him from leaving behind a stray hair or flake of dandruff. The jacket's surface, slick and waterproof, didn't absorb blood, so it was easy to clean. So were the high-topped rubber boots and the water-repellent hiking pants.*

*Not that he needed to clean any of his stuff very much. From the distance of a shovel handle, he usually managed to stay clear of spatter, and the shovel blade itself was easily cleaned. Most of the blood came off while he was shoveling dirt over the still-warm corpse.*

*As the investigation cooled down, everything would leave his house, one piece at a time. Freshly washed with bleach, it would all be donated to charity or packed into garbage bags thrown deep into far-flung dumpsters. He got rid of the shovels quickly, after taking a sledgehammer to them. He'd gotten very good at making it look like they were going to the dump because they had finished their useful lives. As far as he was concerned, they had.*

*All of this care didn't mean that there wasn't a dangerous window when the police might show up with a search warrant. He was smart enough to understand that he could never know when his tools were clean enough to fool a lab. The answer to that question was "Probably never."*

*It was far more important to fool the people doing the investigation. Evading their attention was what he did best. If they never got close enough to his trail to send evidence out for testing, then how could their forensics labs ever uncover the truth?*

*After a kill, while the police were trying and failing to find him, his nervous itch had always subsided for a while. He could live for weeks, months sometimes, on the lingering thrill. It distracted him from the paycheck that was too small and the bills that were too large.*

*But not this time. He'd been robbed of the climax to Frida's murder. Another woman had come to save Frida, stealing his tender ritual of laying his victim's limp form in the grave. She had left him hungry, and he was dangerous when he was hungry.*

He had followed the interloper, lurking close enough to see the warmth in her dealings with Frida's little girl. The sight of Frida tenderly caring for a child was a trigger for him, and here it was again. Same child, different woman.

Still hungry, he stood in the shadow of a yet another tree, leaning on a shovel and watching the dim light of a lamp through the window of his new quarry's bedroom window… through Faye Longchamp-Mantooth's bedroom window. He knew her name now. Sylvia should really learn to keep her mouth shut, and she should really stop texting all the time. Because of Sylvia, the whole world knew that Faye Longchamp had come upon Frida's grave so quickly that the scent of his sweat must still have hung in the air.

It should have been easy to burst through her window and do what had to be done, but for the steady stream of marked police cars cruising through the campground. Tonight was not the night, but she could remember something incriminating at any time. She had to be silenced.

He hefted his shovel and faded into the woods, knowing that his chance would come soon enough.

# Chapter Eighteen

Frida never left Faye's mind, but work was always a distraction for her. She had thoroughly enjoyed their obvious glee as Ayesha, Stephanie, Richard, Davion, and Yvonna threw themselves into their morning in the museum's archaeology lab. Still, she was counting the hours until McDaniel released the crime scene and they could get started digging.

Dr. Nillsson, the rather staid matron who ran the museum, had greeted them by inviting them to use the lab's microscopes. They'd hung back for a moment, until Faye said, "You're not going to break them. They're made to be used," and that was all the reassurance the young people had needed. The five of them had whiled away an hour checking out the chipped edges of a collection of stone points, having so much fun that Faye was pretty sure they'd forgotten they were working.

Then they'd enjoyed the outdoor exhibits, basically freaking out over the garden where museum staff grew traditional food and medicinal plants.

"You're saying that I can chew on this stick and make a toothache go away?" Yvonna said. "Get out." Then she'd chewed on the stick until her mouth was too numb to talk right.

The vegetables in the museum's teaching garden reminded Faye of Laneer's front-yard vegetable patch, and that reminded her of Kali. She wondered if the girl had started talking to Laneer and Sylvia again. If not, it hurt her to think of the girl sitting in silence, just because there was only one person she was willing to talk to and that person was busy working with old stuff. She promised herself a visit to Kali later in the day.

Jeremiah gave all five students a sprig of mint to chew, then Davion noticed the nature trail leading to the thousand-year-old mounds that served as the centerpiece of the museum's grounds. The group's attention was diverted yet again. After touring the mounds at a run, they were back inside for the afternoon, and Faye was already exhausted. Jeremiah hadn't even broken a sweat.

"Check this out," he said, dragging her over to a large display. "The museum brought in a group of high-schoolers to build this exhibit about their own community. *Our* community."

This was the point where Faye fell in love with Dr. Nilsson. She knew how much dedication it had taken for the museum director to get funding for an exhibit that might seem unimportant to people accustomed to the Met's multi-billion-dollar collection. But those jaded museum-goers didn't grow up in places like the struggling neighborhoods of Memphis.

"Hey! My grandfather went to that high school," said Richard, pointing at a fading photograph.

"Mama says we're part Choctaw," Ayesha said as she peered at a collection of potsherds collected from the very creek where they'd be working.

Yvonna, Richard, and Stephanie stood in front of a display of album covers, listening to music recorded in

Memphis. The sounds seeped out around their earbuds, treating Faye to a heady mix of Beale Street blues, Elvis Presley rock 'n' roll, and Isaac Hayes funk.

The thumping bass of Hayes' music turned Faye's thoughts back to Kali again, and to Laneer, too. Everything seemed to remind her of Frida and her bereaved family.

"Jeremiah," she said, drawing close and letting the music cover her voice. "You're from around here. You knew Frida. You know the people who live here. Have you talked to any of them? Who do they think killed her?"

He hesitated in his answer. Instead of letting him gather his thoughts, which she knew was the polite approach, she pressed ahead. "Who do *you* think killed her?"

He was still slow in answering, but this time she didn't push him and he eventually spoke.

"No, I haven't had a chance to talk to anybody. Well, I'm on Sylvia's long list of people to gossip-text, but she hasn't said anything you don't already know. She's ready to lock up all of Frida's exes, and I can't say that I blame her, but that can't be a surprise to you. Other than Sylvia? I'm too busy with all this." He gestured at the five eager young archaeologists in his care.

"As for me?" he went on. "I don't like to think about it. I don't like to think that I know somebody who could do that to Frida. Even Linton. He slapped her once, yeah, and Kali saw it happen. It cost him his marriage. I will hate him forever for that. I—"

His voice broke. He cleared his throat and tried again. "I'm not going to pretend that I don't know a soul with a criminal record. I do. I wish I didn't know the past of everybody in my neighborhood, but I do. Their stories aren't all pretty. But mostly? We're talking drugs. Petty theft. Breaking-and-entering. Stuff like that."

Faye wasn't buying it. "You're telling me that nobody ever uses a gun or a knife when they do their breaking-and-entering or petty stealing? Nobody's dangerous? That seems like a stretch."

"Well, my stepbrother's doing time for pulling a gun on Mayfield at the corner store, which is damn stupid when you think about how little money Mayfield usually has in his drawer. Didn't pull the trigger, thank God, but that didn't keep him out of prison, not with a record like his. And he belongs in prison. He really does, because he's dangerous. But he's not beat-a-woman-to-death-for-no-good-reason dangerous. At least, I don't think so. Anyway, he didn't kill Frida, not when he's sitting in West Tennessee State Penitentiary."

Faye tried not to think about what it must be like to sit in a penitentiary, waiting for the years to go by. She watched the young people around her, learning to operate a microscope while they grooved to music that was older than they were, and she wondered if they were any older than Jeremiah's stepbrother.

"Just because he got caught, it doesn't mean that they all do," she pointed out.

"True. But here's something else for you to think about when you're judging who's dangerous and who's not. People are good at fooling themselves. If you could peel back their skulls and look inside their heads, how many people doing time in the pen really thought they were going to use that gun? Not many, I don't think. I think they see it as a shortcut."

Davion was back at one of the microscopes, using the hand with the wisdom tattoo to make a fine adjustment. Faye couldn't imagine a man his age living behind bars for years on end.

"A shortcut? You think they look at a gun and see a shortcut?"

"Yeah. I think most of them pick up a gun, believing it'll make all the people standing between them and some money just step aside. Like magic."

"Guns are magic? I guess maybe they are, when you want something that belongs to somebody else."

"I'm not saying it's right. My stepbrother belongs where he is. He could've killed somebody or got himself killed. That's why we have laws—to keep everybody alive. And hopefully happy. I'm just saying that I don't think many people leave the house thinking 'I'm gonna kill somebody today, and I'm gonna enjoy it.' That's who killed Frida. Somebody who doesn't think twice about anybody but themselves. Somebody who left his house that morning planning to kill somebody and enjoy doing it."

"Do you know anybody like that?"

"I certainly hope not. And I hope you don't, either."

# Chapter Nineteen

Three hours at the museum had proven to be the limit for Faye's crew. Attention spans waned and, as the morning passed, blood sugar levels dropped. Tempers frayed. When Stephanie leaned toward Davion, locked eyes with him, and deliberately flicked out a finger that knocked a twenty-five-hundred-year-old spear point out of his hand, Faye knew that it was time to go.

They all rode in Jeremiah's car, which was old enough to have bench seats in both front and back, complete with seat belts. Nothing else, short of a van or a big SUV, would have carried the whole crew, but this tank did. Faye had thought that he'd need her car to help with transporting personnel, but Jeremiah was a self-sufficient man.

Less than half an hour after Stephanie's spear-flicking move, they were standing in the parking lot of the motel that would be their new home. Faye had grown more depressed by the mile after they left the museum's verdant grounds. As they neared downtown, they sped past tourist-trap motels, chain restaurants, and strip malls for people desperate to shop. Spindly trees planted in parking lots were a sharp contrast to the trees they'd left behind, and it made Faye sad to look at them struggling to grow.

After parking their cars, Faye and Jeremiah headed toward the motel lobby to check in, and also to make a decision that might be the most important one of the day: Where were they going to eat lunch? Faye judged that the blood-sugar situation was growing dire, so this decision couldn't wait.

The aging motel had a generic two-story façade and overflowing trash cans on either side of a front door that creaked as they passed through it. The lone clerk was slow to answer the bell, giving Faye time to look around the small lobby, where dirty footsteps crisscrossed a floor covered with small gray 1980s-era tiles grouted in black. Dusty silk flowers decorated the counter where she waited. Faye could hear her grandmother's voice saying, "You get what you pay for."

Her heart fell when she thought of how happy her crew had been with their cabins, and their outdoor meals, and their burnt marshmallows. She'd taken a lot away from them when she'd decided to play it safe and move them here.

She handed over her credit card. As she waited for the clerk to make key cards for them all, Jeremiah asked, "Where do you want to eat?"

Faye had counted five overpriced and boring chain restaurants within an easy walk of the parking lot where her crew stood. Gesturing in their general direction, she said, "How much money did you save from the training budget? Can we afford to eat at any of these places?"

"Maybe, if we make them to stick to soup. But no worries! I know a barbecue joint, not too far from Beale Street. It's walking distance from here, and I get the family rate."

"You're related to the owner?"

"Not by blood, no. But that don't mean we ain't brothers. Armand and me? We go way back. Get me?"

"Armand? Didn't Frida—?"

An unidentifiable look flickered over Jeremiah's face. "Come to think of it, yeah. Frida started working for Armand a few months ago. Does that mean you wanna eat someplace else? It's not really fair for Armand to lose business because of what some asshole did to Frida."

"No, it's not. Let's go." Faye said this in a this-totally-doesn't-weird-me-out tone of voice, but there was a place at her center that was shaken to think of walking in the workaday steps of the woman she'd only known while she was dying.

She shook it off.

"You're telling me that Armand knows how to do barbecue right?"

"Massage the pig pieces with a dry rub. Cook it low and slow. Serve it just like you cooked it. No sauce. Ain't no other way to do it that's worth the time."

Joe, who was a fan of beef barbecued after a long marinade and served with lots of sauce, would have begged to differ, but Joe was not there.

Within minutes, Faye and the others were following Jeremiah toward Beale Street like a line of ducklings trailing after their mother. The closer they got to the historic music district, the more people they saw who were obviously on vacation.

"I know it's hot, but you gotta step it up." Jeremiah barked. "It's a Saturday and it's July. The tourists are out. If we let them get to the barbecue first, there won't be a rib left to gnaw on."

As they hustled to catch up, he enticed them by explaining why they were passing restaurant after restaurant as they walked in ninety-five-degree heat.

"At Armand's, you gotta get the ribs. Or the pulled

pork. If you're not real hungry, get the pulled pork sandwich. And, oh God, wait until you chase it with a bite of Armand's slaw. Really mustardy. Dr. Longchamp-Mantooth gave me a nice lunch budget, and Armand likes me, so we're getting dessert, too. Lemon cream pie. Chocolate fudge pie. Peach lattice pie. You're sweating now, but you're all gonna thank me when we get where we're going. I'm serious."

• • ● • •

Armand was as suave as his name. His high-top fade haircut looked like it was precision-cut weekly, and it set off his sensual mouth and strong bone structure very nicely. Faye might have been married, but she still had eyes.

Armand's name was on the "Armand's Rib Palace" sign, but Armand didn't cook nor wait tables nor tend bar, not that Faye could see. He greeted guests at the door. He snapped his fingers at waitstaff and pointed at glasses and bread baskets that needed filling. He moved easily from table to table, visiting with his guests without intruding on their conversations or overstaying his welcome.

Faye's nose was telling her that the food at Armand's Rib Palace was every bit as good as Jeremiah had promised, but she didn't think that the food alone explained the huge and overflowing dining room. Armand's Rib Palace thrived because of the expansive charm of Armand himself.

When Armand leaned down close and, in a husky whisper, asked Faye, "Do you have any questions about the menu?" she had two thoughts. The first was that she remembered hearing Laneer say that Frida had been dodging advances from her boss. And the second was that there had to be a reason that Frida had been reluctant to go out with this handsome and charismatic man. Laneer and Sylvia had said that Frida had been trying to learn from her earlier mistakes with men. The evidence suggested that Frida had seen Armand as one more mistake to be avoided. Why?

Since Faye had no intention of going out with him, she felt free to enjoy the superficial charm of a man hoping she enjoyed her meal enough to come back and bring her six employees with her. Good food was Faye's drug of choice, so an hour spent scarfing down ribs, slaw, and beans, while having the undeniable pleasure of watching Armand be Armand, was a happy hour for Faye. She felt the fear and pain of yesterday lift a little. It would be back, but in the meantime, she intended to fully enjoy being a carnivore.

Her happy mood lasted her all the way through her plate of ribs and a slice of peach pie a la mode. When that happiness cratered, she was standing at the cash register with her back to the dining room, checking over the bill. She was also thinking that the bill would have been a lot lower if Richard hadn't had three beers.

"Would you stop looking at me?"

Faye didn't have eyes in the back of her head, but she knew Ayesha's voice. The young woman was slightly built, but her pipes were strong enough to silence the rest of the packed room enough to let everybody hear Richard's more muffled response.

"I didn't mean nothing by it."

Faye felt like she was turning around in slow motion. She heard the conflict more than she saw it.

She heard "Get your hands off me!" and, again, she knew that she was hearing Ayesha's voice. The twin female voices saying "Take your hands off her!" had to belong to Stephanie and Yvonna.

She was still turning, trying to find the conflict and focus her eyes on it. A strong male voice was saying "Settle down, everybody. Settle down," so she knew that Jeremiah was taking charge.

Out of her own mouth, she heard, "This is unacceptable. Everyone sit down and be quiet this instant."

This was what she said when Michael and his preschool friends fought on the playground, so it was what she naturally said in a time of conflict. The surprising thing was that it worked just as well on this group of people who were a lot older than Michael. Silence dropped over the room like a blanket.

Faye took a deep breath as her eyes focused on the overflowing restaurant. Armand's regular customers were physically drawing away from her crew, scooching their chairs away from them and refusing to make eye contact. This thoroughly embarrassed Faye, as if she had somehow become their mother and was responsible for any childish behavior.

She moved on Richard, who sat at the center of the disruption.

"Are you drunk?" she hissed at him.

He tried to stand but staggered and fell back into his chair. Ayesha laughed and stuck out a hand to give him a stiff push. Richard couldn't maintain his balance against even that slight force. He slumped against the wall.

Jeremiah stood over Richard. He shook his head in disgust as he turned to the others, which was his mistake.

"We're going back to the hotel. Now. Go outside with Dr. Longchamp-Mantooth while I get this idiot—"

Richard's hand shot out and grabbed Jeremiah by the wrist, twisting hard. He might be too drunk to sit up straight, but he was still conscious and he was still strong. Jeremiah yelped in surprise.

"Don't ever call me an idiot." Richard's words were slurred, but he was able to get his point across.

Faye could see by Jeremiah's face that Richard's grip hurt and it hurt a lot. Richard's other hand snaked out and put still more pressure on Jeremiah's wrist. Faye's hand went to her phone. She could dial 911 by feel, but she could also reach McDaniel, whose number she had on speed dial, with a single keystroke.

The noise in the room was suddenly deafening. All the bystanders backed away from the fight, dozens of chair legs dragging across the concrete floor with a groan. Yelling above that din, Ayesha, Davion, Yvonna, and Stephanie's voices implored Richard to let their boss go. Only Richard and Jeremiah were silent, saying nothing, but eyeballing each other as if planning for an all-out fistfight.

And then Jeremiah brought up his free hand, snaking it between Richard's forearms to immobilize him. Twisting his ensnared wrist, he easily yanked it out of the drunk man's grip. Then he clapped Richard on the shoulder with a hand that looked gentle but still meant business, and he said, "We're leaving now. Get up slowly and don't try anything. I'll make you regret it."

Faye looked around the room for damage and saw none, so she threw down some extra tip money and headed for the door. As she herded her employees out, she locked eyes with Armand and telegraphed a mute apology for spoiling his restaurant's mellow vibe.

She reached the others waiting on the sidewalk as Jeremiah guided Richard out the door. Sometimes his hand on the younger man's shoulder steered, and sometimes it kept him from toppling over. There was no way Richard could walk all the way back to the motel under his own power.

Faye beckoned to Jeremiah, who sat Richard's sagging form on a bench that looked sturdy enough to hold the inebriated man up while Jeremiah spoke with his client in private.

Holding the bill out for Jeremiah to see, she pointed at the line item for Richard's beers. "It isn't possible that he got this drunk on three beers."

"You got a point there." Jeremiah shrugged. "He's twenty-one. It's not like I searched their suitcases. Maybe he packed more liquor than clothes. It looks to me like our boy had ethanol for breakfast, then kept drinking."

"I can't tolerate this. I have to fire him."

"Hold on! Don't do anything hasty. Besides, you can't fire him. He works for me. You can tell me not to assign him to your job, or you can terminate your contract with my organization, but you can't fire Richard." The expression on his face was almost insubordinate, but not quite.

"You're his boss? Okay. So you're his boss and he just assaulted you. Why aren't you firing him?"

"He didn't hit me. He grabbed my wrist. Big deal."

"He tried to twist your hand off. He didn't manage it because you're big and you can apparently handle yourself in a fight. If he did that to me, I'd have a broken arm right now. Ayesha, too."

"But not the other women?" Jeremiah's eyes were squinched up like a man about to laugh. Faye was not amused.

"I think Yvonna and Stephanie can probably take care of themselves, but I do not want to see them try. You're willing to risk everyone's safety on the chance that Richard will stay sober and peaceful? Why? There are plenty of people who would love to have that job and all the training and perks that come with it."

Jeremiah's eyes looked less amused now. "Sure there are, but they're not interchangeable. Richard is a human being and he deserves a chance. He's not perfect, but I'm not ready to throw him away. Are you?"

Faye struggled to keep her voice down, because her crew definitely did not need to hear this conversation. "Who said anything about throwing human beings away? Who called them interchangeable? This is an important contract and it needs to be staffed by people who take it seriously. Why is it so important to you for Richard to stick with a job that he may not even want to do?"

"Where would I be if nobody ever gave me a chance when I screwed up? I was real good at that, you know. Screwing up, I mean. Everybody needs somebody to hold their feet to the fire."

Faye didn't know what to say, but she knew that it wasn't, "*Tell me exactly what you did to screw up, and when.*" Jeremiah and his past was not her current problem. Richard was. When she weighed Richard's future against the safety of those around him, not to mention the success or failure of her contract, she wasn't sure what the right answer was.

"He's staying in my room with me, right?" Jeremiah said. "That fabulous room you're paying for because you think a murderer is out to get us?"

Faye tried to protest, but he just waved a hand and said, "Joking."

Faye wasn't laughing.

"I'll talk to him. I'll search his suitcase for liquor. I'll watch him like a hawk," Jeremiah promised. "I'll tell him that I don't give three chances to people who screw up, but I do give them two. One more screw-up, and he's out. And I'll tell him all those things again when he's sober enough to understand me."

Faye hesitated, not sure that she was willing to buy into Jeremiah's management style.

He took her hesitation as a sign that he'd won. "Now, why don't you walk the others to the hotel and then drive back over here to get me and Mr. Can't Hold His Liquor? I bet Armand will bring me a glass of sweet tea while I wait. Maybe one for Richard, too, but it looks to me like he's already sloshing inside. He doesn't need to take in anything wet for at least a week."

Faye had just witnessed a small miracle and she was grateful.

The miracle had occurred after she'd dropped off the women and driven back for Richard and Jeremiah. After she'd successfully loaded them into her car and headed back to the motel, Richard had miraculously managed the entire five-minute ride back to the hotel without throwing up in her car. He had even managed to walk the ten steps to the trash can outside the motel's front door before vomiting. Given the circumstances, Faye called that a win.

As for managing the aftermath of Richard's drinking spree? Faye called that Jeremiah's job. She was so angry at both men that she dropped them off at the hotel lobby, parked the car, then used the back entrance so that she could get to the privacy of her hotel room without looking at them. But when she finally reached the door to her room, she paused at the door for a moment and turned away. Her new roommate, Yvonna, was sitting in there with Stephanie and Ayesha. She didn't want to be part of their conversation, not until they were thoroughly tired of talking about Richard's behavior. They should reach that point in…oh…four or five hours.

She turned away from the door and went back to the concrete staircase that had brought her to it. Checking to make sure that she wasn't sitting on a tarry bit of old, chewed bubble gum, she settled herself on a handy stair and pulled out her phone. It told her that the barbecue debacle had only seemed to take up the whole afternoon. It also told her that she had no missed calls.

Halfway to the motel from Armand's, she'd remembered that she hadn't talked to her husband in twenty-four hours. When she was away from home, her habit was to call every night at bedtime, and he really deserved to hear from her more often than that now, considering that she was surrounded by a murder investigation. Well, at bedtime the night before, she'd been having an uncomfortable conversation with the man running that investigation, so calling Joe had slipped her mind.

The fact that she'd neglected to let her husband know that she'd survived a full day without falling prey to Frida's killer was not the thing most disturbing for Faye at that moment. She was far more disturbed to realize that Joe, a practical man who didn't pick fights over things like forgotten phone calls, hadn't just pulled his phone out of his pocket and called her when she failed to check in.

But what did his failure to call her really mean? She was reasonably sure that it did not mean, "Go ahead and get murdered. See if I care."

If she had to guess, she'd say it meant, "I can't think of anything nice to say to you and I don't want to argue."

She studied her phone's face for a moment, looking at the photo of Joe and the children that she used for wallpaper. If she put a video call through, she'd be able to see his face and she needed that badly. But she would also be able to see his fear and his anger, so she opted for an audio call instead.

It went straight to voice mail, which was no surprise. Joe always spent summer Saturday afternoons at the beach with his children and it would never occur to him to take his cell phone and let it interfere with the fun. Subconsciously, or mostly subconsciously, she had known this when she picked up the phone, so the call had been strategic. She'd reached out an olive branch without actually having to talk to her angry husband. The next move was up to him. Score one for the wife.

Still holding the phone and refusing to admit it was because she was hoping Joe would dial her right back and say, "I took the phone to the beach in case you called," she stared at a large stain on her pants leg.

Peach pie. It was definitely peach pie. She wanted to lick her pants leg, just to get one last taste of Armand's peach pie, which had been so good that she'd wanted to kiss him. She'd also intended to buy another piece to save for Kali, because she wanted to fatten the little girl up. And also because she was pretty sure that Armand would rather have her money than a kiss from a married woman with no plans to stray. Instead of giving him that money, she'd spent the next hour trying not to let Richard vomit on her, totally forgetting to buy Kali a piece of pie.

She was already planning to check in on Kali that afternoon. Should she go get the little girl and take her to supper at Armand's Rib Palace? No, not when the little girl's late mother had worked there. That would have been too weird.

Fortunately, she knew of another Memphis ritual that Kali had surely never experienced. There was no place in the world like The Peabody Hotel for a special afternoon with a child. Faye had taken her own kids to The Peabody's Orlando branch for afternoon tea and some time with its famous in-house ducks, and it had been magical. How much better must the duck parade be here in Memphis, at the original Peabody with its Jazz Age opulence?

She looked at her watch. If she left now, she could spend a little time visiting with Laneer before taking Kali downtown. Should she do it?

Her phone told her that the Peabody didn't serve tea on Sundays, making it a full week before she and Kali would have another chance to enjoy cream scones and cookies if they didn't go that day. Faye decided to yield to impulse. But she'd have to hurry.

Here was a chance to sweep Kali far, far away from her problems to a place where children had tea parties and communed with live ducks, and Faye could think of no downside to that plan. As quickly as that, Faye made her decision and picked up her phone. First, she used it to make a reservation for tea. Then she dialed Laneer's number.

"Can I borrow Kali for a while this afternoon? Yeah? Fabulous. I'll see you in a few minutes."

Faye hung up and went back to her room. She was ashamed to admit it to herself, but she was relieved to see that Stephanie, Yvonna, and Ayesha had left. Tossing on a sundress that she hoped was Peabody-worthy, she left, and she didn't bother with good-byes beyond a text to Jeremiah telling him she'd be back after dinner. He could deal with a sometimes-fractious group of young adults. She had a date with a little girl and some ducks.

# Chapter Twenty

"I wish I knew why my sweet Frida was so dressed up when she passed." Laneer's hand shook as he held out a cup of coffee for Faye. "But I just don't. I can't stop wondering who that precious soul wanted to look so pretty for. How did she spend her last night on this Earth?"

Faye took the cup quickly, but not quickly enough to keep him from sloshing a few drops into the bone china saucer. He had offered to feed her lunch, poking around in a pantry stocked with jars of vegetables he'd canned himself, and not much else. Faye wasn't about to take food that he needed for himself, and for Kali.

"I had an early lunch before I came, and I'll be eating again at The Peabody, but thank you for offering," she'd said quickly. "I just came to pick up Kali and to check on you."

And, apparently, on Sylvia, who had appeared at the front door before Faye had even passed through it. She must live somewhere on the same street as Laneer. Faye wasn't sure which house was Sylvia's, but she was pretty sure the woman spent her life at her front window, waiting for something interesting to pass by. This afternoon, Faye's car had been the interesting thing that got Sylvia out of her house.

If Faye's car hadn't budged Sylvia from her window, then the car pulling into Laneer's driveway would have. It was a 1990s-era Cadillac, as blue as the sky and well-waxed, and it moved like a barge. Faye watched out the window as Walt Walker stepped out of it, sharply dressed in khakis and a flame red shirt that clashed with the small pink backpack in his hands.

Laneer greeted him at the front door, saying, "Come in. There's lots of coffee and it's hot," but his eyes said, "Why are you here?"

Ever affable, Kali's schoolteacher smiled at the wary Laneer as he held out the pink backpack. "I hope I'm not intruding, but it occurred to me that I made a bad mistake yesterday. I stopped by because I was worried that Kali didn't pick up her food for the weekend, but I didn't bring her the food. That was a bit stupid."

Laneer said, "We thank you," and took the backpack. "Like I said, the coffee's hot."

As Laneer sat with Faye, Sylvia, and Walt, sipping coffee, Laneer jerked his head in the direction of a closed door. "She's been in that bedroom all morning. I told her that if she went out the window, I'd come get her and then I'd nail it shut. So far, she's stayed put, but she won't come out here and talk to me. Meantime, I just had to answer the phone when Armand called to find out why Frida didn't come to work last night. He said he'd been texting her all day. It was so hard to tell that man what happened to her."

"I met Armand today," Faye said. "He seems nice. Charming, certainly."

"Well, he was fussing from the time I picked up the phone 'cause he had to clean his own restaurant his own self. It shut him up when I told him what happened. He took on pretty bad when he heard about Frida. He said not to worry about her paycheck, nor the next one. Said he'd clean the place personally all the rest of the month, just so's he could afford to send me Frida's whole check. One last time."

They all sat silent for a moment, then Sylvia put her hand on Laneer's. "People can be kind, sometimes."

"Yeah, sometimes." Laneer passed around the coffee cups, managing to control his jittering right hand long enough to pour Sylvia's coffee.

"This china is so pretty!" Faye said, holding her own cup and saucer up to the light. Garlands of pink roses encircled both pieces.

"My mama painted it, long time ago."

He set out another china cup and filled it with a little coffee and a lot of milk. A lot of sugar, too.

"Kali! I made you some coffee the way you like it, and it's in your favorite cup. Come drink it with us." The little girl's cup was as pretty as Faye's cup, only the roses were yellow. A single red rose bloomed on the side of the cup he'd handed to Sylvia.

Laneer had pulled two dun-brown mugs out of a yellow-painted kitchen cabinet for Walt and for himself. Faye felt self-conscious drinking out of her beautiful cup when her host's mug was dull and chipped, but she would have felt even more self-conscious if she'd insisted that he or Walt take it, calling attention to the fact that he didn't have enough of his special china to go around.

Faye's grandmother had always said that nice china was meant to be used. Faye could hear her voice proclaiming, "Life is worth celebrating. Good china makes things taste better." Taking a sip of her coffee, Faye decided that her grandmother was right. She raised it as if toasting Laneer and said, "This is delicious. Thank you."

Sylvia turned her eyes to Kali's closed door. "She ain't said a word since you left. Ain't ate a thing, nor drunk anything." Sneaking another spoon of sugar into the little girl's coffee, she called out, "Kali, come on! We made your coffee the way you like it, and it's getting cold."

"I miss my girl talking to me," Laneer said. "We've been buddies since she was a little bitty thing. She talked to you, Faye. Why'd she want to talk to you but not to me? She don't even know you."

"Don't matter why," Sylvia said crisply. "The only thing that matters is Kali and making sure she's happy. If she likes Faye, you can make coffee for Faye every day of the week and you can be happy about it. I'll bring the Milk Duds."

Pretending that she didn't see the silent Kali as she slipped through a barely open door, Sylvia reached deep into her apron pocket and pulled out a yellow box. Laying a napkin on the table, she dumped out the contents of the box. Hard brown balls hit the napkin-cushioned table with a clatter. "Dig in!"

"Lots of people are doing nice things for you, sweetheart," Sylvia said, patting the seat of the chair next to her and setting Kali's coffee cup in front of it. "Your Uncle Laneer gave you permission to go to The Peabody Hotel to have tea with Miss Faye, and he made you a nice cup of coffee. Take a good long drink. And Mr. Walker here brought you a backpack full of food like you usually have to walk a long way to get. These people are real nice to you, don't you think?"

Kali didn't respond, but a little hand shot out and grabbed a handful of candy. Faye could see that Laneer had already told her about Faye and her invitation to afternoon tea, because she was wearing a dress. It was orange knit, printed with gray elephants, and the juvenile fabric was subtly wrong on her. Kali was still a little girl, but she was standing at the edge of the gulf between child and woman. Already, the childish elephants on this dress, which would have been adorable just a few months before, made her look awkward and unsure.

"Would ya look at that?" Laneer said, squinting at the candy going into her mouth. "She ain't opened her mouth for nothing, not for talking and not for food, since her mama....not since yesterday. But she's eating now."

Kali chewed her Milk Duds, but she didn't look up from Laneer's bright red tablecloth, not even when Walt started to speak.

"It's me, Kali. Mr. Walker. Your teacher. You talked to me every day, all school year long. Won't you even look at me?"

"Neither one of you is asking the child what she wants. This ain't about you," said Sylvia. "Do you want to talk to us, honey?"

There was no answer. To be fair, Faye noticed that the girl's jaws were glued together by firm, sticky caramel.

"You do what you're gonna to do, Kali. You don't have to do any talking," Sylvia said, catching the other adults' eyes in a signal that they should ignore the girl. Without looking at the Milk Duds or at Kali, she used her left hand to shove a few duds in the child's direction. "Us grown-ups can talk to each other. Faye, why don't you tell us about what kind of stuff you're digging for?"

So Faye did.

Kali avoided Faye's eyes as she spoke, focusing instead on unloading the backpack Walt had handed her. Faye was under no illusion that the man had gone to the playground on a Saturday and loaded up a backpack. Unless he had a key to the food storage closet and the refrigerator, it would have been impossible. He'd bought that backpack and packed it himself, no small gift for a man living on a teacher's salary.

Kali was unloading a lot of things from the stuffed backpack, and it didn't all look like food people gave away for free to keep children healthy and alive. There was yogurt and granola in there, it was true, but there were little toys and cupcakes, too, even a set of colorful plastic barrettes.

Everybody but Kali seemed interested in hearing about the archaeology Faye was doing in their very own neighborhood. Since she knew Kali was listening, she ramped up the drama in her monologue, doing her best to make the long-ago discovery of a mammoth's skeleton in a Memphis creek the most exciting story she'd ever told. She got no response, other than the sounds of smacking lips and small teeth gnawing on hard caramel.

As Faye came to the dramatic conclusion—"And now the skeleton is on display at the museum, where anybody can see it!"—Kali was ready to speak. She must not have been remotely interested in Faye's exciting but nerdy stories, because she interrupted, speaking right on top of the fascinating mammoth skeleton story.

"I'm going outside. Wanna come?"

Kali walked out the back door and let it slam behind her. Faye took advantage of the absence of little ears to say, "I'll be at the funeral tomorrow. I'm giving my crew time off, because I know Jeremiah and Richard will want to come."

Then she checked her watch. She and Kali had time

to take a short walk before leaving for the Peabody. Her instincts told her to do whatever the girl wanted her to do, even if it meant missing tea. According to Sylvia and Laneer, the handful of words Kali had just used—"I'm going outside. Wanna come?" were the only words she'd spoken since she last saw Faye, and a full day had passed since then.

Why did Kali respond so well to a stranger? Maybe it was simply because Sylvia was old enough to be her grandmother and Laneer could have been her great-grandfather. Kali had lost her mother, and Faye had experience in that area—having lost her own mother—but Faye suspected that her bond with Kali went beyond being bereaved daughters. Faye was a mother, and she supposed it showed.

Kali led Faye out Laneer's back door and to the back of his deep, narrow yard. The back gate opened onto the bank of the creek.

Land on the opposite side of the creek belonged to the state park, as far as the eye could see, and Faye knew that a well-marked trail wound in and out of the wooded parkland. She and Kali had nothing to follow on their side of the creek but a faint path that wandered through scrubby underbrush. It wasn't much of a path, but it stuck to higher, drier spots, keeping Faye's semi-nice sandals from most of the mud. Maybe the path had been worn by Kali's small feet.

Walking would have been easier on the other side of the creek, where the park's trails ran along the edge of a bluff, but the creek was deeper here. Kali didn't even seem tempted to wade across it and scale the bluff. Instead, she followed the faint path that she had walked so many times, picking her way downstream toward her own home.

When Faye had begun to think that Kali would never speak, she spoke.

"It's hot, but it's still nice out here by the water. Didn't think I could stand sitting in that house one more minute. Uncle Laneer likes to listen to the gospel station. Plays it from getting up to going to bed. It's like living in a church. Which I guess is better than living in a bar with music that's just as loud, but still."

Faye laughed, but she wondered how Kali knew what a bar sounded like. She decided to take the risk of going straight to a tough subject. She thought the girl would respect her for not beating around the bush.

"Your Uncle Laneer and Sylvia tell me you haven't said a word to them since I left yesterday. How come you're talking to me now?"

Faye counted how many steps she took before Kali spoke. It was seventeen.

"Want me to stop talking again? I know how to shut up, you know."

"I do know that, and no, I don't want you to shut up."

"I'm talking to you 'cause I got stuff I want them to know, but I can't stand it when Uncle Laneer cries. I'd rather stay in my room forever than say something that makes him cry. I need you to tell him something."

"Anything."

"I want to pick out the flowers for my mama's funeral. And her dress. I want to pick the dress they bury her in."

This time Faye was the one who stayed silent for several steps. How was she supposed to talk to a child about her murdered mother's funeral?

Finally, she said, "Okay. I'll do it. If you don't want to talk to them about those things, I will."

More silent walking took them downhill as the bank

got lower and lower. By the time they reached Kali's back yard, they were so near to the creek's level that the path was wet. Water stood in the ruts below the unused swingset.

Faye picked her way around the path's puddles, wondering how high the creek rose with heavy rain and whether water had ever seeped into the house. Mold was so bad for little children.

When Faye was convinced that Kali had sunk back into her quiet grief and that she wouldn't be hearing the child's voice again that day, the girl spoke. "She liked carnations. Pink ones. And she looked really pretty in yellow. There's a yellow dress she used to wear. I really liked it. She had silver shoes and a necklace and earrings and everything. I want her to wear that. You tell my uncle."

Faye promised to tell Laneer, hoping against all hope that Frida had owned more than one yellow dress. She would rather walk through fire than say, "We can't bury your mama in her yellow dress, sweetie. You see, she was murdered in that dress, and it will never be whole again."

Kali had turned toward the creek crossing and strode in, shoes and all. Faye stuck with the handy rocks that kept her feet out of the water but she hurried across them to keep up with the girl. She could see where Kali was going and she didn't want her to go alone.

They made better progress along the park-maintained trail, reaching Kali's hideout quickly. The trail took a hard turn there but Kali didn't follow it. Instead, she stepped into the grass and rushed to her special place. She was in such a hurry to get there that she ran the last few steps. After tossing a few sweetgum balls aside, she dropped to the ground. Sitting with her arms clasped around her bent knees, Kali leaned against a tree. Faye found her own tree and assumed the same position. The spot was so small that their feet bumped together when they sat. Kali carefully rearranged herself so that she was touching nothing but the ground beneath her and the tree at her back.

Not far outside this cozy spot was a terrible place. It was invisible from where Faye sat, hidden by trees and greenery, but she knew it too well. It was a rectangle of disturbed soil where Frida had been left to die. Nothing that Detective McDaniel and his crime scene technicians could do would ever make that spot right again.

Kali had chosen to sit facing away from her mother's first grave. Her body was stiff, taut, electric with tension, and she didn't say a word. Had she already said all she wanted to say? Had she asked Faye to join her just so that she could tell her about a yellow dress? Did she invite her because she was afraid to be here alone? Or did she wish Faye would go away and leave her in peace?

There was no way in hell that Faye was going to leave this child alone here. And there was no way in hell that either of them would be staying here much longer, because the reality was already sinking in for Faye that they shouldn't be this far from help when there was a murderer at large.

"First of all," Kali announced, "you can tell the policeman that I know who Mama's date was that night."

"Do you want me to call Detective McDaniel and put you on the phone?"

"No, I want you to tell him. I think he likes you."

Faye wasn't so sure.

Kali continued with a series of announcements that she'd clearly been thinking about all day.

"I don't want wanna talk to the detective. I wouldn't mind talking to Laneer and Sylvia, but I ain't got anything to say that won't make them cry. That's why I don't talk these days. It hurts too much. Hurts me. Hurts them. Just hurts."

Faye kept her eyes off Kali, and she kept her mouth shut. The girl needed to speak in her own time. To give her eyes a place to be and to keep her hands busy, she started building a mound of sweetgum balls. The trees over their heads had been shedding those round, pointy seed balls for a very long time, so Faye was in no danger of running out of them. She handled them with care, protecting her fingertips and remembering barefoot summers when hardly a day went by without sweetgum balls wounding the soles of her feet.

Kali leaned her head back against her tree. Faye thought she was finished with her revelations, but she was wrong.

"I heard him."

"Kali. Who did you hear? What are you saying?"

"I didn't know what I was hearing, but it was awful. Thumps. Bumps. Slaps, too, but I know what it sounds like when somebody gets slapped. It was the thumping I didn't understand."

Faye wished she didn't know how Kali knew the sound of a slap.

"After a while, there was some screaming. That's when I figured out that the thumping sound meant that somebody was getting beat bad. I told you about the meth heads. I thought maybe some of them were having a fight. Guess I was wrong." Her eyes were still closed. "Maybe it was a meth head that did that to my mama. Naw. They woulda got caught by now. It's hard to plan ahead when you're messed up like that."

Faye tried to think calm thoughts, without a lot of success. She needed Kali to keep talking, because she could be the witness that would put her mother's killer away. But she also needed to handle this moment well. If she didn't, Kali could draw into herself again, forever damaged by what she'd heard but not willing to reach out for help.

"Did you see the person hurting your mother?"

Kali shook her head. "No. Well, I crawled through the bushes and found a place where I could tell I was looking at a big man, but I never saw his face. Coulda been anybody, long as it was a man and he was big."

"Did you hear him? Did you hear his voice?"

*Calm down. Ask her one question at a time. Don't scare her.*

Kali gave another shake of the head.

"Did you know you were hearing—"

"My mama? No." For the first time, Faye saw tears on the stubby eyelashes. "No, it didn't—it didn't sound like her a bit. When I got home and she wasn't there, I thought maybe. Maybe it was. But I didn't know for sure that she was dead until the minister told me so."

Faye looked into Kali's eyes and saw fear there and more. There was something else the girl wanted to say. "Tell me what's bothering you."

"What if he saw me? What if he knows where I'm staying? I think he's gonna come get me."

"Do you think he saw you? Did he look your way?"

"No. No, he didn't. I just—Faye, what if he comes to get me?"

"I don't think he will. He knows the police are after him, so why would he take any chances? And also, you have your Uncle Laneer to look after you."

"He's old."

"That doesn't mean he won't take care of you. And you've got Sylvia."

Kali rolled her eyes. "She's not very scary. I need somebody scary. You're not scary, but you're scarier than her."

Maybe Faye shouldn't have laughed, but she did.

"Uncle Laneer and Sylvia need me to take care of

them." Kali's voice was insistent. "That's why I don't sleep any more. Somebody's got to look out the window and see if he's coming."

Somebody needed to know that this child wasn't sleeping.

"I'm scared about you, too."

Faye was confused. "Why are you scared of me?"

"No. No, I'm not scared of you. I'm scared he wants to hurt you, too."

"You don't need to worry about me, Kali. Why would he want to hurt me?"

"I saw you. I saw you climb up out of the creek and start digging up my mama. If I saw you, maybe he did, too."

Kali was shaking her head. "Been thinking all day today. He didn't have to see you for you to be in trouble. Everybody knows it was you that found Mama. Sylvia made sure. Text, phone, people on the street. She told 'em all. She doesn't know I was out there, so she hasn't told 'em that, but she sure did tell 'em about you."

"Why does that worry you?"

"Because it means it don't matter if he saw you. He knows you were there. And he knows that maybe you saw him."

Faye supposed she'd known this all along, but she hadn't let herself think about it. Maybe she should listen to Joe and run for home, but Kali didn't have that option.

Kali was stuck in this neighborhood, whether it harbored a killer who was looking for her or not. Or rather, she was stuck in this neighborhood if she was lucky. Any day now, a social worker could decide Laneer was too old or too poor to be a suitable guardian, swooping in to park her with a family of people who were strangers.

To be honest, this could happen anyway. At Laneer's age, he was a heart attack away from dying or from being too sick to take care of a little girl. Next week, Kali could have a brand-new address, but that wouldn't save her from a killer who probably knew her name.

Faye considered the evidence. Unless McDaniel was sitting on something explosive, there weren't many clues that she knew about, but Faye felt comfortable making a few assumptions. An attack as violent as the one that killed Frida didn't come out of nowhere. This man had hurt people before. Maybe he had a criminal record that could tie him to this crime. And maybe he had hurt Frida before.

If he knew that Frida was alive when he buried her, then the possibility of a criminal record only grew. A man didn't start a criminal career by burying people alive. He worked up to it, or so it seemed to Faye, unless he was completely unbalanced. And maybe he was. If she were to play amateur psychologist, this act rose to the level of sociopathy displayed by the most famous serial killers. Ted Bundy. Danny Rollins. Aileen Wuornos. The BTK Killer. Jeffrey Dahmer. All of them had made a final misstep and been brought to justice, but not before killing scores of innocent people among them.

Faye looked at little Kali and tried to imagine walking away from her, knowing that there could be a Jeffrey Dahmer on the loose right here in her neighborhood. She couldn't do it.

Kali hugged her knees tighter. "I'm scared, Faye. Aren't you?"

# Chapter Twenty-one

*He liked women in dresses, because there was so much pleasure to be had from arranging the sumptuous folds of their skirts in the final minutes before he said good-bye and laid them in the graves he'd carved from the earth, just for them. Straight sides, flat bottoms, perfectly square corners—he was meticulous about the forever beds that he made for the women he loved, all of them.*

*And once he'd lowered them into those graves, he gave them the care and attention they deserved. He crossed their hands beautifully on their still bellies. He straightened their legs, even when they'd been broken, making sure their dainty feet rested side by side as he fanned their skirts about their battered thighs. Once, when he was young and brash and believed he could never be caught, he had taken the time to paint a dead woman's fingernails, washing her face and applying fresh lipstick while he waited for the nail polish to dry. It bothered him still that Frida had lost a shoe in their flight toward her open, waiting grave.*

*The archaeologist, a woman who loved to interfere in the lives of children and the burials of their mothers, had surprised him and he'd had to flee. He'd been forced to throw Frida in her open grave and shovel hard.*

*Faye Longchamp-Mantooth was delicately formed, small and slender, and that was the way he liked his women. His attraction to women who wore their hair short was inconveniently weak. However, when he looked past the manly clothes she favored—olive drab work pants, button-up shirts styled for men, heavy boots—he could see that she had the large eyes and full lips that always caught his eye. If he needed her dead, and he was fairly certain that he did, he felt sure he could muster up the enthusiasm to make it so.*

*His enthusiasm would be more heartfelt if she were wearing the dresses he favored, and fate was going to fix that for him. Sylvia had announced to the world that the "doctor woman," was taking little Kali to afternoon tea. The archaeologist was worldly. She had class. Any fool could see that Dr. Faye Longchamp-Mantooth would not darken the door of the four-star Chez Philippe in trousers.*

*He would be waiting for them outside the Chez Philippe, hidden in a faceless crowd. Then, after they'd sipped their tea and nibbled their party sandwiches, he would...what? Grab them both off the streets of Memphis or out of one of the city's dark, lonely parking garages? Kill the child, too?*

*This was a problem. Killing a child was a line he had yet to cross. He had thought of it, of course. He was not immune to the premature charms of a girl who was rocketing toward womanhood but didn't know it yet. Those premature charms had never driven him to action, but now the novelty appealed to him. In fact, he was surprised by his enthusiasm.*

*Had he been bored? He wouldn't have thought so. There had been safety in repetition. Hunt. Stalk. Kill. Bury. He knew how to do these things and, as evidence showed, he knew how to do them without getting caught. Would adding a second victim, a very young one, to the mix change that? Could he do it?*

*He didn't know, but the more he thought about the question, the more he wanted to know the answer.*

# Chapter Twenty-two

Kali walked out of the bathroom and past the dining room table where Faye, Sylvia, Walt, and Laneer sat. She didn't speak, although she did acknowledge Laneer with just a slight wave in his direction. She was moving fast, but not fast enough to avoid being embarrassed by her great-great-uncle and her candy lady.

"So pretty…" Sylvia announced loudly. "Don't she look pretty?"

Laneer nodded forcefully. "That's my girl. She's growing up."

Kali was almost running as she stepped out the front door.

Sylvia picked up the backpack that Walt had brought. Peering inside, she said, "Is she wearing the barrettes you gave her?"

Smiling broadly, Walt said, "Yes, she is. And she's carrying the little purse I brought her, too."

"She could've thanked you," Sylvia said, and the tone of her voice told Faye a bit of what it meant to be a child's candy lady.

"She already did by using my gifts. It makes me so happy to see that she liked them."

Sylvia snorted and muttered something about gratitude being seen *and* heard.

Faye rose and said, "I'd better get moving. There's a girl with a very pretty new hairdo waiting in my car, and downtown Memphis is waiting to meet her."

"Hold on."

Faye felt a hand grab hers. She looked down and saw that it was Laneer's. He rose slowly to his feet to speak.

"Did she talk?" he asked. "When you were on your walk, did my girl say anything to you?"

She put her other hand on top of his and squeezed it. "She talked a blue streak. She seriously hasn't been talking to you?"

The old man shook his head. "Not a word since you left. Doesn't leave her room except to go to the bathroom." She felt his hand tremble between both of hers. "I need to talk to Kali 'bout her mama's funeral. Maybe there's hymns she wants played or bible verses she wants the minister to read, but how can I start talking about things like that when we ain't even said good morning to each other?"

"I don't know anything about hymns or bible verses, but Kali says she wants her mother to be buried in a yellow dress."

"She was wearing her yellow dress when—" Laneer's voice broke. "I saw it when the police took me to identify her. Oh, Lord."

Faye's hope that Frida had owned more than one yellow dress crumbled. "I'll go buy one tonight after I bring Kali home. It'll be my present to all of you."

She squeezed Laneer's hand again. "Do you hear me? Take this off your list of worries. I saw the dress she was wearing, and I'll go find one as much like it as I can. I'll bring it to you tonight. Go over to her house and look at the dresses in her closet, then text me Frida's size."

Laneer didn't answer, and Faye wasn't sure he was able. She looked at Sylvia. "Can you text me those sizes?"

Sylvia nodded. "I can do that. Thank you."

Laneer's hands trembled as always, and sorrow had caused his tremor to spread to his arms and trunk, but he was still standing tall. Faye respected that.

"I thank you, Faye," he said. "We all do."

Faye took a trembling old hand and squeezed it. "We won't tell Kali about the dress. If we're lucky, she won't notice that it's a different dress. I can't fix anything else that has happened here, but maybe I can fix this."

Kali waited until Faye merged onto the interstate highway before she spoke.

"Where are we going?"

"Sylvia and Laneer didn't tell you? Then I think I'll leave it for a surprise."

"The signs say we're going to the Mississippi River bridge."

They passed a big green sign that said just that. "Well, we're going downtown, and that's where the bridge is, but we're not going over it."

"I want to see the river. I always wanted to do that."

Faye almost said, "You've lived all your life in Memphis and you've never seen the Mississippi River?" but she managed to stop herself.

"Mama was always too busy to take me on the bus. Laneer don't have a car, neither, and he never wanted to go. Sylvia says the river's pretty much like my creek, just bigger, so why do I need to go look at it? But that's why I want to see it. It's big."

"Yes, it is. It's really, really big."

"I tried to walk there once."

Faye remembered their hike down the creek. "I bet you did."

"I followed my creek downstream all the way, and it dumped into something pretty big. I thought I'd got there. It looked like a river to me. I came back and went straight to Sylvia. First, she said she'd tell my mama if I ever did anything that dumb again. Then she said I'd only gone to Nonconnah Creek. Just a creek!"

"I've seen Nonconnah. It's a big creek, but the Mississippi will make it look like nothing."

"Get out."

"Yep."

"Can I see your phone? So I can look at a map of where we're going?"

Faye handed it over.

"I told Sylvia I was going to try again. I said, 'All the water I saw in Nonconnah Creek has gotta go somewhere. Probably it's the Mississippi River. Next time, I'll just keep walking.' Then she got out a map. She showed me where I started and where my creek runs into Nonconnah Creek and where it runs into some lake. I forget the name. To get to the river, I'd have to get across that lake and then across a big island."

Faye pictured the map of Memphis that she'd studied to get ready for this job. "It's a long way from here to the Mississippi on foot, sweetie."

"No joke. I'm not gonna lie. I cried. But I was only eight then. I ain't eight no more."

"No, you're not."

Faye topped an overpass and got a good look at downtown Memphis and its tall buildings. She knew that the

Mississippi River and its bridge were just on the other side of them. "I'd take you to the river right now, but we have reservations in a few minutes."

"We have what?"

"Reservations." Faye got a blank look, so she tried again. "We have an appointment for your surprise and we can't be late. But when we're finished with the surprise? We'll walk down to the riverfront, so you can see just how big it really is."

Another sign caught Kali's eye. This time it was a billboard announcing that Armand's Rib Palace was the place to be. Specifically, it said "Get Down with Armand's! Mouthwatering Ribs with A Funky Downtown Vibe!"

"Mama used to say that Armand would sell anything for a buck. That's why she kept telling him no, she wouldn't go out with him. Until she did."

"Wait. She went out with Armand. On a date?"

"I started to tell you that in the woods, but we got to talking about something else."

"Your Uncle Laneer doesn't know that. Neither does Sylvia."

"I know. She didn't have much of a chance to tell 'em. She didn't even get a chance to tell me how her date went. He came and picked her up, but she never came home. I know because I checked her bed that morning."

Faye's hands spasmed around the steering wheel, clenching tight. "You're saying that she was out with Armand on that last...on Thursday night?"

Kali nodded once.

"Do you mind if I call Detective McDaniel and tell him that? Can I call him right this minute?"

Again, Kali nodded once. "I want you to call him. That's why I told you."

So Faye did. When she hung up, Kali said, "Guess she changed her mind. About going out with Armand, I mean. Tell me something. When I grow up, am I gonna start doing dumb things because of men?"

Faye couldn't help smiling. "It happens to most of us. And they do dumb things because of women. It doesn't always turn out bad."

Kali rolled her eyes. "Coulda fooled me."

Faye stood in the lobby of the Peabody Hotel, surrounded by marble and bronze and the trappings of wealth, and she knew that she had made a mistake.

Standing just outside the doorway of Chez Philippe, the Peabody's flagship restaurant, she lingered in the grand hotel's lobby, surrounded by hundreds of tourists who weren't even dressed as well as she was. In comparison with their touristy shorts and sneakers, Faye's clothes might even be called upscale. This was not the case inside Chez Philippe, where there were children wearing shoes that cost more than she had paid for her wedding dress.

When they'd entered the hotel's lobby from the street, a throng of people had blocked their view of the grand fountain rising in its center. Carved from a single block of granite, the fountain dominated the room, but she and Kali couldn't see much but the towering mound of fresh flowers that topped it. Monumental chandeliers shone down on the fountain and its flower crown.

"What's everybody looking at?" Kali had whispered, but Faye had said only, "Keep looking."

Holding the child by the hand, Faye had snaked through the crowd and secured them a spot so close that they could feel the cool air rising off the fountain's flowing water. This choice viewing spot had put them less than an arm's-length from the five mallard ducks paddling nonchalantly in the fountain. Kali had nearly had a spasm when she saw them. Their soft feathers and bright beaks had been so unexpected amid the lobby's opulence that Faye had almost joined the girl in jumping up and down, flapping her hands, and squealing. Among the overexcited tourists, Kali's exuberance had blended right in. Above them, more tourists had leaned over the mezzanine's railings to get a look at the Peabody's famous ducks, swimming unperturbed among the tumult around them.

Kali had laughed every time they paddled their feet, rose out of the water and flapped their wings. She'd cooed over their broad yellow feet, slick and leathery. When they had quacked, she had quacked back.

Faye had hung back and let the girl entertain herself as long as possible, but she'd been lucky to land the last reservations of the day, and time was getting on. Dallying too long would cost them their tea at Chez Philippe. When she'd tugged Kali's hand, the girl had given the ducks a final longing look, then she had followed, looking around for the door that had brought them in from South BB King Boulevard.

"I can't wait to tell Uncle Laneer about those ducks. They were so cute! Did you take pictures?"

Faye nodded and said, "You're not ready to go home yet, are you? I know where we can get a special meal before we go. Then maybe we can see the ducks again."

Kali's face had brightened. "And the river?"

"Yes. I promised you a river. A big one."

Their trek across the lobby to Chez Philippe had been arduous. The lobby's many tables, all occupied by tourists wearing shorts, fanny packs, and souvenir t-shirts, had stood in their way.

The t-shirts and their ribald slogans had added an extra element to the trip. By Faye's observation, the younger the tourist, the edgier the t-shirt's caption, so the slogans on the chests of teenagers had ranged from suggestive to obscene. Wishing Kali couldn't read, Faye had led her on a twisty path between the tables, eventually getting them to the doorway of Chez Philippe, where they were on the reservation list for afternoon tea. And now, here she was at the gilded doorway to the finest restaurant in Memphis, realizing that she'd made a mistake.

Faye peered through an imposing doorway into the most sumptuous room she'd ever seen. She wore a trim beige sundress and a pair of flat leather sandals. Her hair was slicked down with a bit of pomade. She even wore a smear of cinnamon-brown lipstick on her lips. If she'd been at home in the Florida panhandle, she would have blended in at a restaurant, a church, a business, a bar, anywhere. Here at Chez Philippe, she was painfully underdressed.

Kali, in her orange-and-gray elephant dress, stood out even more. Seeing the girl in this light, among these people, Faye saw things that hadn't been obvious before, not even under the sun's unforgiving light.

Kali's dress was faded from repeated washings. The soles of her shoes were worn at the heels. The colorful barrettes in her hair, though brand-new, adorned the hair of a ten-year-old who had combed it herself. Faye personally saw nothing wrong with the way Kali's hair looked, but none of the children in Chez Philippe wore the hair of ten-year-olds. They wore hair that had been blow-dried and flat-ironed and hair-sprayed into submission, and Faye hated herself for not helping Kali more. The difference between Faye and the parents in this room was that Faye thought Kali looked beautiful the way she was and she, quite frankly, thought the other children dining at Chez Philippe looked a little plastic.

Faye and Kali hadn't been the only people of color when they were standing in the Peabody's lobby, and they weren't the only people of color in Chez Philippe, but Faye was realizing with the sting of a physical slap that socioeconomic prejudices hurt, too. When the maître d' approached to ask whether they had reservations, she answered, "Yes, we do. We do have reservations," and she said it just a little too loudly. The restaurant's heavy draperies dampened the sound and none of the people sitting beneath them appeared to notice her faux pas. She would have been relieved by their failure to notice her error, but feeling that she was beneath their notice hurt, too.

Faye took a deep breath and reminded herself that her name was on the reservation list and that she had the money to pay for their meal. Well, she had a credit card.

She had as much of a right to be at Chez Philippe as anybody in the room, and so did Kali. She just wished that she'd remembered to shave her legs and polish her toenails.

# Chapter Twenty-three

*The door to Chez Philippe looked like a wrought-iron fence painted gold. He'd never been inside, but he'd looked it up on the Internet and he knew that it was equally opulent inside. He also knew that this was the only way out.*

*Fancy mirrors lining the restaurant walls served as fake windows. Fancy curtains fostered that illusion, but, in reality, nobody inside the restaurant could see out and nobody outside the restaurant could see in. Chez Philippe's dining room was constructed like a blind canyon. This was the only door routinely used by the public.*

*Oh, there were probably exterior doors labeled "Emergency Exit," because fire marshals held sway everywhere, even over the Peabody. But the odds were small that his quarry would use any door other than the one in front of him.*

*He liked it that the metalwork adorning Chez Philippe's main door looked like a fence. He liked it even more that the restaurant's layout made everyone inside sitting ducks, just like the pampered birds that swam in the restaurant's fountain and lived in a penthouse that was finer than the homes of literally everyone he knew. The ducks even had a freaking pool. He knew this, because he had ridden the elevator up there and looked.*

He knew that there were security cameras on him, because places like this had them everywhere. Good luck identifying him from any video in this brand-new hat, pulled low over his eyes, and this oversized new jacket that he would never wear again. He'd even bought new shoes, a size too big, in case they found footprints beside the grave sized for two where he'd be putting little Kali and her interfering new friend.

He didn't know where the grave would be yet, and this left him feeling unbalanced. He'd always been so deliberate. Drive to a new town. Scope out a deserted spot. Dig a grave. Find a woman. Put her in that grave and drive away, disposing of the evidence as he passed from little town to little town. What had come over him to kill Frida, someone he knew, and to do it here where he lived?

He had always idealized Ted Bundy, who had used his charm to lure women to their deaths. Bundy could make a woman disappear while walking down a public hallway, and so could he. But Bundy had lost control at the end, rampaging through a sorority house like a man begging to be caught. Was he losing control, too, just like Bundy?

No. He was proceeding logically, as always. Or perhaps he was just pretending he was still in control of his actions, as he planned to charm a woman off the streets of a major city in broad daylight. If Bundy could do it, he could.

# Chapter Twenty-four

The maître d' had the unflappable bearing that comes with working at a superlative restaurant, so he'd answered Faye's nervous assurances that she had reservations with nothing but "Madame." Then he had ushered her to a table that was perfectly lovely.

As he led them to their table, Faye forced herself to take the first step into the restaurant's intimidating dining room. Putting a hand on Kali's back that said, "I've got you," she moved forward and, in so doing, propelled the child into a space that was terrifyingly ornate. Ceilings of dizzying height were rimmed with gilded molding and supported by gilded columns. Small staircases with golden railings ushered them from level to level. Deep green walls were hung with mirrors and draperies, and marble was everywhere.

Faye was grateful when they reached their table, where they could sit down and hide half of their inappropriate clothing under its richly draped tablecloths.

Chez Philippe's afternoon tea seemed to be a popular place for well-heeled mothers to take their daughters. Every one of those daughters had a cell phone in hand. Some of them were shooting photos of their food, probably to post on social media so that everyone would know they'd been to Chez Philippe. Some of them were taking selfies, probably for the same reason. And some of them were slumped in their chairs, using their thumbs to scroll or to play games.

Faye slipped her phone under the table and laid it on Kali's lap, so that it wouldn't be obvious that the girl didn't have one. The girl took a selfie of the two of them with a burnished wall sconce in the background.

"You do that well. My selfie skills aren't the best," Faye said.

"Sylvia lets me use her phone sometimes."

They had hardly placed their order when the first tiered tray, silver-toned and shining, landed on their table and Kali said, "Those are the fanciest sandwiches I've ever seen. Uncle Laneer has just gotta see these."

She would have put some in her purse for him, but Faye talked her out of it. "Take a picture."

"Can't taste a picture."

"You can make him some. It's not hard. I know a good chicken salad recipe."

Kali examined the morsel from all angles. "I think you're right. It's ain't like it's hard to cut off the crust and make little triangles." Then she put the whole triangle in her mouth and reached for another one.

The next course was blueberry scones with marmalade and clotted cream, and Kali approached the crumbly pastries with the same strategy: Admire them, declare that she could make them, and devour them. Faye saw culinary school in Kali's future.

She wished she could believe that Kali had forgotten that she was out-of-place here among the well-dressed women who were sending their food back half-eaten, but she saw a small hand reach up every now and then to straighten a barrette. She saw the lively eyes dart from table to table, checking to see whether the other girls were eating their sandwiches with their fingers or their forks. She might even have compared the small diamond engagement ring on Faye's left hand to the massive rocks on the other women's hands and earlobes, but maybe Faye was the one chafing under the conspicuous weight of the other women's jewelry. She wished she could tell whether they were judging her for her clothes or for how much she was eating.

Maybe these women who belonged here had already dismissed her as unworthy. Or maybe they hadn't noticed her at all. Faye wasn't sure which one was worse.

No, they were looking. She could see them now, mother and daughters, their appraising eyes raking over a woman in sensible sandals and a girl in a faded dress dotted with elephants. She hoped Kali hadn't noticed, but a girl who cared enough about her appearance to sneak into the bathroom and decorate her hair was old enough to feel the pressure of social judgment.

The scones distracted them both from the scrutiny of their peers, and that was a good thing.

"Best biscuits I ever had, but they're just biscuits with blueberries stirred in. Don't know why they call 'em scones. Laneer grows blackberries. Reckon I could make these with blackberries instead of blueberries?"

Faye said she thought that would be delicious, but Kali was already musing that Laneer's plums would make marmalade that was just as good as the orange marmalade ladled over her scone. And then another towering multitiered tray arrived, this time loaded with desserts, and Faye decided that she and Kali were going to rise the challenge of eating every last one of them, calories and all, and to hell with any judgment that might radiate from the social-ites around her.

• • ● • •

*He was not surprised to see his quarry exiting those cage-like doors, side by side and right on schedule, because Chez Philippe didn't serve afternoon tea forever. He had a gift for predicting the motions of people who didn't know they were being watched and, sure enough, Faye and Kali turned to walk down a short passageway, just as he'd expected. It led to the exterior door he had known they would use.*

*He rose, put some cash on the table, and headed for another door nearby. From there, he could easily trail them from BB King Boulevard to their car. This was going to be easy.*

*He had spent the afternoon waiting for a sign. If Faye had ever once left Kali's side—to go to the bathroom, perhaps, or to pay a bill while the girl watched the ducks—he would have snatched her then, knowing that he was meant to kill the woman and spare the child.*

*This hadn't happened, so the converse must be true. He was meant to kill them both.*

• • ● • •

As Faye approached the door to BB King Boulevard, her step slowed.

"Kali, did you want to take a taste of what we just ate to your Uncle Laneer and Sylvia?"

"Don't have anything to take them. You told me it wasn't polite to put anything in my purse."

"It's not. But the hotel's got a bakery in the lobby over

there. I bet they sell the same stuff, plus a lot more."

Kali turned on her heel and said, "Show me where."

● ● ● ● ●

*It was as if the woman and child had dropped down a rabbit hole, and he really didn't think there were any rabbit holes in the Peabody's grand lobby. They had been mere steps from the BB King door when he last laid eyes on them. By the time he exited his own door, they should have been right where he wanted them: close enough to tail but far enough away to be sure they wouldn't see him. Soon enough, he would judge that the time was right. They would see him but it would be too late.*

*He risked stepping back into the lobby a single time, scanning the area around the fountain, in case the little girl had demanded to see the ducks one more time. Woman and child were not there.*

*When his prey were dead and buried, it would do him no good to be visibly obvious on the Peabody's security cameras, prowling around the lobby mere moments after his victims were last seen. He couldn't afford to keep looking for them, but they had to leave the hotel sometime. Until then, he needed to content himself with hovering on the sidewalk in an unobtrusive spot, waiting for them to emerge.*

● ● ● ● ●

Having secured a big bag of goodies for Laneer and Sylvia, Faye looked at her watch. "We can't go yet! You have to see this."

The crowd around the fountain had grown too much to get near and Kali was grousing that she couldn't see the ducks, but Faye said "Hang on," and situated them in an area near the elevators where the crowd was thinner. Within seconds, a recorded Sousa march blared and Faye patted herself on the back for her good timing.

A red carpet stretched from the elevator's gleaming door to the stone fountain, and it carved an opening in the crowd, because nobody dared to step on the carpet. As the music played, the five mallard ducks descended a set of carpeted stairs and sashayed down the carpet, flicking their tails and waddling with determination. Faye thought that Kali might actually die of joy as the ducks proceeded along their triumphal route.

Perhaps ducks can read human minds. Faye was telegraphing unfocused thoughts at the ducks that said mostly, "Make her happy," and the green-headed drake seemed to have heard her. He stopped right in front of Kali and rose up tall, flapping his wings and looking her right in the eyes. Then he followed the four females into the elevator and its heavy door slid shut behind him.

Kali looked suddenly deflated, as if she'd been left physically smaller when her excitement seeped out. "Is it time to go home now?"

Faye knew that their exciting afternoon had to be over sometime, but she was happy to be able to tell Kali that they weren't finished quite yet. "Did you forget? The river."

A short walk later, they were standing in Tom Lee Park, looking at a breathtaking amount of water fleeing to the Gulf of Mexico. Faye judged that it wasn't quite a mile wide, but it was close. She knew that it carried a full load of the sediment that earned it the name "The Muddy Mississippi," but it looked more blue than brown. From their vantage point on the bluff, the river looked almost peaceful. Ripples covered its surface, but they were so gentle that they gave no indication of the unimaginable power beneath.

Faye considered saying all of these things to Kali, but trimmed it back to one obvious statement. "I told you it was big."

Then she showed Kali the monument to Tom Lee, an African-American man who had rescued thirty-two survivors of a wrecked steamboat in 1925 in his small boat, despite not knowing how to swim. They settled onto a bench nearby, taking a little time just to watch the river roll. Its elemental power led Faye's thoughts to life and death. From there, they went straight to Frida.

The river put Faye in mind of Frida's killer. It was deadly in and of itself. The river didn't seize its victims out of hatred. They merely found themselves sucked into whirlpools because drowning people is what rivers do. Why was that her impression of the killer?

Maybe it was because Frida's murder site seemed like an odd place for a woman to be killed out of passion. It was her impression that women who were killed by lovers died in their homes and at their jobs and as they went about their daily business. Frida's ex-husband certainly knew her comings and goings, so it seemed like this would have been Linton's approach. Mayfield, too, could easily know Frida's routine. Faye had seen him strolling down her street just the day before.

If the murderer was Armand, then he had kept Frida out all night and killed her at the end of their date. If so, then the murder site made a strange kind of sense. Perhaps Frida had refused to invite him into her house and he had lost his temper, dragging her into the woods and killing her in a fit of rage. But how did that explain the carefully dug grave? Either it had been dug before he took

Frida out or else he'd somehow acquired a shovel. Since he would have been physically dragging Frida to her fate, he couldn't have had a shovel in his hand, so it would have had to have been waiting for him by the creek.

No matter what suspect she considered, the grave and the shovel that had dug it argued against a crime of passion. They argued for premeditated murder by someone who had already chosen the spot where he would bury her.

As someone who dug for a living and occasionally encountered buried bodies, Faye found that she couldn't quit thinking about Frida's meticulously dug grave, straight-sided and square-cornered. Those square corners spoke of murder committed by a cold-blooded someone who was simply doing what killers do. Faye believed to her core that Frida's murderer had no more remorse than the Mississippi and he had no more of a soul. He was a man who was practiced at killing, a man who would jump at the chance to do it again.

She stretched an arm along the back of the bench. It didn't touch Kali but it encircled her. Maybe her motive was to comfort Kali, but Faye felt more inclined to protect her. The river didn't care much about what happened to little girls.

After a time, Kali squinted upriver at Mud Island, sitting well off the river's east bank.

"It don't look so far to that island. I got a lot of experience wading in the creek. I think I could walk there. What do you think, Faye?"

Faye started sputtering things like, "It's farther than it looks," and "Deep! It's deep!" and "You can't imagine what the currents are like," until Kali started to laugh and couldn't stop.

"I'm not stupid, Faye. You're a real smart person, but

you need to learn how to know a joke when you hear one," she said. And then she laughed some more.

● ● **●** ● ●

*The disappearance of his prey was disorienting. It knocked his mind into an unfamiliar groove. Or perhaps the mounting panic wasn't unfamiliar, but he had successfully held himself together for a long time. With occasional outpourings of fear and rage, he had managed himself quite well, and he was proud of it, but frustrations like these brought out the unwelcome thoughts. They brought out the voices. His father's voice was a roaring thing that told him he was no good and never would be. His mother's voice was a tenuous screaming that reminded him of the times his father wielded his belt on both mother and child.*

*His hands were shaking and that wasn't good. He jammed them in his pockets and stood on Union Avenue, wondering where all the security cameras were.*

*A series of big potted streetside shrubs showed that the city had put some effort into beautification. He chose one and stood close, practically hugging it, while pretending to talk on his phone. Bush, phone, and hat would obscure his identity on surveillance videos and he liked that.*

*Where were they? He had asked the universe for a sign. When this opportunity had presented itself, he'd believed that the response had been, "Kill them both," but maybe he had misunderstood. Maybe the message had been "Spare the girl and kill the woman, even if it means you have to try again another day."*

*He waited beside the bush for an interminable period, far longer than was safe, but he used the waiting time to his advantage. By the time he left, he had thought through five scenarios that would extricate him from this situation. All of them left Dr. Faye Longchamp-Mantooth dead and buried.*

• • ● • •

If a bird, perhaps a duck in flight, could have looked down at the Peabody Hotel, nestled in the heart of downtown Memphis, it would have seen a woman and child leave via a door on South Second Street, then head south. It would also have seen a big man in a hat and a jacket too heavy for the summer day, waiting patiently near the corner of Union Avenue and South BB King Boulevard. The man would have stood motionless for quite a long time while the woman and child moved steadily away from him, making their way downriver and west.

The bird would have seen the woman and child approach Riverside Drive, cross it, and find the walking trail that parallels the great Mississippi River. The pair's journey would take a while and, after some time, the bird would see the man begin to pace, looking from time to time at the hotel's grand entrances in consternation. After more time passed, the duck would see him walk away, unlock his car, and leave. When the man's car began to move, the woman and child would be finding a park bench and settling down for a little rest. As he faded from sight, they would still be sitting comfortably on that bench, watching the river do what rivers have always done.

The duck, who dived and swam for its supper, would have known that the rivers show different faces as you go deeper. The surface waters are riffled by the wind, and the direction the ripples go has no bearing on what the water beneath is doing. The deepest water hugs the bottom of the river and the underside of its bluffs. Its undercurrents tug at the carcasses of dead trees and the broken bellies of sunken boats.

The deeper you go, the colder the river water grows. It wants to suck the heat from your blood. It wants to drown you. It wants to tug you downstream, deeper, until it makes you realize that you will not go on forever, but the river will.

# Chapter Twenty-five

It had been a mistake for Faye to rush back to her car after taking Kali home, hurrying to place a phone call to the detective. She was a deliberate woman, usually, and she liked to gather a small mountain of facts before she acted on important matters. When the facts were there, though, she didn't hesitate to share them and then to act. The details of Frida's case had led her to an unsettling and unlikely conclusion, but facts were facts, so she'd laid her argument out for McDaniel and waited for his response.

Now she was listening to him dismiss her ideas, using his years of experience as a bludgeon. She couldn't compete with his experience, but that didn't mean that she was wrong.

"You think a serial killer killed Frida? Everybody thinks their case is the biggest and baddest, Faye," he had said. "Everybody thinks they're chasing a serial killer. This man may have killed people before. He may kill again. I agree that he's dangerous. But I have no reason to think that he was the kind of deranged serial killer you see on TV."

McDaniel's tone was respectful, more or less, but he was putting Faye in her place. He was the experienced detective and she was not. He was happy to use her to open communications with a community that distrusted him, but he didn't want to consider her input.

His voice was firm when he said, "The only thing special about this case is that she was buried alive."

Faye drove slowly as she talked, peering into the evening shadows on either side of this street where a dead woman had lived. They were deep and dark enough to hide anything or anyone. "Being buried alive is pretty special, don't you think?"

Her almost-obsolete cell phone only distorted McDaniel's chuckle slightly as he said, "You got me there. I agree that it would be special if I thought he buried her alive on purpose, but we don't know that he did. Maybe he got in a hurry because he heard you coming. There may even be a shred of evidence that he did hear you coming."

"What makes you think that? What evidence?"

"Frida wasn't raped and her purse was found nearby, with money still in the wallet. If he planned to rob her or molest her sexually, you interrupted him, so he covered her up and ran away."

Faye considered that a good thing, sort of, but its goodness was mostly counterbalanced by Frida's death. "Maybe he wasn't a rapist. What if he never intended to do anything but kill her? What if he is a serial killer and all he wanted was the experience of snuffing out her life?"

"If I thought the Zodiac Killer was prowling around Sweetgum State Park, I would have brought the FBI into this way before now. If you really think some phantom killer is running around this part of the South, why haven't you run home to Florida?"

What could she say to McDaniel? Maybe the truthful answer was "I'm still here because of Kali."

Or maybe the right answer was, "Deep down, I don't

think I'm in any more danger now than I was when I agreed to do a job in a tough neighborhood."

The rock-bottom truth might even be "I need this job, my employees need this job, and I'm not scared enough to cancel it. Yet."

Instead of answering his question, she bounced it back at him. "If you were in my shoes, would you run back home to Florida?"

McDaniel was silent for a moment. Then he said, "Well, we can't exactly evacuate everyone in a five-mile radius of a crime scene, or even a one-mile radius, not even for a little while. We certainly can't clear them all out indefinitely. And I do think the killer knew Frida and had it in for her, specifically. I honestly don't think he's prowling around those woods looking for somebody new to bludgeon. So what would I do in your shoes? Hmm...well, I do think I'd stay and do the job."

"Even if it means keeping five community college students within that five-mile radius? I'm responsible for them, you know."

His answer was quick and sure. "I'm sure you had them sign releases."

"Morally responsible. I'm the adult here, and I have to balance the good that this job is doing them, personally and financially, against any danger I'm putting them in."

"So you're balancing a job that could put them on a path to an education and a lifetime of steady employment against a theoretical danger that comes from a killing that happened more than a mile away? Faye, you're giving a chance to young people who haven't had many of those. One of them lost a father to murder, right?"

"Two. Richard and Stephanie." Having lost her own father, Faye ached for them.

"And one of them has a juvenile record?"

"Davion. Jeremiah says he was arrested years ago for a bar brawl." Faye didn't like the way that this information stamped calm, thoughtful Davion with a label that said, "Dangerous," so she hurriedly added, "But he hasn't been in any trouble since."

"Faye, if you want to know the truth, I think you're doing the Lord's work. I say you keep these kids on the job. You were smart to move them to that motel downtown. Institute a buddy system, for sure. Murderer or not, you don't want any of those kids prowling the Beale Street bars all alone. And I'll do my part by sending officers to drive by your worksite and the hotel several times a day. You'd be amazed at the impact of the sight of a black-and-white on your average criminal."

"Thank you for that, but do you really think Frida was killed by an average criminal?" Faye felt compelled to disagree with that position, one more time and for the record. "I don't think there was anything average about her murder."

It crossed her mind to ask if he'd be so sure that Frida was killed by an average everyday murderer-down-the-street if she'd died in a ritzier zip code, but she squelched that impulse.

"Honestly? I think she was killed by a mean, vindictive ex-boyfriend. Or ex-husband. She had more than one mean, vindictive ex, so it may take me a while, but I'm going to find out which one killed her, and I'm going to nail his sorry ass to the wall. In the meantime, I think you and your crew should enjoy sunny Memphis in July. You couldn't have come in October? Or May? It's beautiful here in May, but I advise staying in your air-conditioned house in July."

"I can't afford to do that. Amazingly enough, my phone company expects me to write them checks every July."

"Mine, too."

A factory outlet store near Laneer's house had sold Faye a yellow dress in Frida's size. It was the same sunny shade as the one the murdered woman had worn on her last night. The bodice was supported by slender straps, just like Frida's had been. She had almost gotten a pair of strappy silver heels, but she'd remembered at the last minute that "open casket funeral" really meant "half-open casket funeral." Frida's body would only be visible from the waist up, so the shoes weren't necessary, and Kali would never know if the skirt of the dress was all wrong. It just might be possible that this dress would fool her.

Laneer met her on the front porch, so that Kali wouldn't see her deliver this yellow dress. When Faye handed it to Laneer, still in the shopping bag, she said, "People will send a lot of flowers. Tell the funeral home to put some in the casket with her. You know—to cover up the dress as much as possible. If we're lucky, Kali will never notice the difference."

She said good-bye, then turned back to the old man. "I forgot. There's another dress in the bag, a black one for Kali. I went ahead and got it, because most little girls don't own black dresses. Children like happy colors."

In her car, yet another dress waited in a second shopping bag, black and in Faye's size, because she didn't travel with funeral-appropriate clothes. As she opened her car door, one last thought occurred to her.

"Laneer," she called out. "The flowers. Tell the funeral

home to use pink carnations in the casket with Frida. They'll tell you that they won't look good on a yellow dress, but you insist. They're what Kali wants."

● ● ● ● ●

Faye was drifting into a troubled sleep when a ringing phone brought her back to a troubled reality. Her first thought was that Joe was calling to nag her to come home, but the voice that answered her was female. She threw on a robe and crept out into the hall, so that she could talk without waking Yvonna. Faye pretended she didn't know that Yvonna was her new roommate because she had lost a game of Rock, Paper, Scissors. Yvonna really needed to learn to pick paper sometimes.

Settling herself in the stairwell that had become her impromptu office, Faye said, "Sylvia? Is that you? Is something wrong? Is Kali okay?"

"Kali's fine. Everything's fine. She's stretched out on Laneer's couch, sleeping like a baby. I think you tired her out with that walk and that trip to the fancy hotel restaurant. When she starts talking to me again, I'm going to get her to tell me all about it."

Faye didn't want to ask, "If everything's fine, then why on Earth are you calling me after midnight?" so she floundered for something friendlier to say.

Sylvia didn't wait for her to respond. She talked fast, like a woman with no time to waste, but then Sylvia always sounded that way. "I need for you to tell the police some things."

Faye still wasn't sure yet why this merited a middle-of-the-night call, but Sylvia was talking about the police, so she must be getting to her point.

"I can do that, Sylvia, but why don't you tell the police yourself? It sounds like you know something important, so they're going to have questions for you that I can't answer. It's way easier for you to do the talking."

"I don't talk to the police."

"I've seen you talk to McDaniel. He's not a bad guy."

"I answer questions from the police when they get asked. I know how to be polite and respectful, when I need to be, because it's the people that act nasty who they remember. But I don't offer them anything extra, and I sure don't call up the police to pass the time of day."

This debate was going nowhere, and Faye hadn't lived Sylvia's life. Who was she to say whether the woman's suspicion of police officers was warranted or not? If the woman had information that needed to be passed on to Detective McDaniel, the smart thing for Faye to do was to listen.

"I'll tell him whatever you want me to tell him, Sylvia."

"First of all, tell him that Mayfield and Linton ain't as dumb as they look."

"What are you saying?"

"I'm saying that Mayfield is smart when he wants to be smart. When he was in high school, he used those long arms and legs to be the best quarterback we ever had. Good grades, too. Woulda gone to college if his rap sheet didn't scare off the scouts. Mayfield ain't dumb. Dumb people make bad quarterbacks."

Faye wasn't much of a sports fan, but this sounded true. "What about Linton? Was he an offensive lineman or something?"

"Don't know what he did in high school, but I know what he did after. Seems like he made a big score on some test the Navy gave him and they were gonna train him to do electrical work on nuclear submarines. He could've worked for them for his whole life, or he could've done his time and got out, ready to be an electrician. That's a good job. You can be your own boss. Hire some people to help you. Build up a good business."

"Then why is Linton working at the convenience store?"

"Couldn't keep his fists to his self. The Navy only likes you to hurt people when they say so."

McDaniel was going to want some proof of the things Sylvia was saying, but Faye had no doubt that he could get it. Surely, he had underlings who could check the local high school yearbook for its football rosters.

Sylvia wasn't finished talking. McDaniel would be fit to be tied when he realized how much helpful information he couldn't get because his badge scared people.

"Tell him to talk to Arkansas. And Mississippi."

Faye let a beat of silence pass while she processed that statement. "Well, now, you've got me stumped. How is McDaniel supposed to talk to two whole states?"

"To their police. To their sheriffs. Their highway patrol. Hell, I don't know who's who when it comes to people in uniforms with guns. Just tell him to talk to the people who are out there hunting for missing girls and pulling dead women out of dumpsters."

Faye fought back the memory of two hands thrusting up from the ground, grasping for help. There were people who saw things like that all the time.

"What are you saying, Sylvia? Do you know of someone in particular? Someone who was killed? Someone missing?"

"None of those things. I'm just saying that our policeman needs to talk to the other people who are looking. Or who should be looking."

"Who? It will help him do his job if you can tell me who."

Faye was shocked to hear Sylvia sobbing. She had been so calm, even when coming to terms with terrible news about a young woman she clearly cared about. Faye recognized the sound of someone who had been strong for other people until she just had nothing left.

"Laneer is in his house, crying himself sick, because that detective called to tell him how Frida died."

"He got the coroner's report? Since I was there with Laneer?"

It had only been a few hours since Faye left Laneer's house and McDaniel had spent some of that time talking to Faye. Since she doubted that the coroner had called at eleven p.m., McDaniel had known the cause of death when he spoke with Faye, and he had made it a point not to tell her. Maybe he'd known more than that and he was keeping it from her. This information rankled.

"Yeah. You hadn't been gone an hour."

"He must have called right after he hung up from talking to me."

"He didn't tell you nothing about it, right? With you helping him every way you know how? And you wonder why I don't talk to the police. Everything they say and everything they don't say—it's all a lie."

Faye's mother had taught her to trust and even revere the police, telling her to run to them when she was in trouble. She felt that lifelong trust begin to crack. "Mississippi and Arkansas. What were you going to tell me about them?"

"Tell the policeman to call the minister at Clay Creek Baptist Church in Corinth."

"Corinth, Mississippi?"

"Yeah. My sister goes there, and they spent six weeks last

year praying for a woman what never came back. Somebody buried her in the old graveyard out behind her own church, and they never did find out who done it. They ain't used that cemetery since the Depression and nobody noticed that somebody'd dug an extra grave out there. Marked it with a big rock, he did, like people used to do when they didn't have money for a headstone. Blended right in with the other old graves."

"How was she killed?"

"That coroner said there hadn't been no gun and no knife. She'd been beat with something, but he didn't know what it was."

"Why do you think McDaniel should know about that case?" Faye asked, hoping the answer wasn't that the poor woman in Mississippi had also been buried alive.

"He told Laneer that the devil what killed Frida didn't use a gun nor a knife. Said she was beat with something big and wide. And heavy. The way her skull was cracked and—"

Sylvia choked and tried again. "And the way the marks on her face was curved, well, they make him think the bastard killed Frida with a shovel."

"The shovel he buried her with?"

Another choking noise sounded and then, "Most likely. I thought we was going to lose Laneer when he found that out. He took to his bed. I know he's awake in there, 'cause I hear him crying, but he won't answer when I knock on the door. If he won't come out tomorrow, Kali won't know what's wrong, but there ain't no way we need to tell her every last little thing about what happened to her mama."

Faye agreed, without reservation. "What happened in Arkansas?"

"Laneer's second cousin knew about a woman south of

Earle who went missing and turned up dead. Two years back, I think. Beat to death, and they never found the one that did it. Found her buried in a state park, and the killer had done a fine job of covering up the grave. Even laid out some grass seed. They only found her by accident. Some little kid picked that spot to dig a fort, and ain't that a terrible thing?"

"Worse than terrible. And it makes you wonder how many times he covered up the grave so well that nobody ever found it."

"Exactly."

"What else makes you think the Arkansas murder is related to Frida's?"

"The police never did turn up a murder weapon. Never even decided what it was. Laneer's cousin would tell you she didn't think they tried too hard, but maybe that's just her."

Faye tried to retain her objectivity. Lots of murder victims were buried by their killers, or so she thought. Maybe they were almost all dumped without a burial. How would she know? She didn't have McDaniel's experience, which is why Sylvia should have been talking to him and not to her.

She supposed a good percentage of those lonely corpses, buried and unburied, were beaten to death by unidentifiable weapons. It was hard to make a case that all murders accomplished by bludgeoning were related.

"Can you think of anything else, Sylvia? Anything that would make you think that the same person did all the killing?"

"The only other thing I know about is that all three of 'em turned up right around the Fourth of July."

It crossed Faye's mind that bodies, even well-buried

bodies, might be easier to find in July, when the heat would make odors more noticeable. To people…to animals…to insects and larvae and worms…

She stopped her mind from traveling down that path. "I'll tell McDaniel everything you've told me, Sylvia. I'll tell him right now." She almost said, "You should talk to him yourself. I think you can trust him," but she didn't, because she was no longer sure that it was true.

She said good-bye to Sylvia and dialed McDaniel, trying and failing to make herself feel safe in the spartan but well-lit stairwell.

When he answered, Faye got right to the point.

"Sylvia called and she told me some things that can't wait until morning. She wanted me to tell you about an unsolved case in Corinth you should check out. A woman was found buried in an unmarked grave in a church cemetery."

"I'm already on it. Not a lot of clues that I know of, but I've got the case file in my stack of things to read."

"What about the woman found near Earle? In Arkansas."

"Don't know about that one. What did Sylvia say about it?

"She said that the body turned up buried in a state park."

Faye could almost hear McDaniel sit up straighter as he said, "Another state park?"

"Yes."

"Murder weapon?" he asked.

"None found. They don't even know what he used to beat her to death."

"I'll get on the phone with folks in Earle first thing in the morning. Tell Sylvia thank you for me. And tell her that she could have told me this herself. I don't bite."

"It never occurred to me before how important it is for people to trust the law. The people, I mean. Laws aren't much good without trustworthy people to enforce them."

He didn't answer her right away. Finally, he said, "Maybe I'm missing your point, because I am really, really sleepy, but do I hear an accusation in what you just said? And a passive-aggressive one, I might add? Because honestly, Dr. Longchamp-Mantooth, I didn't sleep last night and I don't expect to sleep tonight. It wears on my nerves to think that I'm working myself to death hunting Frida Stone's killer, but her family still doesn't trust me. Or you."

"Trust goes both ways." Faye was flabbergasted to hear her voice tremble. Where did her unflappability go? If she couldn't hang onto that, she was in uncharted waters.

"What are you saying? That I should have told you how Frida died before I told her family?"

"You're in charge of how information flows. It's your case. But you asked me to help you, then you talked to me for the better part of an hour and didn't tell me something really important. Critically important. It's hard for me to tell Frida's family how trustworthy you are when, at the very same time, they can see that you're keeping things from me."

"As you said, it's my case." His voice had dropped in pitch. Faye couldn't tell whether she was hearing his anger or whether she was hearing an effort to soothe hers. "Faye, I can see that you care about Frida's family. Why wouldn't you want to help me help them?"

"I do. And I will. But sometime when you're not working night and day, you might think about whether you could help people more if you made sure they knew that you respected them."

Faye wasn't sure what it was about McDaniel that

pissed her off so. He had listened to what she had to say. Yeah, he still clung to his theory that Frida was killed by one of her exes, but he'd also asked her about the women found in the Mississippi churchyard and the Arkansas state park. He hadn't completely dismissed her concerns about a serial killer.

"Sylvia wanted you to know that those two women weren't stabbed or shot. They were beaten with something that was never identified. When Laneer told her that Frida was beaten with a shovel, she immediately wondered if that's what had happened to them."

She only knew what Frida's cause of death was because Sylvia had told her. Faye was pursuing this line of conversation for Sylvia's sake, but also because it conveniently reminded McDaniel that she wasn't dependent on him for information. Or for anything at all. And her confrontational tone of voice let him know that she was pissed that he hadn't told her himself.

Should McDaniel have told her everything he knew as soon as he knew? Maybe not. It wasn't required of him, but he needed her. In the space of just a few hours, Kali and Sylvia had told her things that they would never have told him—important things that he needed to know.

"I guess it might have been good to tell you about the shovel, now that I think about it. You work with shovels every day of the week," he said, and his nervousness was audible. It slowed his speech and accentuated his Tennessee drawl.

"You were under no obligation. But telling me would have been a gesture of cooperation. And respect."

And there it was, the uncomfortable thing that had been nibbling at her psyche from the moment she met Detective Harold McDaniel. Minutes after she had given her all to save Frida's life, he had treated her like a suspect. He had been self-aware enough to back away from that presumption, even going so far as to ask her to be his go-between with Frida's family. Yet there was the undeniable fact that, even after all that, he had chosen not to tell her how Frida died.

How did he expect her to help him if he couldn't be straight with her? In all their conversations, she felt a stiffness, a formality, a barrier.

Was that barrier really based on something as simple and undeniable as her skin color? Kali and Jeremiah had been forthright in saying that she didn't fit into their neighborhood, presumably due to her education and her middle-class pocketbook. They didn't see her as one of them. Yet McDaniel did, despite the fact that Faye probably had about as much money as he did and her doctorate presumably put her far ahead of him in education.

Faye put a hand to her cheek. Without looking in a mirror, she knew that it was brown. She always knew that it was brown. Was she touching the one and only reason that McDaniel had chosen not to trust her? There was no way for her to know.

And this meant that she couldn't afford to trust him, not fully. There was no such thing as one-way trust. There just wasn't.

Sometime between puberty and becoming a mother for the second time, Faye had gained confidence that was often hard for very young women to come by. She'd lost the need to believe that other people thought she was pretty, because she liked the way she looked just fine. She'd also lost the need to be liked by everyone, because she had true friends who loved her the way she was.

After the need to be liked and the need to be desired

fell away, it had become far easier for Faye to see what was important to her now, as a full-grown woman. She needed respect, and she had learned to demand it or walk away.

Detective McDaniel might not like her, and it was completely immaterial to her whether or not he thought she was attractive, but if he wanted her help, then he had damn sure better learn to take her seriously.

Respect goes both ways.

# Chapter Twenty-six

Faye crept back into the motel room so quietly that Yvonna never stirred. Grabbing her laptop off the nightstand where it was charging, she returned to the stairwell and opened it. After poking around in her bookmarks for a minute, she found a link to the article she wanted and clicked it. If McDaniel wanted to keep things from her, maybe she could keep a few things from him without breaking the law.

The article was called "An Algorithm to Die For," which was a dumb headline, since it was about a woman who had developed an algorithm that could save lives. A sexier title like "The Woman All Serial Killers Should Fear" would have gotten more clicks. Faye had read it a week before, and its message had stuck with her.

The article was about a data scientist who believed that lives were being lost because investigators were too busy to share information. And maybe because they didn't trust each other enough to reach out to someone who could help. And maybe because they had evolved to be suspicious and territorial. The reasons didn't matter. The dead did not care why the people working for justice didn't make the best use of the information that they had.

The woman all serial killers should fear was seventy-two years old, short, slight, and wheelchair-bound. Phyllis Windom was a data scientist who had spent her retirement chasing notorious serial killers without ever leaving her house. A lifelong lover of true crime books, her fascination with unsolved murders had blossomed into something much more when she realized that her skill with interpreting data was uncommonly useful in tracking down serial killers.

She had reasoned that a single killing generated a lot of single data points—time of death, murder weapon, age of victim, and so on—but that a murderer with multiple victims committed a series of data-generating events that repeated themselves. To a woman like Phyllis Windom, each serial killer was operating under a personal algorithm that was hard for human beings to perceive in the pile of data generated by all of America's killers. But if she turned all that information over to a computer? She believed it would find patterns in those data sets that could be used to track down some of the most terrifying people who ever lived.

No. That was wrong. She didn't just believe that she could find patterns that identified serial killers. She knew it for a fact.

She knew it because she had found the most notorious serial killer in North Carolina by combing through publicly available data, and she'd done it from the comfort of her bedroom. Much of her information came from the FBI's Uniform Crime Report, which was like a playground for a data scientist with a certain morbid mindset. Once she was comfortable that her work was solid, she'd built a website and had given her database and search algorithm to the public for free.

The article on Faye's screen gave Windom's website address, saving Faye the trouble of searching the Internet for it. She entered through the public login portal and started working her way through Windom's database, using search strings and drop-down menus.

She found the Corinth murder immediately and spent some time studying the file. The victim had been petite, female, African-American, and in her mid-twenties, just like Frida, but so, tragically, were a lot of murder victims. Everything Sylvia had told Faye was correct. The unidentified woman had been found in July in a church graveyard and she'd been bludgeoned with an unidentified weapon. She had not been raped and there had been no evidence for robbery as a motive.

The victim buried in an Arkansas state park, however, did not come up in a search of Windom's database. This was not a surprise. Windom herself had put a big "Help Wanted" banner on her home page, with a caption saying:

Police budgets are tight. Reporting often falls through the cracks. None of the databases I've tapped to build my own data set is complete. If you know of a case that should be here, WRITE ME. "Big Data" is nothing but individual data points. Send me your data, and you may save lives.

Faye shot off an e-mail to Phyllis Windom, telling her everything she knew about the Arkansas murder victim and about Frida. Then she started exploring Windom's database.

First, she searched "Unsolved murders in Mississippi," "Unsolved murders in Arkansas," "Unsolved murders in Tennessee," just to get a sense of the scope of the problem.

Her answer? The scope was big, too big for any one person or any one police department. Once a serial killer began roaming over a wide territory, it just might take an algorithm like this one to find the tracks the killer had left through the data.

Faye was no data scientist, so she just kept entering search strings and pushing go. What was she hoping for? A miracle, probably.

> Missing women in Mississippi
> Missing women in Arkansas
> Missing women in Tennessee

There were just so many of them. This fact alone made Faye want to crawl into bed and resign from the human race.

The clock had rolled on past three when she started another round of random, fruitless searching.

> Unidentified bodies in Mississippi
> Unidentified bodies in Arkansas
> Unidentified bodies in Tennessee

Again, there were just so many. She was getting nowhere and her body needed sleep, so she stomped on her desire to filter those searches by "Unidentified murder weapon" and "Body disposal by burial."

Instead, she navigated back to the WRITE ME button and dashed off a second e-mail to Phyllis Windom.

> I know of three women murdered and buried within an hour's drive of Memphis. They were all bludgeoned in the summertime, one with a shovel

and two with unidentified weapons. I'm working
with your database, but I don't know it well and I'm
slow. One of the murders happened two days ago,
so the clock is ticking. Can you help?

She included a signature line that identified her as a
PhD archaeologist, which she hoped gave the subtle message of "I'm not crazy." After pressing send and closing her
computer, she wanted to sleep, but she couldn't wipe her
mind clean of all the unsolved killings she'd seen on her
silent, glowing screen. Who did such things? More importantly to Faye, who had done such a thing right here in
Memphis? And was it possible that the person who killed
Frida had struck before, many times, and would strike
again?

Or maybe McDaniel was right. Maybe Frida's killing
had been an isolated crime, committed by someone who
knew her. If this was true, she would say that Linton was
the prime suspect. He had a history of violence, both in
the Navy and toward Frida herself. She could still feel the
unwelcome touch of his finger on hers.

But there was something deeply disturbing about
Mayfield's sullen eyes.

On the other end of the charming-to-sullen continuum,
it was hard to suspect the smooth and handsome Armand,
but he was the last man known to have been near Frida,
and that counted for something. Besides, serial killers were
known for being charismatic. Ted Bundy lured dozens of
women to their deaths with nothing more than a fake
limp, a cane, and his satin-smooth patter.

But Faye's mind wouldn't stick with the three obvious
suspects. It strayed. It considered every man she'd met
since coming to Memphis.

There was Jeremiah, who was certainly big enough to overpower a woman Frida's size. What did she know about him anyway?

There was also Kali's teacher, Walt Walker. It made Faye feel unkind and suspicious to suspect a man who had given Kali nothing but kindness, but unkindness and suspicion came easily after two a.m.

Kali's minister, Reverend Atkinson, came to mind as a sign that Faye's ability to suspect people knew no bounds.

Her suspicious mind even turned to Detective McDaniel himself. Wouldn't a job as a homicide detective be a convenient one for a serial killer?

And now Faye realized that she was straying far from what she knew to be true, tiptoeing alone out onto a precarious emotional ledge. She needed stability. She needed calmness and love. She needed Joe.

She pulled her phone out of her pocket to check her notifications. It wasn't like Joe to wait so long to answer her call.

And he hadn't. She had turned her ringer off hours before, afraid of disturbing Chez Philippe's intimidating silence and its intimidating diners, and she'd never turned it back on. Joe had called at bedtime, and she smiled at her mental image of him in a rocker on their front porch, reaching out to her from Joyeuse Island's familiar trees and blue-green water. Her home grounded her. There was a reason that she rarely strayed far or stayed away long.

She could see that Joe's call had been a video call, probably so that Amande and Michael could join in. Michael was long asleep, and Amande was in her room, either asleep or doing whatever seventeen-year-old girls liked to do on their favorite social media sites, all of which were too cool for the likes of Faye. She went to the stairwell and hit return on the video call anyway, because seeing her husband's face would make her feel better. Or maybe seeing her husband's face would put her in a car heading home. She wasn't sure.

He answered on the first ring and she wasn't surprised. While she was away, Joe always kept his phone on at night with the ringer maxed out. And she could tell by the dizzying scene on her screen that he had indeed been sleeping. She saw their bedroom walls and ceiling careen by as he pulled his phone first to his ear and then to his eyes.

"Hey, Faye. Damn, you look good."

Her short, straight black hair was glued to her head with nervous sweat and her skin was shiny-bare, so she took this statement as evidence of love. Or sleepiness. Joe was lying flat on his back in bed, holding the phone up toward the ceiling. He probably couldn't see much through those drowsy eyes.

"How's the job going?" he said.

She noticed that he had not said, "Did they find out who murdered that woman?" so she joined him in avoiding the sore subject.

"Real good," she said. "We did some training at the museum this morning, then we had some fabulous barbecue for lunch. And peach pie. Good heavens, we had some amazing peach pie. I should have gotten you the recipe. Then we moved to this fabulous motel that you see before you."

She waved the phone around the cheery gray stairwell and Joe laughed. Neither of them mentioned the reason she had needed to move her crew.

"After that, I took Kali to The Peabody for tea."

*Danger, danger*, cried the voice in her head, because mentioning Kali opened the door to talking about her mother's murder. Joe looked too comfortable for her to disturb him with death and fear. She changed the subject and he let her.

"One of my employees—Richard—got stinking drunk at lunch. My guess is that he was nearly stinking drunk when we got there and then he took advantage of my credit card to the tune of three beers. Those three beers pushed him over the edge. I wish you'd been here to see him make an idiot of himself."

"Did you fire him?"

"Jeremiah talked me out of it, but I have my eye on him."

Joe grunted and she knew that he meant *Damn straight. You better keep an eye on that one.*

"In the end, it was pretty funny. A twenty-one-year-old man is an adult, for sure, but when you get one staggering drunk? All of a sudden, he might as well be a middle-schooler who's been sneaking drinks out of his daddy's liquor cabinet. It's not a good look."

Joe laughed, but not very loud. It wasn't the half-hearted laugh of a man who doesn't like other men behaving poorly around his wife. It was the laugh of a man about the change the subject, because he wasn't going to let her get away with changing the subject.

"What about that poor woman? Have they found out who did it?"

"No, but they found out how he did it."

"You gonna tell me?"

"Shovel. Beat her with it, then she died of the injuries."

"God."

"Yeah, I know."

Silence between Joe and Faye was usually a comfortable thing, but not now, not when they both were thinking about what Frida had suffered.

"You're going to be really careful until they catch that guy?"

"You know I always am."

"Oh, yes, I do. I know you can do anything you set your mind to, all by your own self. You could roll back the Mississippi and walk across it, if that's what you needed to do. Might be easier on you if you let me help you more." He softened his words with a laugh, and it was the drowsy laugh of a man who needed to go back to sleep.

So she let him do that. She told him to sleep well and to call her soon, and then she blew him a good-night kiss. When his face was gone from her screen, the emergency lighting in the dank stairwell made it seem even danker. She sat there and wallowed in its charmlessness for a while, then she went back to her room.

Yvonna sighed and rolled over in her bed as Faye eased her body under her own covers, pulling them over her chin. It was time to sleep. She just wished she believed that sleep would actually be coming for her.

# Chapter Twenty-seven

*He usually slept like an innocent. Like the dead.*

*On those times when sleep played coy, leaving him alone with himself, certainty dawned and he knew it was time to act. Tonight, the blood lust had roused him, sending him hunting for the woman who had frustrated him that very afternoon.*

*Faye Longchamp-Mantooth had been wise to pick up and move. If she'd stayed another night alone in the state park cabin, she would already be a dead woman. Instead, she'd moved to this motel that was no more defensible, except for one thing. He had no way to know which of its dozens of windows was hers.*

*She had parked near the stairwell, so the location of her car told him only that she was sleeping on the side of the building where he was parked. Sitting in his car with a pair of binoculars, he waited, hoping for a miraculous parting of the draperies that would show him where she slept. Just that one stroke of luck would seal her fate.*

*Even if the barely parted curtain revealed that she wasn't alone, he still would go in. Ted Bundy had done some of his best work in a sorority house full of women, walking out to freedom after killing two of them and critically injuring two more. No one had heard a thing.*

*By comparison, killing a woman—two women, even—would be easy in a motel so crappy that odd sounds were simply part of the low-rent experience.*

*The voices in his head argued with each other and with him. One urged restraint. The other demanded that he barge in and go door to door, bludgeoning anyone who answered his knock.*

*For the moment, he had chosen restraint, but there was no guarantee that he could maintain it much longer.*

# Chapter Twenty-eight

Joe lay in the bed, his six-and-a-half-foot frame stretched out from headboard to footboard. The covers on Faye's side were undisturbed. The smooth, unrumpled bedspread and linens made him lonely for her, and he supposed that was why he never disturbed them when she was away. He wanted to be lonely without her. He never wanted to get used to her being gone.

Faye had just blown him a good-night kiss and his phone was still in his hand. He studied its blank screen for only a moment before he came to a decision. He shot a text to Amande.

U awake?

She responded immediately. Joe wondered where kids learned to type so fast. He wasn't even thirty-five and his children made him feel like an old man.

Yeah, but I can't believe u r. Wut's up Dad?

Joe was a deliberate typist, but he tried to return her message quickly. An image of his daughter tapping her foot and saying "Any day now, Dad…" gave him speed, but speed lit his dyslexia on fire. Maybe she could read it anyway.

Need hepl bying a plain tiket

Crap. That looked awful. He wished he hadn't already hit send.

Even with his learning differences, Joe could tell the difference between trendy text abbreviations and embarrassing mistakes. This was why he needed Faye—not to do things for him, but to remind him to take his time.

He heard Amande's light, firm tap on his door, which meant that he could stop typing and start talking,. Praise God for that. He would have walked down the hall and knocked on her door in the first place, but sometimes it was a little uncomfortable to be the father of a young woman. It was better for her to be the one to decide how she wanted to be seen at this time of the morning.

"Come on in," he said.

She entered the room in an oversized tee-shirt and gym shorts, golden-brown curls tumbling over her shoulders. Crossing the room in one long-legged step, she flopped across the foot of his bed.

"A plane ticket? Where are you going? Can I come? What website's giving you problems?"

"Ain't even pulled one up yet. I figured you could do it in half the time."

"I love you, Dad, but it'll be a lot less than half the time."

He handed her his phone to use, but she waved her tablet at him. "I'll use this. So seriously…where are you going?"

"How quick can you get me to Memphis?"

"You're going to see Mom? Does she know? Is it a surprise? I guess you do have an anniversary coming up...." Her voice drifted off and she cocked her head to the right, studying him. "What's wrong?"

"Well...hmm." Amande was nearly grown and she'd led a hard life before he and Faye had adopted her. Joe figured he didn't need to beat around the bush. "Your mama tried to save a woman's life yesterday. Well, I reckon I should say she did save her. She called 911 and she did CPR, and the lady was still living when the ambulance took her. It ain't really your mama's fault that the hospital couldn't keep her alive."

"So you want to go up there and spend some time with her, in case she's upset about the poor woman. Dad, that's really sweet. What happened that Mom needed to do CPR? Heart attack? Stroke?"

"Somebody showed her the business end of a shovel."

"She was beaten with a shovel? Bad enough to kill her? Dad. You have to go."

"Considering that the person who did the beating is still running loose and your mama won't come home, yeah. I have to go."

Amande was too busy tapping on her tablet to answer him. She was also mumbling, but Joe judged that she was mostly talking to herself and didn't need any answers from him.

"Tallahassee's the closest airport, but the 5:40 a.m. flight is booked solid. So's the one that leaves at six. The 6:20 makes two stops and takes thirteen hours to get there. That's not counting the time to rent a car and get to Mom."

"That's what? Twenty hours from now? That's way

too long. How come the airplanes take so blamed long? They're supposed to be fast."

She peered at him through the lashes of lowered eyelids, then she pecked around on the tablet a little more. "I could get you something out of Mobile, but it would take just as long, with the drive time and all."

"The woman your mother found? She was buried alive. I need to be there now. I mean right now this minute."

Silent, Amande tapped out a few more keystrokes and hit the enter key. After a moment's reflection, she typed a while longer, then pounded the enter key like someone who was done with passive research and was ready for action.

"It's a nine-hour drive from the marina in Panacea to Memphis. Add in time to throw some clothes in a bag and take the boat to the marina, plus a few minutes to stop at the Sheriff and Magda's house, and I'd say we can be in Memphis by lunchtime, easy. Wait! We'll gain an hour with the time change. If we ignore the speed limits, we can have a late breakfast down the street from Elvis' house."

Joe felt control of the conversation slipping away from him and he did his best to stop it. "I like the idea of driving, but you can just quit saying 'we.' Who'll take care of Michael?"

"Why do you think we're stopping to see the Sheriff and Magda? Because we miss them? Well, I do miss them, but that's not why."

"No. I'm serious. I'm going to Memphis because it scares me that your mother is there. What makes you think I would take you?"

"Dad. You haven't slept and now you're talking about driving the rest of the night and into the morning. You'll die in a flaming car if I let you do that."

Joe said, "No, I won't," but she was still talking and she showed no signs of taking a breath.

"Plus, I'm sorry to say this out loud, but it's true. We both know you drive like an old man. I can drive it in nine hours or less, but it'll take you ten. Or more. And also, I wish you'd let me show you how to use your GPS again. You could find your way out of a Panamanian rain forest without a compass, but you're useless on the highway. I don't want to answer my phone and hear you saying that you're not sure how you wound up in Dallas."

Joe was, for the first time in his life, beginning to like the idea of corporal punishment.

"We'll swap off driving so we can both get some sleep. I'll drive the legs that go through Montgomery and Birmingham." She squinted at him. "And Tallahassee. You'll be fine on the straight stretches. As long as you don't have to deal with any city traffic. Let me check the traffic reports." She lowered her head and went back to tapping on her tablet.

"We're not talking about the driving. We're talking about me going someplace dangerous. Like, murder-level dangerous. Without you."

"I just want to get you to Mom fast, and I want you to get there alive. Once we get to Memphis, you can…I don't know…get us a motel room far away from the murdering spot and you can warehouse me there. You'll have the car, so I can't go anywhere you don't want me to go. I'll have cable TV, which I'd like to remind you that we don't have here, and I'll have the Internet. Wait. Hang on. Let me find us a place with free Internet. And free parking."

Joe felt himself crumbling under the barrage of words that, if he were to be honest, did make a lot of sense. "Your mother said she'd moved her crew to a motel that was pretty far from the scene of the crime. It would be simpler if we got a room there. You know she wouldn't have picked a place that charged for Internet. Parking, neither."

"Then why aren't we packing our bags?"

Joe didn't have a good answer for that, so he said, "You be ready in ten minutes or I'm going without you."

Amande was instantly on her feet. He watched her head for her room with the high-stepping lope of a victorious running back enjoying his moment in the end zone, and he knew that Faye was going to kill him for bringing their daughter to a place so dangerous that a young woman had ended up dead. But then, she was already going to kill him just for coming to her and she couldn't kill him twice.

# Chapter Twenty-nine

The phone was loud, really loud. Faye was floating in a dreamless place, a place without fear or pain, and she hadn't been there long. She wished the phone would shut up, because she didn't want to be awake in the bed where she had tossed and turned the night away.

The phone rang again. Yvonna groaned as she threw her sheets over her head, and Faye returned fully to reality. She reached for the phone and her bad shoulder yelled at her for disturbing it.

Detective McDaniel's voice sounded remarkably alert. "I hope I didn't wake you, but I wanted to tell you this while it was still early enough for you to do something about it. It's good news."

She still wasn't fully conscious, but she was awake enough to respond to the promise of good news. "You found the killer."

"I wish. No, my news isn't that exciting, but you should like it. My forensics people say they've done all they can do. They did all they'd planned to do yesterday, but they wanted to do one more walk-over today. Unfortunately, there was a terrible storm early this morning. There's just no point. The odds that there's still any physical evidence that didn't get washed away are zero. They told me to go ahead and release the site to you."

"There was a storm?"

"You're a hard sleeper. Yes, there was a storm. Thunder. Lightning. Wind. Hail. Will the wet ground make it hard for you to work? I'm hoping you'll keep me posted on what you all find at that old CCC site. I've always thought that archaeology was fascinating."

He sounded eager, even ingratiating, like he was hoping she'd stop being mad at him now.

Was she mad at him? Not particularly. He merely made her uncomfortable, unsure, as if the world could shift under her feet and leave her talking again to a man who didn't believe her when she spoke.

Faye couldn't shake the drowsiness. She really needed to sleep all the way through the night sometime soon. "You're saying we can work at the site today? In—" She squinted at her phone. It was six o'clock. "In two hours?"

"Whenever you want to start. You can wait until tomorrow, if it's better to stick to the original plan, but the site is yours when you're ready."

Faye thought through her disorganized plan for the day, which had been to take her crew to the university library and then to…well, honestly, she had been planning to give them Sunday afternoon off. She didn't know about the others, but she would be going to Frida's funeral, and she knew that Jeremiah would want to be there. It made her nervous to leave the group unsupervised after Richard's drunken display, but it wasn't right to require them to go to the funeral of somebody they didn't know.

She was walking a fine line with managing this team. She couldn't work them around the clock because that would put her afoul of about a million labor laws. There was just no way around the fact that they were going to spend a lot of hours unsupervised. Richard's drunken trip to Armand's barbecue joint was evidence that idle hands were an open invitation to Lucifer, but it couldn't be helped.

"Wait until tomorrow? No, I don't want to waste the day. We can get a lot done before I turn them loose so I can go to Frida's funeral," she said to McDaniel. "Tell your forensics people I said thank you for giving today back to us." Then she told him good-bye and dialed Jeremiah to tell him that they had work to do.

Mobilizing the crew had gone smoothly, because everybody was anxious to start the project. Faye and Jeremiah had rousted them out of bed. They'd gotten dressed. Everybody was loaded in the vehicles.

Faye was patting herself on the back for her efficiency, until Jeremiah pulled her aside.

"We need to feed them and I didn't make a grocery run."

Food. Faye knew she was stressed when she forgot about food.

"Oh, yeah. Food. Hmmm."

She tried to picture the state park and the area surrounding it. She couldn't remember any fast food, nor a grocery store, but she knew there was a shabby convenience store, staffed by an unpleasant man. It would have to do.

"I know a place, just a few miles away from the site, and they have a big sign advertising their chicken biscuits. We can stop there and buy chicken biscuits for breakfast, plus some bread and some sandwich meat that should cover lunches for several days."

"Bread. Meat. Ice for the cooler, water, chips. I've got mayonnaise and mustard. That'll make lunch, and it won't cost all that much."

Faye nodded her agreement and they got underway. She hoped they weren't going to be buying their supplies from the sullen and creepy Linton, but even if he had the day off, the odds were good that his replacement would be Mayfield, who didn't seem much better.

Creepy cashier or not, the store was convenient and she didn't have time to waste on looking for another one. If luck completely eluded her, one of Frida's unpleasant exes would be on duty, and the other would be waiting for his shift to start, so that she could enjoy spending time with both of them.

And, because she'd burned all her good luck that day when she received access to the site a day early, that's exactly what she got. Frida's two exes were waiting for them. Mayfield was sitting inside, waiting at a table near the store's lunch counter, and Linton was working the cash register.

Stone-faced and silent, Mayfield watched each of Faye's workers, one by one, as they passed in front of him. She was pretty sure that his eyes lingered longer on the women than the men, which pissed her off and scared her, all at the same time, but he studied the men, too. Jeremiah passed in front of him last and received the same treatment—no talking and lots of looking, despite the fact that Faye was pretty sure that they knew each other.

When Jeremiah proved her right by nodding and saying, "How you doin', Mayfield?", Faye sensed that he wasn't just passing the time of day. He was trying to provoke the silent man.

Mayfield didn't say a thing.

Faye passed him last and she received even more scrutiny than the younger women had. He had looked their bodies up and down, but he kept his eyes only on her face. His aggressive body language—forward-leaning with hands flat on his thighs—made her jumpy. She wondered why he'd chosen her as the target of his intimidating glare. Was it just because she was an outsider?

Linton, on the other hand, seemed to have grown a personality since Faye first saw him. Maybe she'd just caught him on a bad day. He assumed his place at the food counter and began taking orders for breakfast biscuits.

"So that's one bacon-and-egg biscuit for you," he said, pointing at Yvonna, "and chicken biscuits for everybody else but Yogurt Girl."

He pointed to Stephanie, who seemed to have offended Linton by ordering yogurt instead of something he cooked.

"Two chicken biscuits for you," he said, pointing to Davion, "and three for the big dude." He pointed at Richard. "Good job, Big Dude. You're gonna like my biscuits. What about your boss lady and ol' Jeremiah? Where are they at? Do you think they should they get to eat?"

Faye stepped past Davion and Richard, who were standing between her and the counter. "I'd like scrambled egg on my biscuit."

"Hot sauce?"

"If you've got it."

Linton, grinning, plunked a tray on the stainless steel counter. It was loaded with six kinds of hot sauce. "Pick your poison."

"Don't go for the one with purple flames on the label," Jeremiah told her. "Trust me. You'll regret it."

Jeremiah's patronizing air made her want to choose the

purple flames to spite him. Faye knew that this was not a mature response. The man was only trying to be helpful, and spiting him could cost her the lining of her entire digestive tract. Still, the purple flames were calling out to her.

As Faye perused the sauces, she heard an unfamiliar voice behind her. There was only one unfamiliar person in the store, so it had to be Mayfield.

"Same old Jeremiah. Pretending to be important when he's really just a sack of shit."

Eight heads swiveled his way. Faye knew that this was what Mayfield had wanted, and she wished they hadn't given it to him so easily. The man knew how to get people's attention.

Linton grabbed everyone's attention right back. "Takes a sack of shit to know a sack of shit," he said, but somehow he made it into a joke. On her last visit, Linton had been sullen and silent. She would not have expected him to have charisma, but he did. All eyes were on his handsome face.

Finally, Faye could see why Frida had married him. Remembering his cold eyes on her when she first saw him, she also had a pretty good idea why Frida had divorced him.

Mayfield stopped talking and turned his back on Linton. Unbothered, Linton threw some bacon onto the hot griddle and some chicken breasts in the basket fryer, before filling several toaster ovens with biscuits. As everything sizzled and browned, his eyes darted from face to face.

While the food cooked, Linton focused on Jeremiah. "You coulda called me. I know you got one of these." He pulled a smartphone out of his pocket and held it out on an open palm. "Don't you?"

Jeremiah's eyes flicked down to the phone in his hand. "Haven't called you since eleventh grade. Why do you think I oughta do it now?"

"Because I shouldn't have gone a day and a night without somebody telling me my wife was dead."

"She was your ex-wife. The rules are different when you're divorced."

Jeremiah sounded like he was spoiling for a fight and Faye thought he was overreacting. She also thought he would be smart not to challenge Linton. He was marginally bigger than the man cooking his breakfast, but Faye would have predicted that Linton would come out on top in a fist fight. She wondered how much thought Jeremiah had given to the wisdom of provoking this man.

Not much, apparently, because he was still talking. "Besides, Sylvia did the calling. If she thought you should know, you'd know."

"Sylvia never had any good reason to hate me. But she did."

"All you had to do was to make Frida happy. Then she would've liked you."

"Frida always—" Linton stumbled on his words like a man who was realizing too late that there was no good way to criticize your recently murdered ex-wife.

Standing there searching for words, Linton looked like a Greek god, but not the Hollywood kind made of washboards, sinew, and zero percent body fat. No, Linton was built like the old statues of Zeus, the ones with thick chests, thick arms, thick necks, and heavy-lidded faces. Even his slick-shaved skull looked heavy, as if forged of bronze.

"Frida couldn't afford a lawyer. I didn't want to afford a lawyer, because I wanted to be married to her. No papers got signed. She was still my wife till the day she died."

"Well, she's dead now and the funeral's tomorrow," Jeremiah said, taking a step closer. "You planning to come? If you do, folks will expect you to help Laneer pay for it."

"I can chip in, now that I won't be paying anybody rent every month."

"Where you planning to live that won't charge you rent?"

"My house. The one that's mine, now that my wife is dead."

Jeremiah took a big step forward, fists clenched, and Linton hustled out from behind the counter. "You wanna fight? We can fight, but we gotta take it outside this store. I don't want to break anything important with your head."

Neither man moved toward the door. To Faye, it looked like Jeremiah and Linton didn't really want to fight. Not yet. They just wanted to stand face to face and yell at each other.

"Frida's house?" Jeremiah demanded. "That she got from her grandmother? You think that's your house now?"

The bronze-heavy head nodded once. "The law says it is."

It had never occurred to Faye that Frida had owned her home, not seriously. Frida hadn't even owned a car. If she truly had owned the house, it changed everything. Kali still needed to live with Laneer but, properly invested, the money from renting or selling that house could send her to college. Or cooking school. Faye could totally see Kali in cooking school.

But if Frida's possessions went to Linton, house and all, Kali would have her clothes to start her new life, and that was about it. Faye had only known for a moment that inheriting the house had even been an option for Kali. Now, she felt the loss almost as keenly as if it were her own.

"Don't be thinking that Laneer will let you anywhere near that girl," Jeremiah said.

"She's my stepdaughter. She can live with Laneer if she wants to, but she don't have to. If she lives with me, I'll feed her and make sure she's got clothes. Make sure she goes to school. All those things that dads do, I'll do 'em. Laneer ain't got no reason to keep me away from her."

"He thinks he does."

Linton gave him the tiniest possible shrug. "Let him think what he thinks. I got a lawyer looking into things. He says it won't be long before I can move in. Can't wait to kiss my landlord good-bye. Really can't wait to have all that extra spending money."

Mayfield broke into their conversation like a class clown breaking up a fight between the captain of the football team and the surprisingly fierce president of the chess club. "Didn't you hear the timer go off? The biscuits are ready."

Then he settled back into his chair and watched Linton hand out breakfast orders. Jeremiah and Linton didn't look his way, but they stopped arguing.

"Biscuit, biscuit, two biscuits, biscuit, three biscuits, biscuit," Linton said, counting the well-browned pastries. "Where's Yogurt Girl?"

Stephanie raised her hand and he pressed a container of strawberry yogurt into it.

"What's your name, Yogurt Girl? Want some coffee? Coffee comes with everybody else's biscuits, but I'll give you some on the house."

Faye remembered that Sylvia said Mayfield had behaved the same way with Frida, giving her free stuff as part of an obnoxious courtship ritual. She was wondering if she should step in when Stephanie solved her own problem by refusing the coffee brusquely and backing away from him.

Mayfield laughed at Linton's failed flirtation with Stephanie, and Faye could see that his amusement pissed Linton off.

Jeremiah was more sophisticated. Smoother. He only let a flickering smile slip, but Faye could tell that he wanted to laugh just as loud. Davion and Jeremiah were grinning, but not Ayesha and Yvonna. Their faces were expressionless as they each sidled closer to Stephanie. If Linton didn't get out of their friend's face, they were going to get in his.

Faye found her voice. "Everybody go pick out some sandwich meat, and some fruit if you want it. I'll get the chips. Oh, yeah, and somebody get some water, enough to last the week. Jeremiah, load up the ice chests. We need to get moving."

As they left, Mayfield was taking over the register and starting his shift. Linton still stood right where he'd been, staring at Mayfield, a man who'd tried to date the late wife whom he had still loved.

# Chapter Thirty

Once Mayfield and Linton were in their rearview mirror, Faye's attitude improved and her crew perked up. Ayesha and Davion had chosen to ride with her, and their rapid-fire questions had bounced off the windows of her car all the way to Sweetgum State Park. Now, the whole group was hauling equipment through the woods and across the creek, and they looked happy to be doing it.

Faye loved the early days of an excavation, when everybody involved still believed that maybe they'd uncover the American King Tut's tomb, or something very like it. Maybe something better. Unpacking equipment, walking the site, laying out a sampling grid and finally, finally, breaking ground...these were the days when the whole crew wore smiles and walked with a spring in their steps.

In a couple of weeks, they'd all have ground-in dirt decorating the knees of their new work clothes. There would also be dirt ground into their cuticles and into the calluses on their palms. On the rare occasions that Faye treated herself to a manicure, the manicurist earned every cent, because she had, for all intents and purposes, spent the past twenty years giving herself dirt tattoos on both hands.

In a couple of weeks, this perky and hopeful crew would be grateful to find any chip of stone or seed that might be worth cataloging. Reality would set in at about the two-week mark, but Day One was always golden.

Watching Jeremiah in action made her laugh. He was so invested in the success of his protégés that he was running in circles like a sheepdog barking instructions.

"Where's your field notebook? Ayesha? Your notebook? You, too, Davion."

"Yvonna, those sandals just won't do it. I know you have boots. We all went boot-shopping together and I packed everybody's boots in my car. Go find yours."

"Stephanie? This way!"

Faye assessed her workers for about the hundredth time since she had met them. She was keeping a close eye on Richard. He smelled like yesterday's liquor, but at least he did not smell like fresh liquor. The odor of his hangover followed him around, and it smelled like sweat, beer, and gin, but he was not drunk today. If he managed to survive a sweaty day under this cloudless July sky, then she might not have to demand that Jeremiah fire him. He would be handy, if he stayed and if he applied himself. He was Jeremiah's burliest employee, with only Stephanie coming close to him in size. Jeremiah himself was bigger than them all.

Faye wondered if Jeremiah relied on his size to keep his employees in line. She didn't have that advantage, but in her observation, physical intimidation only went so far in managing a crew. Faye would never be physically intimidating, but she could project a fearsome attitude and she knew how to earn her team's respect through sheer professional competence. So far, this approach had been good enough.

Davion wasn't as big as Richard and Jeremiah, but he had a wiry strength and he struck Faye as alert and thoughtful. He and Ayesha seemed like the group's natural leaders, so she put Ayesha in charge of organizing all the gear, and she sent Davion and Stephanie out with machetes to delineate the study area. The site was big, but only parts of it were covered with thick underbrush. Her machete-wielders had a shot at finishing their work before lunch.

In the meantime, Faye walked the site with a GPS receiver, marking interesting features she'd observed on aerial photos. After they'd all been at their tasks for an hour or so, her phone rang. She found a shady spot and answered it.

She still hadn't heard from Joe, so she absent-mindedly answered without checking to see who was calling, figuring it was him. Instead of her husband, she heard a woman's voice, old and quavery, saying, "Dr. Longchamp-Mantooth? This is Phyllis Windom. You're telling me that you've been playing with my database?"

"I have, and I was impressed. Please call me Faye."

The woman took a wheezing breath, and Faye remembered the news article detailing her health problems. "What's your story, Faye? Your e-mail didn't give me the impression that you were one of those murder groupies that gets obsessed with a crime. I hear from a lot of those and I try to handle them with a quick e-mail. Something about your message made me want to pick up the phone." She paused and Faye heard a cough. "If I'm wrong and you're crazy, please tell me, so that I can hang up and go on with my day."

"I'm not crazy. Truly." Even as she said it, Faye realized that the words themselves made her sound unbalanced. "I have a personal interest in a case, and I don't think the police are pursuing all their options."

"Of course, you don't. People who think the police are doing everything right don't use my database to do an end run around them, now do they?" Faye heard a laugh so uninhibited that she would have called it a cackle. This made her wonder whether it was fair for this woman to be calling other people crazy.

"The victim's name was Frida Stone and she died here in Memphis on Friday. One of her friends told me about similar cases of women beaten to death in north Mississippi and east Arkansas."

"Easy drives from Memphis."

"Exactly. The police here didn't know about the Arkansas killing, which makes me wonder what else they don't know. I've been poking around your database, but it's going to take me some time to get up to speed, and I don't have it. I'm starting a big contract today. Complicated. Big crew. Getting conversant with the software to search your database is going to take time."

"What kind of crew?"

"Archaeology."

"Oh, yeah. That's what it said in the signature line of your email. Anyway, I'm not surprised to hear that you do archaeology. You sound like someone who takes a scientific approach. You also sound like a seeker. Seekers are always busy."

Faye was stupidly flattered by praise from this woman who could apparently suss out her prideful weaknesses pretty darn fast. She could see Ayesha approaching with an I-have-a-question expression. "You have me pegged. I'm stupidly busy all the time. In fact, I don't even have a lot of time to talk right now. Maybe thirty more seconds before I have to turn back into a boss. Can you help?"

"Give me thirty more seconds of information and I'll try."

"Frida was in her late twenties. African-American. So were the other two women. Great care was taken with the other two burials, but Frida was buried quickly. And alive, but that may be because I interrupted the murderer."

"You do have a personal interest in this one. Wow."

"No kidding. What else? Oh, yeah. All three victims were found in July. None were raped. All three were beaten to death. They think Frida was killed with a shovel but they don't know about the other two."

Ayesha arrived, looking expectant. Faye didn't want her to hear this conversation, so her thirty seconds were up. She held up a hand to say, "Hang on just a second," then told Phyllis Windom that she had to go.

"Can I text this number?" Windom asked.

"Yes. Please send me anything you find."

"Will do. Have fun seeking, Madame Archaeologist."

• • ● ● •

Davion, Stephanie, and their machetes had done a masterful job of hacking out the boundaries of the study area. There was more machete work to do as the team laid out a sampling grid, but only in a few places. Much of the area was shaded by trees that kept the underbrush down, and there was a sizeable flat area at the center that intrigued Faye. If she were the director of a CCC program who needed to house hundreds of workers, this is where she would have put them.

No pictures or descriptions of the workers' quarters had survived, which was in itself noteworthy. Many CCC crews working together for months and years during the Depression had produced community newsletters, but the history of the Sweetgum State Park workers was lost in silence. Faye suspected this was because this crew, in the segregated 1930s, had been all African-American.

Other newsletters had pictures of large barracks used for housing. If a structure that size had been built here, Faye stood a decent chance of finding remnants of it. But maybe something ephemeral like rustic cabins or even tents had been considered good enough for a black crew, and there wouldn't be much left of those for her to find.

Faye could hear her own African ancestors whispering in her ear. "You like a challenge. Find something that will bring those forgotten people back to the world's memory."

Their voices echoed in her head while she followed Davion and Stephanie, listening to them tell her about their machete work. Accompanying them all was a softer voice, and Faye was pretty sure that it was Frida's voice in better days. It was a sweet voice, without the rasp of pain that Faye had heard in her groans, and it was saying, "Find the answers. Remember us. Remember us all."

GPS receiver in hand, she walked the site boundaries with Stephanie and Davion, who were rightfully proud of their long, straight cuts through the underbrush. With such good machete work, the walking was easy until Faye felt her left ankle roll under her.

Her boots saved her from a broken ankle or even a sprained one, but nothing could save her from the inevitability of inertia. Her toe was caught on the edge of the depression that had turned her ankle, but her body was moving forward and Faye's flailing arms weren't going to stop it. She was going down.

Her right knee struck the ground, followed quickly by her left knee and the palms of both hands. The right one still held the GPS and she had a sick feeling that she was about to break both her neck and an expensive piece of field equipment. For a moment, she thought she had a fighting chance to keep from doing a face-plant, but no. Her chin hit the ground hard as she finished crumpling.

Ayesha and Davion were kneeling beside her in an instant, calling for help all the while.

Faye was more jolted than hurt, but she was moving slow as she gathered herself. Head swimming, she was able to rise to her hands and knees, but then she had to linger in that position until the trees stopped spinning around her.

She handed the GPS to Davion who said, "Stop worrying about the equipment. It's fine."

The uneven earth that had tripped her was palpable under her hands, a straight-edged raised line. Faye's dazed eyes still weren't working quite right, but she was perfectly capable of recognizing something this obviously man-made by touch. She groped to her left and right, following the line as it extended beside her and behind her. It made a perfect rectangle, long and narrow.

Faye reached for her pocket. By feel, she poked the button on her phone that would take her to Detective McDaniel and was quickly rewarded with his voice saying, "Hello, Faye."

"I've found something. I'm in the woods, so far from the creek that I have to be well outside your crime scene, so your people didn't check it out. You need to see this."

● ● ● ● ●

The grave—and that is what it was, a grave—was old, and there was no evidence of recent activity associated with it. Faye and McDaniel had put their heads together and decided to wait the morning out before deciding if her project could continue. Faye was holding out hope.

"It only makes sense that you'll want to focus on the area surrounding the old burial. We can start our survey far, far away," she said to him. "You'll hardly know we're here."

"I'll think about it, Faye," he had said. "But no promises."

She looked at her crew, huddled around Jeremiah and looking like they needed to do something or explode. "I guess I'll take them back to the motel and...oh, I don't know...pony up a few bucks for pay-per-view."

"Can you send them with Jeremiah?"

Her face must have spoken for her, and it must have said a resounding "Why?", because he explained himself quickly. "I could use you here."

Faye said, "Then I guess they can watch pay-per-view without me." She called Jeremiah over and sent her workers away with instructions to make themselves a big pile of sandwiches to eat in front of the TV.

Standing in the parking lot and watching them go, McDaniel said, "Now that I have your undivided attention, how old is that grave?"

"Don't know for sure, but I have some ideas."

In her trunk was her briefcase packed with an extensive sequence of historical aerial photos of the area around Sweetgum State Park. She spread the photos across the hood of her car and gave him a visual tour of west Memphis history. The photos covered eighty years at varied intervals—1938, 1951, 1963, 1973, 1987, 1997, 2002, and 2010. Using a magnifier, she showed him what she'd learned while preparing for the project that she was apparently never going to get to start.

"Look right here. The grave was in an area that was wooded just after the CCC crew built the park. It stayed that way for a long time, but then see what happened in the late 1990s?"

"Somebody cut a lot of trees."

"Yep. A good chunk of the study area was cleared and it stayed cleared until well into this century. I asked around and people tell me that those trees were cut in preparation for a lodge construction project that never happened."

"Like now. You're here because they want to build a lodge, right?"

"More like a campground with mostly cabins. Anyway, the park kept the area mowed for a while. People even put up some unauthorized volleyball nets, but the vegetation eventually came back in and they stopped coming here. It's not much fun to play volleyball in a blackberry patch. Since then, the area has been slowly going back to nature. You can see the trees growing in over time on the later photos."

"And this tells us what?"

"Not very much, from your standpoint. I'm thinking that this wasn't the best place to hide a body when people were using it for recreation, so that's something useful to know. I'm also thinking that if the grave had already been here while they were coming and going on a daily basis, somebody would have noticed it. It would have been sinking, and somebody besides me would have tripped over it."

"If a volleyball player was running in to set the ball, and she took a fall like you did, she'd have broken every bone in her face."

"Exactly."

His eyes roamed over her face. "Speaking of that, how are you feeling? Bruises? Cuts? Do I need to get you to an emergency room?"

Faye waved the question away. "I'm fine. But let me finish telling you about the photos. My best guess is that the grave was dug after people stopped playing volleyball here. Say, maybe sometime after 2010 or so. But it wasn't dug yesterday. It's had time to sink, and it was covered with a thick layer of pine straw and leaf litter when I found it. Well, when my clumsy foot found it."

"You did better than we did."

She gave him another dismissive wave of her hand. "I got lucky. How were you supposed to find a shallow dent in the ground, covered in leaves and way outside your search area? You certainly defined a reasonably large piece of ground for your search. What were you going to do? Search the whole park? All of Memphis?"

"Maybe. If that's what it takes. I should have searched more than I did."

"We don't even know if the bones your people found in that grave are related to Frida's death."

A woman approached them, stripping off her protective gloves and goggles. Her blond-and-gray hair was pulled back in a short, no-nonsense ponytail. As McDaniel jogged in her direction, he called back to Faye, "If my forensics people are any good at all, they're about to answer that question."

His tone of voice caught Faye's ear. He sounded like maybe he didn't think his forensics people were any good, and this was the first time she'd heard him even suggest such a thing.

He jogged a few more steps, then stopped short. Turning around and walking back toward Faye, he said, "The evidence here is a grave full of old bones. That's what you do for a living. That's my forensic archaeologist over there, telling me to hurry, but two heads are better than one.

Would you like to come with me and take a look at this skeleton she dug up?"

• • ● • •

Faye was pretty sure that Dr. Margaret Broome did not appreciate her presence. Professional jealousy was the norm in their business, and it probably was the norm in everyone's business, but Dr. Broome truly had nothing to worry about. Faye did not want her job. She most certainly did not play the one-upmanship games that would prompt her to make her colleague look stupid in front of Detective McDaniel. To signal that she was no threat, she stood by quietly as Dr. Broome spoke, trying to ignore the fact that the woman was a nitwit.

Dr. Broome was nervous. She moved too fast. She spoke too fast. Faye admired scientists who were deliberate and imperturbable, and Dr. Broome was neither.

Nervous scientists forgot things. This could be forgiven if they took careful notes, so they could backtrack when they needed to jog their memories. Dr. Broome didn't even do that. Her field notebook had been dangling unused at her side since Faye first laid eyes on her.

Nervous scientists also missed things. While Dr. Broome blathered on and on to McDaniel, repeating herself and even contradicting herself, Faye's attention was focused on a small object a few feet behind the nervous archaeologist. It was barely dime-sized, protruding from the side of the spoil pile of soil removed from the old grave. The spoil pile was only light dirt-brown. The object was dark dirt-brown and it called to her.

Faye walked over to the spoil pile, careful to touch nothing and to step in areas already networked with footprints. She could feel Dr. Broome's eyes boring into her back, but she was only going to stop what she was doing if McDaniel said so. He kept his silence.

Pulling a magnifier out of her pocket, she crouched down to look at the object.

McDaniel's curiosity finally got the better of him. He called out to her. "Whatcha got, Faye?"

"A flower. Dried. About two centimeters in diameter. Maybe a little less."

Dr. Broome's gray eyes raked across the ground around them. It was dotted with the lavender flowers of horsemint, growing in dappled woodland shade. "There are flowers everywhere around here. Your point is…?"

"My point is that this looks like a flower you'd buy from a florist. There's only a stub of a stem, but it's stiff, and you can see that there was a substantial crown of petals. And it's still showing a lot of red, like maybe it was dyed. It looks like a chrysanthemum to me."

Dr. Broome's lips pursed in…what? Tension? Anger? Frustration? Embarrassment?

Faye couldn't tell, but she was relieved to hear the woman's response, which was the correct one. "We're going to need to sift that backdirt. Pronto."

# Chapter Thirty-one

It was too much to hope that Dr. Broome would let Faye or her crew help with the backdirt-sifting. She had insisted on doing it herself, as if determined to atone for something that truly could have happened to anybody. The flower she had missed was, after all, very small, and it was the color of dirt.

Faye might not be welcome to help but she sure as hell wanted to watch, and McDaniel had said okay. They had settled themselves in two folding chairs several feet away from the slowly dwindling spoil pile, and they were watching the warring emotions on Dr. Broome's face as she found one tiny object after another. The woman obviously hated herself for dropping the ball. Rightly or wrongly, she almost certainly hated Faye. If Faye hadn't found the chrysanthemum, she would have never known that she had failed.

The finds that were embarrassing Dr. Broome so much were all flowers, tiny ones that anyone could have missed. Every one of them was dwarfed by the faded red chrysanthemum that, after years of withering, was now smaller than the end of Faye's pinkie finger. They looked to Faye like individual blossoms of baby's breath, a flower usually seen as a cloud of tiny white blooms. Like the dyed red chrysanthemum, babies' breath would almost certainly have come from a florist.

"You're going to hate me." McDaniel's eyes stayed on Dr. Broome, but he was talking to Faye.

"For what?" She also kept her eyes on the forensic archaeologist, because she, too, could do the play-it-cool-and-don't-make-eye-contact thing.

"I told you that I'd try to fix it so that your people could keep working. There's a lot of territory between this body and the creek. It made sense that you could be doing archaeology over by the creek while we did our work way back here. But now—"

"Now you're thinking that you didn't cast a wide enough net after Frida died and you can't afford to do that again."

"Yeah." Still no eye contact. "I need to throw everything I've got at this, and I need everybody out of this part of the park. I'm sorry, Faye. I made a mistake last time and, because of that, I missed this burial. I can't afford to make the same mistake again. What if I miss clues that will nail the person who did this? Or the one who killed Frida?"

"You don't think it might have been the same person?"

"I can't jump straight to that conclusion. I know you love your serial killer theory, but I don't see it."

"But the women in Corinth and Earle. Same age, same race, not raped—"

"Don't hate me when I say this, but this is what I do for a living and I'm going to tell you straight. A lot of young black women get murdered in this country. It's a damn shame and it makes me sick inside, but they do. It's my job to make it stop, and I can't. That makes me sick inside, too."

He quit talking and his gaze dropped to his hands,

one on each thigh. He looked like he wanted to be doing something useful with them.

He finally looked at her again, catching her eye as if wanting to be sure she heard and understood. "How can I say this to you? You look at a cluster of murders of young black women and see a pattern that maybe takes in Mississippi and Arkansas. I look at the same thing and I see a pattern that takes in the whole country. You want to believe there's one killer, because that means we can find him and make it stop. I just wish that were true."

"But the ones in Mississippi and Arkansas showed an obsession with burial—"

"Two or three killers got their shit together well enough to dig a good grave, instead of dumping their victim in a ditch. Big deal."

"It's a coincidence that they were all found in July?"

"One out of twelve murdered women, or something like that, get buried in July. Actually, more, because murders peak in the summertime"

"Are they usually raped? Robbed?"

"No, not always. I just don't see a pattern that says 'serial killer.' I know you want me to, but I don't."

He flicked his eyes her way in what she thought might possibly be a hint of apology. But she also saw the look of a man who was confident in his experience and proud of it.

"You're the expert," she said, because it was true, but not because it made him right.

"Well, you're the expert in bones that have been buried for a long time. How long do you think this body's been in the ground? You said 2010 or thereabouts before. Now that you've seen the bones, does that opinion still stand?"

"Based on the condition of the body and the look of the soil? In addition to the activity I saw on those old aerial photos? I'd say five years, give or take a few years, so yeah. There's nothing here to change the opinion I gave you before."

The eyes finally flicked her way and they were frustrated.

"It's not an exact science," she said. "I'm sorry. Your forensics lab may be able to narrow that date range down."

"I've got people searching our missing persons data to try to figure out who the victim was. I'll tell them to pay close attention to that time window. So by your logic, I should be looking at missing persons from 2010 all the way up to now, since this supposed serial killer has been active for five years, seven years, maybe more?"

"I sure hope not."

He looked around them, at the open woodland and the thicket beyond. "Well, this isn't a bad place to hide a body. There could be others out there. Maybe the same killer put 'em there. Maybe not. Either way, I need to search this whole end of the park. How would you do that?"

"Dr. Broome probably has ideas. It's her project."

"I asked you."

Now he definitely was not making eye contact. He was watching his own forensic archaeologist, whose professional judgment he was clearly beginning to doubt.

"Ground penetrating radar comes immediately to mind. LIDAR—that's short for light detection and ranging—is great if you've got the budget for somebody to fly around in an airplane."

"If you're right that there's a serial killer crossing state lines, it'll be the FBI's budget. They can afford whatever they want to afford. Until then, I'm not sure how much money I can pry out of the department. And if I'm going to lose jurisdiction on this case, I'm not sure I have the time to drag in the fancy equipment beforehand."

"What about drones? They're cheap. Put a camera on one and you can see a lot. You can still do the GPR and LIDAR later, but drones give you quick-and-dirty information. You don't have to wait for someone to come out and operate them, because you can do it yourself. And you don't have to wait for them to interpret the data, either. The best thing? You can get a drone at the toy store, if you have to."

"A toy store. Get out." Now he was laughing. "The department probably has something I can use. If they don't, I'll go to the toy store." He stacked up the historical photos they'd been studying. "You don't seem to have any right-this-minute aerial photos. If drones are so great for checking out a big piece of land, how come you're not using one?"

"Tennessee state law includes requirements for hiring somebody with the right insurance and such. But there's a clause in the law that specifically says it's okay to take a picture with a drone for law enforcement purposes. That's you."

He slapped both thighs and laughed. "Yes. It is."

"My crew is cooped up in a motel room, eating bologna sandwiches and watching movies. If you want to make that up to me, you'll give me a copy of that drone footage so I can use it for my project."

"You've got a deal."

Ayesha, Richard, Davion, Stephanie, Yvonna, and Jeremiah stood in the motel lobby looking expectantly at Faye. They were all so young and innocent, even Jeremiah, who obviously considered himself far older and more worldly than the rest. Since she'd last seen them, they had watched a movie together and eaten sandwiches and nobody had, to her knowledge, gotten drunk or misbehaved. From a managerial standpoint, today was a much better day than yesterday.

"I'm going to Frida's funeral and I'll be happy to give a ride to anybody who wants to come." At the mention of Frida's name, Jeremiah lowered his eyes. Faye's own eyes were burning.

"I'm taking my car, too," he said, "if anybody wants to ride with me."

"It's no secret that the police uncovered another body today," Faye continued, "so you won't be surprised when I tell you that they are barring us from our worksite again. I can't say that I blame them, given the circumstances, but this may mean that we have to put the project on hold. There's just not much more we can do without access to the site. Our contact with the state of Tennessee is aware of the situation. He was already planning to be here tomorrow to monitor our work, so we'll be able to talk face-to-face then about how, or even whether, we will go forward. But we're not going to do that today. Today is a day to pay our respects to Frida."

Faye was still trying to grab hold of the day's events and change her world view to fit them. Only in this moment was she realizing that she had a bigger reason for closing down the project than mere scheduling and budgeting.

"Let me back up a bit and try again. I'm not at my best today and my thoughts are all jumbled up. It really doesn't matter what the state's representative says tomorrow. I've got to shut this thing down. I have no other choice."

Jeremiah shifted on his feet, like a man who was trying hard not to argue with her.

"Yesterday," she went on. "I based my decision to keep you here on the police department's belief that the attack on Frida was personal. They believed that the killer was someone who knew her and wanted to hurt her, and I had no reason to doubt their judgment. Over the past day, evidence has surfaced that made me think otherwise. Our discovery of a hidden grave today convinces me that there has been a serial killer at work here in Memphis and the surrounding area for years. I cannot in good conscience keep you here. Frankly, I'm running for home myself, as soon as Jeremiah and I do what has to be done to shut this project down. I wish none of these things were true, but they are."

Now Ayesha, Yvonna, and Stephanie were standing with their arms around each other, weeping.

"Look after each other. Try not to be alone until you're all safe in your homes. Well, you can be alone in the shower, as long as your roommate is outside watching the door."

She was relieved to hear that they were still able to laugh.

"We'll gather after the funeral for a good-bye dinner, then we'll talk about how we're going to get you all home."

# Chapter Thirty-two

*They'd found another of his women. He had never known her name, but he remembered the act of saying good-bye. It had been Christmastime, so nobody had blinked at a man buying a bouquet from a grocery store's florist counter that was bloody with scarlet flowers, all of them tied with spruce green ribbons. He remembered how lovely the red chrysanthemums and white baby's breath had looked as he placed them in her limp hands.*

*His neighborhood's corner of Twitter was alive today with the discovery of her bones. Everyone on Faye Longchamp-Mantooth's team had been sworn to secrecy, but at least one of them had lied. That person had told Sylvia and she had told the world.*

*That person had also told Sylvia that the archaeologist was closing down her project. This was good, since she seemed to be better at finding his women than the police were. However, the end of her project meant the end of the archeologist's time in Memphis, and he didn't intend to follow her to Florida just for the pleasure of silencing her. Today was the day. It had to be.*

*What flowers should he buy today? Perhaps he should go buy a bunch of white daisies. Their simplicity made him think of Faye Longchamp-Mantooth and her effortless grace. He would venture a guess that she loved daisies and would smile if a man presented her with a bunch of them. How much more would they suit her in death?*

# Chapter Thirty-three

Joe was suffering his very first bout of road rage. For Joe, road rage took the form of drumming his fingers on the steering wheel really hard.

Perhaps the highway construction in Birmingham was the reason they were running so late. Amande had thought that they could detour around it, but she had been wrong.

Certainly, the horrific accident on US-319 between Panacea and Tallahassee that had closed both northbound lanes had put a crimp in their plans before they'd gone fifty miles. And perhaps the GPS had complicated things by being overly optimistic with its pre-lunch arrival time. Joe was going with that theory, because there was no way he was going to point his finger at his sweet and well-meaning daughter and ask, "Why in the heck aren't we in Memphis yet? Did you mess up somehow? Did you put the wrong address in the GPS?"

Joe didn't know who or what was to blame, but he knew he was ready to get a good look at his wife and make sure she was okay. He picked up the phone to call her, but remembered that she might hear the road noise in the background and ask him where he was going. He didn't want to warn her that he was on his way, and he wasn't much of a liar. She'd have a harder time being mad at him for coming when she was looking him in the face.

The sight of yet another long stretch of orange cones ahead made him grip the steering wheel until his knuckles turned white. The orange speed limit sign instructed him to slow down on pain of some fearsome fines, so he did so, even though there wasn't a highway worker in sight. Amande was dozing. He hoped she stayed asleep, because she was going to want him to pull over so that she could do the driving through this construction zone. Then she would want to keep the wheel through Tupelo.

Joe was not convinced that he was as bad at driving as his daughter and wife thought he was. He could certainly navigate through a town the size of Tupelo, and he intended to do so. He was too nervous to sit quietly while somebody else, even Amande, took him from this spot to where he needed to be. Even if the state of Mississippi had torn up every road between his car and the Tennessee border, he was hell-bent on getting to Faye by suppertime.

● ● ● ● ●

Faye pulled her new dress over her head. It was plain and sleeveless, and its A-line skirt stopped at the knee. It wasn't particularly flattering but it was black, so it was appropriate for a funeral. It was also comfortable enough to move in, which was a decided plus. She stepped into a pair of flat black pumps, slicked on a subdued shade of lipstick, and called herself dressed.

Letting her hair air-dry, she sat down at her computer to spend a few more minutes with Phyllis Windom's database until it was time to go.

She wanted to try some goofy searches that might not

occur to law enforcement, so she started with the goofiest search of all:

Murdered women found in July

After thinking about it for a minute, she opened the search up with a search string that was going to double her list.

Murdered women found in June and July

Being found around Independence Day might well mean that the killings had happened in June, so she was willing to lengthen her list enough to find more killings that fit the mold.

Now it was time to start winnowing that list down. First, she sorted to find the women who were black and in their twenties. She was able to filter out the ones who were buried, instead of being unceremoniously dumped by the side of the road, and that helped, but the length of the list was still daunting.

It made sense to narrow the search to a two-hundred-and-fifty-mile radius of Memphis, because it was a reasonable distance for a day trip. Why would the killer want to risk being caught by a hotel receipt or a spot of blood left behind in a motel bathroom?

This search cut the numbers to the point that it made sense to start reading the notes, copied laboriously from countless case files. Phyllis Windom must have a herd of volunteers working for her. Faye rather liked the idea of crowd-sourced murder investigations.

Even after narrowing the search, there were still too many murders for her to read about in one sitting. This was too depressing to think about, so she tried not to think at all as she randomly clicked around during the last moments before she needed to leave for the funeral.

Within five minutes, she'd uncovered the case file of a woman in Bowling Green, Kentucky, who was buried in a state park with a rose in her hands. A few minutes after that, she learned that, just the previous June, a woman had been found near Knoxville with daisies in her hair. And the previous March, there had been a murdered prostitute in Birmingham who was found, not with flowers, but with a grocery store receipt. Faye had almost clicked away from this file, but a grocery store receipt was just weird enough to make her look.

She found that the Birmingham police had been particularly diligent in contributing to the database. They hadn't just mentioned the receipt. They had scanned and uploaded it.

Faye clicked on the image and expanded it as far as the image's resolution allowed. It was dated, which gave the last possible date that the woman was alive, June 26. The police had noted the date, but they hadn't thought that the list of purchases was significant. Faye was sure that they'd been hoping for a knife, a shovel, duct tape, and bleach, and they didn't get it. But she was looking for something different, and she most certainly got it.

The receipt said, "Bouquet, Mixed Snapdragons." They had cost the killer fourteen dollars and ninety-nine cents.

Bingo. She had another data point to present to McDaniel.

Yvonna was standing beside her, and there was an insistent rap at the door for the second time. She needed to go. The database would be waiting for her when she got back.

• • ● • •

Faye's phone rang as she was hurrying down the long drab hallway outside her hotel room, late for the funeral. She took it because the screen said "Phyllis Windom."

"Madame Archaeologist?" Windom's voice didn't sound any stronger than it had the time they spoke.

"Yes."

"I've got something for you. I think it might tie the Arkansas and Mississippi cases together."

Faye pushed the phone hard against her ear. The motel's icemaker was loud and the sound of ice dropping into somebody's ice bucket was even louder. Windom's wheezy, airy voice couldn't compete.

"You can tie the two deaths together? How?"

"When you have time to explore my database, you'll see that selected information transcribed from the case files is included in a 'Notes' section. I've got plans to incorporate keywords, so that it will be more searchable. Right now, it is what it is."

"We're on the same page. I found the 'Notes' section a few minutes ago, and I've already found some interesting stuff. What do the notes say for those two unsolved killings? What makes you think they're connected?"

"The Mississippi investigators seem to have been more thorough. If you remember, they properly recorded their data in the FBI's Uniform Crime Report, and the Arkansas investigators working at the state park in Earle didn't do that."

"I remember."

"Well, Madame Archaeologist, I'm willing to say that the Mississippi folks also paid closer attention to the soil in their victim's grave, because they sifted a whole bouquet out of it."

Now she had Faye's attention. "They what?"

"The killer had buried the poor woman with a bouquet of flowers. If you remember, they found her within a few weeks from the time she went missing. This means that the flowers weren't completely rotted and there was still some integrity to the body. They found the stems in what was left of her hands, fanned out across her chest. Carnations, roses, ferns, all of it. And there were hundreds of little white flowers—"

"Baby's breath?"

"Yeah, probably. He'd picked each little flower off its stem and scattered them all over her body. It doesn't make sense that he did all that while he was standing over the body. It would take too long. He must have bought the flowers, then made a bag of the little white ones to bring with him while he was looking for someone to kill. And then he used them to decorate her corpse. Creepy, right?"

"No joke," Faye said. "Or maybe he didn't have to look for someone to kill. Maybe he carried the flowers around while he stalked the woman he'd already chosen as his next victim."

"Exactly right. Some serial killers choose their victims at random. Some prefer to stalk."

Faye pictured an automobile trunk holding a large shovel and a slowly wilting bouquet. What else would he pack? A change of clothes? Soap? Bleach? A small ebony box to hold the soul he had relinquished?

"What about the dead woman in Arkansas?"

"The case file didn't mention finding any flowers, but they were pretty sure she'd been dead for years. The flowers would have rotted with the body. Bits of stem and flower could even have sifted through the rib cage over time and ended up underneath the body. Weird things happen to organic materials left underground."

"Did the note say whether they sifted the soil?"

"No, and who's to say how well they did it, if they did? These are the people who didn't bother filing a report with the FBI. The notes do, however, mention that they found a small plastic ampoule like the ones florists use. You know, the little vial they fill with water, so that they can stick a flower stem in it and keep it fresh?"

She sounded satisfied as she delivered this exciting news, and that made her voice sound younger, healthier.

"I know the vials you're talking about." Faye said. She was thinking that if they'd missed a whole bouquet of flowers, rotten or not, it was a good thing they'd been paying enough attention to find the ampoule. The ones Faye had seen were half the size of her index finger or more. Anybody who missed a piece of plastic that size should probably hang up their trowel.

"So do you think that the bouquet of flowers and the florist's ampoule is enough to say that the same person killed those two women?" she asked Windom.

"Of course not. Any murderer can stroll to the grocery store and buy some flowers, but it seems like a mighty big coincidence. Anyway, it doesn't matter what I say about it. I'm just a civilian with a database. What do you think your investigator is going to say?"

"Considering that his forensic archaeologist just dug up a chrysanthemum and some baby's breath, and considering that I just found three more burials that involved flowers listed in your database, he's going to have a hard time arguing with our hypothesis."

"I love it when that happens."

# Chapter Thirty-four

*Flowers. There were flowers everywhere.*

*And in the middle of them, he saw Frida.*

*She was wearing yellow. Of course, she was wearing yellow. Seeing her there, lying in a satin-lined casket with pink carnations garlanded around her pretty face, she looked the way he had wanted her to look when he put her in the ground.*

*He was nervous. He had attended many funerals in his day, but none that he had personally caused. That was because none of his other women had been Frida.*

*The others had been women of convenience. A woman might be chosen because of the appealing angle of her head as it met her neck. Another might be chosen because of the titillating flutter of her eyelashes when he walked too close to her and she pulled away in fear. They had been random women who had done nothing to merit their deaths beyond standing in the wrong place on a day when he'd pointed his car down a highway and gone hunting.*

*Frida had possessed all his triggers, from the top of her shapely head to the soles of her tiny feet. She had been frail, nervous, pretty, giggly, vulnerable. She'd had the power to trigger a protective pity that was new for him. How Frida had birthed that stony-faced child was anybody's guess.*

*It was dangerous for him to be here, but he was standing his ground. If anyone suspected him, he would see it on their faces, and he would know that he needed to move on. He was proud of how long he'd been able to stay in one spot without being caught, but he'd always had a backup plan. St. Louis seemed like a place where a man like him could get lost.*

*In the meantime, he would enjoy the cognitive clash of being in a room full of people who usually couldn't be bothered to be nice to each other. But just let somebody die and watch the tears start to fall. These people knew the things they'd said to each other about Frida, and they knew how they had treated her, but they were pretending for one short hour that all of that judgment had never happened. None of them had loved her like he did.*

*Frida in her casket presided over them all, like a princess in a fairy tale, sentenced to sleep for a century, or for a lifetime, or for the space of time that it took for someone to figure out that she'd been poisoned with an apple. She was a golden ray of sunshine lighting the room, just as she'd been when he'd last seen her, wearing a yellow dress and begging for her life.*

*This church had its own graveyard. He knew this because he'd kept USGS topographic maps of all of Memphis, ever since he learned that they showed the locations of cemeteries, old and new. America's woodlands were speckled with abandoned graveyards and he loved the poetry of leaving a new corpse among the old ones. It was one of his favorite disposal strategies. Once he realized that Frida would be buried in a graveyard that was a century and a half old, nothing could have kept him from detouring to see it.*

*He arrived at the funeral early, so that he could park at the graveyard's secluded lot, barely a quarter mile past the church, and give himself a personal tour. He was in ecstasy as he strolled the unpaved woodland path that led from the road to the graveyard. From there, another path, stone-paved, would take him from the graveyard to the church, but first he wanted to soak it all in.*

*It was an enchanted place where they would be leaving Frida, an old, old burying ground encircled by massive trees and an elaborate wrought-iron fence. A tall granite obelisk stood at the very center, surrounded by a handful of above-ground crypts, one of them large enough to accept at least a half-dozen members of an affluent family. Its door stood askew and he longed to open it wide, laying eyes on a century of rot.*

*But Frida was not being buried in a rich woman's mausoleum. A rectangular hole waited for her.*

*Someone had dug Frida's grave with a machine. He would gladly have done it for her with his own hands. Her grave was surrounded by flower arrangements on flimsy wire stands. He reached out to one of them and plucked the tiniest possible sprig of baby's breath, delicate and perfect. It rested in his pocket now.*

*With the flower as his hidden talisman, he walked the stone path leading to the church, knowing that he would find Faye Longchamp-Mantooth there.*

*And he did. She was waiting for him and she had dressed appropriately. If his luck held, he could snatch her in the aftermath of the somber ceremony, while she was still wearing a dress, pristine and so black that the blood wouldn't even show.*

# Chapter Thirty-five

Flowers. There were flowers everywhere.

Faye didn't imagine that Frida had known many people with money to spare, yet there were so many flowers. Garlands of flowers covered her casket. Arrangements on wire stands stood in the corners of the room where mourners had gathered to view her body. She had passed through the old church's small sanctuary to get to Frida, and it was festooned with flowers, too. Its old woodwork was an effective foil for their vibrant colors.

She had watched Kali cross the threshold into the room where her mother lay in her casket. The child had taken in a long slow breath. Then, to no one in particular, she had said, "It looks like she's in heaven."

Laneer had taken her by the hand and said, "She is, baby. Somewhere, your mama is walking with the angels."

"No, she isn't, honey," Sylvia told her, patting the little hand she held. "She's dancing with the angels and she's looking down at you."

Faye wouldn't have expected Mayfield to own a suit, nor Linton, but either they did or they had borrowed them, and ties, too. Like Faye, they had come to this room to join the mourners gathered to say one last good-bye to

Frida before her funeral. With their sober clothing and sober faces, they blended in with the other mourners. Mayfield's body, rangy when he wore his convenience store uniform of golf-shirt and khakis, had a model's elegance when wrapped in the wide-shouldered jacket and tapered pants of a dress suit. Linton's jacket emphasized his burly shoulders, hung smooth over his torso, then nipped in at his narrow waist. Even his tie was black, like a streak of grief on his ironed white dress shirt. Their suits were not expensive, but youth and strength don't require custom-tailoring to shine. It came in little glimpses, but from time to time, Faye could see what Frida had seen in these men.

Laneer, too, looked dignified in a black suit with lapels that whispered, "Nineteen-Seventies Chic." He held Kali by the hand, and they stood amid the crowd of hovering grievers, doing their duty by greeting them one by one.

Laneer called them each by name, shaking their hands or hugging their necks, as the case may be. Time and again, he inclined his gray head and responded to whatever expression of grief or sympathy was pouring from a person's mouth.

"It's just so hard."

"I don't know what we'll do without her."

"I do thank you for that wonderful casserole you sent."

Kali was too young to be expected to engage in the language of grief, so she was spared this onslaught, which must have been grueling for a man of Laneer's age. She stood silent beside him, wearing the dress that Faye had bought for her.

The stores are not full of clothes that make little girls look like crows, so Faye had done the best that she could. The child's sundress was made of cotton fabric that was mostly black, but was printed with tiny white leaves and flowers to acknowledge that Kali was still just a little girl. Black grosgrain straps were tied in bows over her shoulders, and a sparkly belt was tied at her waist. Faye thought that, under other circumstances, those sparkles would have made the little girl smile, which is why she bought it.

Laneer or Sylvia had combed her hair into a high ponytail and tied it in a huge white satin bow. The hank of hair should have bobbed when she moved, but she was moving so slow. Kali's ponytail drooped with the rest of her.

Most of Faye's crew had come. Davion had not known Frida, and the expression on his face when he made his excuses had given Faye the impression that he had a morbid fear of funerals. He had stayed at the motel.

Yvonna hadn't given a reason for not going and Faye didn't ask. It was fine with Faye if they wanted to stay behind, and it was fine with her that the other three had come. This terrible murder had made impacts on her crew that would continue to ripple. They were having to deal with mortality at a very young age, and now they were faced with losing this job that had promised them short-term paychecks and long-term opportunities. If Davion and Yvonna didn't want to go to the funeral of someone they didn't know, Faye completely understood.

Jeremiah and his three employees all looked funeral-appropriate, in both clothing and attitude. Jeremiah was wearing his Sunday best, down to a dove gray bow tie. Richard had managed a suit and tie, probably because he had local family who could lend him dress clothes. Ayesha and Stephanie had been forced to make do with what was in their suitcases, but they were dressed in neat button-down shirts and well-pressed work pants.

Walt Walker, whose charcoal gray suit set off a tie in a soft, muted shade of green, was taking long strides across the room toward Kali. She looked up at the man as he surreptitiously handed her a piece of peppermint candy, its nickel-sized disk twisted in cellophane. Faye could tell that he was hoping that she would smile, but he had no luck that she could see.

Reverend Atkinson stood next to the open casket. After people paid their respects to Laneer and Kali, they filed past the casket and paid their respects to Frida. Some people wept loudly and openly. Some reached out to touch the dead woman one last time. Others passed her in tears and silence.

Faye didn't enjoy this part of a funeral, but she knew that people grieved differently, so she joined in the communal act of saying good-bye. The most spiritual moment for her would come during the service, when she felt her own frail voice blend into the congregation's full-throated rendition of old and well-loved hymns. Those were the moments when she felt closest to the loved ones who had gone on before her.

Laneer was nearby, still holding Kali's hand and still responding to the sympathy of others.

"Yes, Kali will live with me. It will be hard to be without Frida, but we love each other very much. We will be okay."

"No, the police don't know who did it."

"Sometimes, I think I still hear her sweet voice."

Faye's turn to pass by the casket and pay her respects had come. She'd been dreading this moment, because she remembered how Frida had looked in the last hours of her life.

She was surprised to see that the mortician had wrought a miracle.

This was not to say that Frida looked good. All the

mourners who were making the obligatory exclamation of "She looks so natural!" were either lying or fooling themselves.

Frida looked like a model of a woman created by a 3D printer—plastic, stiff, and lifeless, and the soft petals of the flowers surrounding her face only made it worse. But the mortician's magic, which Faye knew nothing about and hoped she never did, had done what needed doing. Makeup, internal stitches, prosthetics—whatever they'd done to Frida had been a gift to the guests at this funeral, and to Frida's memory. And it had been a blessing to Kali.

The minister nodded to Laneer as the last few mourners passed the casket, and Laneer took Kali by the hand.

Reverend Atkinson addressed the room, saying, "If Ms. Stone's friends will all take a seat in the chapel, we will give the family a few last moments with the deceased."

Faye joined the line of people leaving the room. She noticed that Linton wasn't leaving. He sat alone in a chair, several steps away from Laneer and Kali. Everyone in a cluster of Frida's other relatives was pointedly ignoring him. As the minister moved to close the door, a thin woman in her forties hurried over to him. She pointed her finger at Linton and whispered something in the minister's ear.

Reverend Atkinson walked over to him and said, "This time is for family only, son."

Linton stayed seated, meaty hands folded on his lap. "Frida was my wife. And Kali is my stepdaughter."

"Not any more," the thin woman said.

"You don't divorce children, and I ain't divorced anyway." He looked to the minister for help.

"Madame," said Reverend Atkinson. "Some charity, perhaps."

Except for Laneer, the cluster of relatives gave a

simultaneous shake of their heads and their spokeswoman put their opinion into a single word. "No."

Laneer took a step toward them. "Catherine, it's not for you to say."

"No" she said again. "Frida didn't want him in her life and her family don't want him here."

Faye could see that Laneer was preparing to speak his piece as the family elder, but Linton didn't let him. He rose from the chair and said, "I won't stay where I'm not wanted. But I want you people to know this and to remember it. Frida was my wife. I made a bad mistake and I paid for it. I lost Frida. I want to do right for Kali, now that her mama can't be here, and I will do right for her. Do you hear me, sweetie? If you ever need somebody, you'll always have me."

Without waiting to see whether Kali would answer, Linton followed the non-family members out of the room, and Faye followed him. She knew that Laneer, the obstreperous Catherine, Frida's other relatives, and Kali were behind her, and something within her couldn't resist turning for a last look as the door closed. Faye studied the little face for a glimpse of how she felt about Linton, but she saw nothing but damp eyes and pursed lips.

● ● ● ● ●

The organist was playing "Rock of Ages" as the crowd sat in the church sanctuary in silence. Faye and her crewmembers who attended—Richard, Ayesha, and Stephanie—sat in the center of the last row, making sure that everyone who had known Frida personally could take a seat in front of them. Linton sat in the second row, directly behind the seats where the family would soon be sitting. Faye could see him clearly in the small church, and it seemed to her that anger radiated off his back. Sylvia also sat on the almost-family row, but she chose a spot several seats away from Linton and she never looked his way.

Mayfield sat a few rows behind Sylvia, and Walt Walker was directly behind Mayfield. Jeremiah and Armand sat together, across the aisle from Linton. As it turned out, Detective McDaniel had felt the same need to hang back as Faye. He dropped into the chair next to her so casually that she was almost convinced that he was glad to see her.

"It's a good thing you're here," she whispered. "I was going to call you. I've been talking to Phyllis Windom. Do you know who she is?"

"Bit of a crackpot, isn't she? Thinks she can use her computer better than we can use ours?"

"Crackpot or not, there are plenty of grateful testimonials on her website from police departments and sheriff's offices that say she can do the things she claims." Now Faye was irritated. She had to work to keep her voice at a whisper. Holding out her phone, she said, "She just called me with information on the Arkansas case that ties it to the bones we found this morning."

"You're kidding. What's the link?" He was trying to whisper, but it came out more like a loud hiss. Sylvia turned and gave him a disapproving look.

"Flowers."

"That's…indicative."

She had the sense that he wanted to say, "That's amazing," or "That's exciting," but that he'd forced himself to find a more noncommittal word.

"You think? And maybe she *is* better with her computer than y'all are. Or anybody else. Just because she's a genius doesn't mean everybody else isn't smart. Guess what I just found in her databases."

"I'm afraid to ask out loud. Sylvia might come back here and rap my knuckles."

"Then whisper. I found three more cases associated with flowers."

"Here?"

"Knoxville. Birmingham. Bowling Green, Kentucky."

"Knoxville's a hike from here. So's Birmingham. Faye, if you reach far enough, you can find anything."

Faye gave him a look that probably had a strong resemblance to Sylvia's please-shut-up glare. "You can drive to any of those places and get back in a day."

"If you hustle."

"The people in Birmingham found an actual receipt for the flowers. Look."

He took a peek at her phone's screen. "A receipt for flowers? Seriously? You found that in the big data pile that Phyllis Windom calls a database? Maybe you're the one who's a genius. You're going to send me that, right?"

Faye cocked an eyebrow. "I don't know if I should. I found it in a crackpot's database."

"I'm thinking of the words 'obstruction of justice….'"

"Oh, okay. If you insist. Here's everything I know." She forwarded him the email thread that had passed between her and Windom, and she heard his phone vibrate in his pocket when it came through. "Now you've got it. Happy?"

"Ecstatic."

A set of swinging doors opened and Frida's casket emerged, escorted by six family members serving as pallbearers. After the casket had been positioned at the front of the sanctuary, the rest of the family came in, with Laneer and Kali entering last, hand in hand. Once the swinging door closed behind the family, Reverend Atkinson took his place at the pulpit. A stained-glass window depicting Jesus in the Garden of Gethsemane provided a glowing backdrop for the minister and his dark clothing. The window sent scattered shards of colorful light to rest on Frida's face.

"We gather today, in the presence of God, to bid farewell to Ms. Frida Stone, who was taken from us so suddenly and far too soon."

A scattering of amens sounded.

"The loss of dear Frida is a reminder to us all that we are made of dust. We must repent daily, because tomorrow is not promised."

From here, the minister launched into a prefab sermon that had nothing to do with Frida, unless one counted intimations that people who lived impure lives should repent early and often, since their lifestyles could attract murder.

This was wrong.

Faye firmly believed that a eulogy should eulogize. It should make the person live again, one last time. She wanted Laneer to hear the minister tell stories about Frida as a little girl who loved ice cream. She wanted Kali to hear about how sweet Frida had been as a young mother pushing a stroller. Instead, they were getting the same hellfire-and-brimstone sermon he preached every time he bellied up to a pulpit. She had been able to resist crying since arriving at the funeral, but now the frustrated tears began to roll.

When Reverend Atkinson got to the climax of his sermon, he shouted, "Yes, ladies and gentlemen, God works in mysterious ways! Everything happens for a reason!"

This was the point at which Kali let the crowd know that she had heard enough.

"No, it doesn't!" she cried, leaping to her feet and into the shadow of Atkinson's pulpit. "It doesn't all happen for a reason. There ain't no reason for my mama to be laying there dead. Is there?" She turned to look at the congregation, evading Laneer's trembling hand as it reached out to quiet her. "Do any of you people think God did this? 'Cause if you do, I don't want to know your God and I don't want to know you."

She was backing away from them all. Laneer was going after her and everybody else was letting him fill the role of comforting caretaker, but he moved so slow. He was no match for a little girl who wanted to say what she was thinking. She darted around the front of the church, always an inch out of his reaching grasp.

"My mama was so good. She was so, so good. She didn't even fight him. Just let him knock her down so's she could get back up, over and over until he heard somebody coming and had to stop. Then he knocked her down into the hole, and she stayed there."

She broke and ran. Laneer lunged forward and actually touched her as she left, but his frail grip could do nothing to stop her.

Sylvia, a generation younger, hurdled the back of the chair in front of her, which was only empty because Kali had left it. Linton knocked Laneer's empty seat out of his way and joined her in chasing the girl, but she had a head start that had already taken her out the sanctuary's side door.

The rest of the room sat still for a moment, shocked into silence and inaction. After an odd delay, the congregation erupted. People were yelling and jumping out of their seats, but most of them just got in each other's way. Laneer kept hobbling forward, far behind Kali's other pursuers, but determined.

Some people rose to their feet but stayed put, muttering with their companions. Others hurried after Linton and Sylvia, close enough to see what was happening but far enough away to ensure that they didn't get involved. Maybe they were trying to help but didn't know how, or maybe they just didn't want to miss any excitement. Faye couldn't tell, but there was no doubt that they were adding to the turmoil.

Still others moved the opposite direction, having decided that the funeral was essentially over and why should they wait while the misbehaving child's elders rounded her up? They had other places to be. These people scattered like sports fans watching a lopsided football game, thinking that if they hurried, they could get their cars out of the parking lot before everybody else.

Faye was caught in the press of people trying to move in both directions. Being shorter than most, she found herself pushed face-first into one person's back and then another person's sternum. Seeing her problem, McDaniel grabbed one of her forearms and yanked her free of the mob in the center aisle. Then he kept dragging her as he headed for the side aisle, then forward to the door where Kali had left the building. They were still dodging people, but there were fewer of them.

He didn't even turn around as he told her why he was dragging her along with him. "The child won't speak to anybody else. If anybody can get her to come back, it's you."

With McDaniel clearing their path, they made progress toward the open door. Faye was grateful for his help, but there would be a ring of bruises around that arm when the melee was past.

As they emerged from the chapel, they found themselves

in a parking lot surrounded by woodlands. Behind the church, a creek much like the one in Kali's neighborhood ran along the back property line. There were lots of people in sight, but none of them was a little girl in a black sundress, a ponytail, and black patent-leather Mary Janes.

Laneer was walking back and forth, calling Kali's name. In the instant since she left his side, he had changed. He had been old before, with a tremor and wrinkles and a head of hair turning white. Now he looked elderly and infirm. And terrified.

"Where is she?" Faye asked McDaniel. "People don't just disappear."

Sylvia looked in no way elderly or infirm, but she, too, looked terrified. "Kali! Where's my girl? You come here to Sylvia right this minute!"

The searchers fanned out. Linton and Walt sprinted into and across the parking lot, then straight down into the creek, splitting up as they crossed it and disappeared into the woods. Mayfield skirted the creek, disappearing behind the church building.

Jeremiah was calling his crew to him. As they gathered, Armand left his side and walked toward McDaniel, asking "What can I do to help?"

Before McDaniel could answer, Jeremiah spoke a few words and Stephanie and Ayesha dropped to all fours. They started looking under cars while Jeremiah and Richard took to the woods. At a hand signal from Jeremiah, the two men split, heading east and west, then deeper into the trees.

Faye's first impulse was to head into the woods with them until, watching Stephanie and Ayesha check beneath one car after another, her heart stopped. Could Kali be hiding under a car? What if someone unknowingly started it up and drove away?

She looked up at McDaniel. "Nobody can go anywhere until we've checked under every one of those cars."

Armand, now standing at McDaniel's side, nodded. "You got that right."

McDaniel turned to Armand and said, "You want to help? Stay right here and keep an eye on these cars. Check their trunks and back seats. I have to go to the lot on the other side of the church and do the same thing."

He ran to the other parking lot and Faye hit the pavement. She started crawling from car to car, gravel digging into her bare knees until they bled.

The asphalt was hot and sticky under her palms and it smelled like hot motor oil. She worried as she crawled, because nearly half of the lot was already empty. Plenty of people must have gotten to the cars and left while she and McDaniel were still trying to get outside.

She told herself that it didn't matter. The grisly truth was that she would have heard the screaming by now if someone had run over the little girl. Unfortunately, another truth was that she would have heard the crowd celebrating if anyone had found her, and she hadn't heard that, either. Kali could have been in the trunk of any of the cars that had already left, and that trunk might also hold a shovel and a bouquet of flowers.

She told herself to stop thinking. Thinking was doing Kali no good. Faye's job was to crawl from car to car, looking for a grief-stricken little girl. So she did, but she didn't find Kali in the parking lot, and neither did anybody else.

All the while, Frida lay in her casket in the stained-glass light of an empty chapel, covered in flowers and waiting to be put to rest for eternity.

# Chapter Thirty-six

*They had looked for Kali until the sun began to fade, and he had helped them. At any number of times during those long hours, he had thought all was lost. They were going to find her before he did, and she would tell them everything.*

*Finally, he knew what he had to do. Kali had seen what he did to her mother, so she had to be silenced, along with the woman who had kept him from finishing the task. Her outburst in the chapel had made that clear.*

*He had seen her footprints. She had been running like someone who would keep moving without a single turn until she dropped from exhaustion, so he had to be running in the right direction. He had obliterated her trail as best as he could while running at full tilt. And as he ran, he asked his mind to chew on a problem for him. He was not, at the moment, armed.*

*It had not seemed safe to load his trunk with a shovel. Instead, he had found a likely spot far away from here, where he had already dug a grave for the archaeologist. A shovel waited there for her. Now he needed it to silence the child, too, but it was there and she was here.*

*Working without the shovel went against everything inside him. Kali was small. So, for that matter, was Faye*

*Longchamp-Mantooth. It would be no big trick to strangle them or beat them with his bare hands. Emotionally, though, he needed the distance of the shovel and its handle. He also needed the protective clothing and gloves that waited with the shovel. They put him in another world. They isolated him from what the shovel was doing.*

*Murder must leave no trace on his person. He knew no other way to do it.*

*Flowers, too, were a necessity. They added grace to the moment. They reflected the woman and her beauty. They fed the earth with the fragrance of their rotting petals. He could do nothing without flowers, but they, at least, were not a problem. He was surrounded by delicate woodland wildflowers.*

*Ripping a fistful of black-eyed Susans from their stems, he thrust them into his pants pocket, alongside the tiny baby's breath blossom he had taken from the graveyard. The flowers' nearness helped him focus. He could do this. He just needed to find her.*

*With the flowers in his pocket, the insight came.*

*The creek. He was looking in the wrong place. A child who waded up a creek every day would not be running through these woods when she had familiar flowing water handy. He would find her there. The creek was a gift, because it would give him a way to do murder at one remove, the way he liked to do it. It would also give him a way to bury her without a shovel.*

*Drowning was the secret. If he drowned her, the water would wash him clean and the water itself would be a kind of grave. Scattering flower petals on its surface would fulfill his final compulsive need.*

*He stared at his hands as he ran for the creek. Could he really hold a living being underwater with those hands? Could he bear to feel the passing of a soul as it left a body?*

*He could do it.*

*Oh, yes. He knew he could do it. He had no other choice.*

# Chapter Thirty-seven

It was well past the time when Joe would have expected Faye to be at the motel, and maybe she was there, but she wasn't answering her phone. She might even be in the room next door to the one where Amande waited, but he had no way to know. He only knew that he couldn't stand lying on an uncomfortable and too-short bed, dialing her number repeatedly. So instead he was wandering around the motel, hoping to see her or to hear her voice.

They'd driven all day, and now his wife was nowhere to be found. There were any number of places where she might legitimately be, safe and happy, but Joe couldn't deny it any longer. He was terrified and he had been since Faye had first told him about the woman who had been buried alive.

Not knowing what else to do, and unable to sit idle, he'd detoured from wandering around the lobby, wandering instead out to the parking lot to look for her car. No luck. So maybe she was working late.

On his way in, he had another idea to distract him from his fear. Well, he had the same idea again. He'd only asked for her at the desk three times. Why not make it four? Maybe this time the clerk would tell him what he needed to know, if he just found the right words to ask him.

When the bored clerk emerged from the office, Joe said, "I know you can't tell me what room Faye Longchamp is in, and I don't want you to, because I'm her husband and I don't want any old stranger to be able to find out where she's sleeping—"

The clerk gave a slow nod. "So you understand why we have rules. That's cool. And unusual."

"But is there anything you can to do help me find her? Do you have a number for anybody else with her group?"

The clerk checked his computer. "I'm sorry. She made the reservations herself through an online vendor. I don't have any information here that you don't already have. I mean, I have her home address, which would be no help since I suppose you live there, too. Or I could call her cell for you, but she's your wife. Surely you know her phone number."

Joe's shoulders sagged. "She's bound to be working late. I'm probably worried for no reason."

He turned to go, but the clerked stopped him with a "Wait. Sir?"

"Yeah?"

"I could leave a message on the phone in her room. Maybe her cell battery died, but if there's a message on her room phone, she'll see the light flashing as soon as she walks in."

"That'll work. Thanks a lot."

"No problem."

The clerk dialed Faye's room as Joe walked away, then called out again. "Wait. Sir?"

Joe turned around again. The clerk said, "I've got her roommate on the line," and handed him the phone.

Joe tried not to snatch the phone, but he grabbed it pretty damn quick. "Hello? This is Dr. Longchamp-

Mantooth's husband. I drove up here from Florida to surprise her. Do you know where she is?"

A young woman's voice came out of the receiver. "A surprise? That's so sweet! You'll have to wait a little while for the surprise, though, 'cause she's at the funeral. It's been a while, so she shouldn't be gone much longer."

Of course, she was at the funeral. That's exactly where he should have expected Faye to be.

A man who wasn't on edge and nearly frantic would have had his anxieties eased by this information. He would have thought, "Great. I'll take Amande for a nice dinner and we'll see Faye soon."

But Joe, whose edginess was rising by the moment, thought, "I don't like the sound of 'It's been a while.' It'll be dark soon and they don't bury people in the dark. I'm going out there."

Once again, he quizzed the young woman, whose name he should probably have asked. "Do you know where they had the funeral?"

"Some old church out in the country. I heard it was where Frida's—that's the dead woman—it's where her great-grandparents used to go. I don't know the name of it."

That was all Joe needed to know. This woman might not know where the old church was, but the Internet did. His daughter knew how to make the Internet sing, and, despite Amande's insults, Joe thought he was pretty good, himself. The website for the Memphis newspaper would have run articles on the murder that would tell him the name of the poor dead woman. With the name, he could find her obituary and that would tell him the location of the funeral.

"Would you do me a favor?" he asked. "If she comes in

or if she calls, would you please, please, please tell her to call her husband?"

Before he used his phone to track down his destination, he called Amande and told her that he was going out and that she needed to stay put. The last thing he needed was to lose both his daughter and her mother on the streets of Memphis.

•  •  ●  •  •

Faye had crawled around a rocky parking lot until McDaniel returned. Now he was telling her to have a seat so he could help her bandage her bloody knees, but she wasn't where she wanted to be. She wanted to be too far away to hear, running headlong through briars and underbrush, looking for a little girl who couldn't be found.

McDaniel handed her a bottle of water, keeping another one for himself. "I know you won't be sitting here long, but please rest here and drink this before you go running off. That's what I'm going to do."

She didn't want to sit still, because then her brain would be free to think. She pulled her phone out of her pocket, hoping someone had texted good news, but all she saw was a voice mail from Joe, and she was too antsy to take the time to listen to it. She needed to tend her wounds and go back to looking for Kali. Joe would understand if it took her a little time to call him back.

This was the advantage of long-term relationships. Most conversations could wait.

She surveyed their work. Four band-aids on each knee were doing a pretty good job of protecting her wounds, but they still stung. The scrapes on her shins were going to have to go uncovered, because she'd given all the other band-aids to her crew. The first-aid kit she kept in her glove compartment had fallen short and she didn't have time to wait for McDaniel to raid his.

"The search-and-rescue team will be here any minute," the detective said as he settled onto the garden bench beside her, facing the woods where Kali must still be.

The ornamental bench with its curves and molded scrolls looked just right in the shady garden behind the church. Its concrete was cool on the backs of her thighs. McDaniel looked like he needed something cool on his sunburned cheeks.

"I hope they hurry," she said, "and I hope they have lights. It's going to be dark soon."

"They're hurrying and they have lights."

"Tell me they have dogs," Faye said, dabbing again at her bleeding shins with a ball of cotton dripping with antiseptic.

"They have dogs."

"If my husband were here, he wouldn't need a dog. He could track her."

"I find it hard to believe that he could do a better job than a dog. No human has that kind of nose."

"Joe doesn't use his nose. At least, I don't think so. He uses his eyes. And when he gets close, he uses his ears. I can't tell you how he does it, but he does it. If we don't find her soon, I'm calling him and telling him to get on a plane."

McDaniel looked doubtful. "Well, right now, we're all we've got. You and your people have checked under all the cars?"

"Yes. And in the trunks. You?"

"I've looked in every cranny of the other parking lot. Nothing under the cars. Nothing in the trunks. But don't you worry. We're going to find that girl, and I'm bringing in all the people we need to do that."

"Do you think Kali might have been in the trunk of one of those cars that left right away?" Faye scanned the parking lot and the people standing in it. "I'd say we lost half of them in the first few minutes after she ran."

"Yeah, half. At least," McDaniel said, and he didn't look happy about it. "They left before I had any clue that it was going to take more than five minutes for a hundred people to find a ten-year-old girl on the lam. Especially when every last one of us saw her leave under her own power, and hardly five seconds passed before people went after her. I want to say that there's no way anybody had time to put her in their trunk before the rest of us came outside. Only I can't say that, because nothing else here makes sense. Where could she have gone?"

"I can tell you that Kali is pretty self-sufficient, especially when she's outdoors. She spends hours in an environment like this every day. I've seen it." She paused to look at the flowing creek and its overhanging trees. Some of them were even sweetgums, just like the ones on Kali's creek. "Should she have been able to evade a dozen or more adults who were looking for her? No. But the fact that I know she can handle herself in a place like this," she gestured vaguely at the trees, creek, and sky, "is helping me hold onto the hope that she's okay. She's just hiding because she's upset and I can't argue with that. She has every right to be upset."

"Everything changes when the sun goes down."

As if in response, the undersides of the clouds hanging west of them began to turn pink. Faye consciously shifted her mind away from her fear of the coming darkness and focused on practical things.

"Do you have a handle on where everybody is? Jeremiah and Davion have come back," she said. "Reverend Atkinson is in the church praying over Frida. Who's still out there?"

"Not them," McDaniel said, gesturing to Linton and Mayfield, who were squatting side-by-side in the shade of a big oak tree, talking on their cell phones and smoking. "Nor him." He pointed at Walt Wilson, pacing the parking lot and looking at the other two like a man who wished he still smoked. Or him," he said, pointing at Armand, who was pacing aimlessly.

Stephanie and Ayesha had positioned themselves on the church's wooden porch, as far from Linton and Mayfield as it was possible for them to be, while remaining safely in sight of Faye and McDaniel.

"Laneer and Sylvia aren't back," he said, "and if they don't show up again, I'm going to go look for them myself."

"They won't come back without Kali. Not unless you send your people out there to drag them."

"Not doing that. But if I tell them they need to let my people and their dogs do their work, maybe they'll listen to reason."

McDaniel's professional opinion was that Dr. Longchamp-Mantooth looked miserable, like a woman born for action who wasn't getting any action. He decided to give her a chance to act. "Did your husband teach you some of his tracking tricks?"

"He did," she said. "I don't have his skills, but I'm better than a lot of people. Even if I do say so myself."

"Maybe I was wasting your talents by assigning you to parking lot duty. Show me those skills."

She led him to the church door, where she stood and mused out loud, "If I were a little girl coming out this door and I wanted to get away from a crowd, where would I go?"

McDaniel saw several directions that he might run, if he were in the little girl's shoes. He probably would have gone to the road, where he could make the best time, and that's why he'd called in some officers to check the road in both directions. Traffic was light, this far out of town. The pavement wasn't too rough. Yes, that would be his first choice if he were trying to run away, but not if he were looking for a place to hide. It was obvious that the little girl was trying to get away from all those sympathetic eyes, but how was she trying to do it? Was she running or was she hiding?

Faye was looking away from the road, toward the creek and the woods beyond. The trees and underbrush were thick there. It was a place for hiding. Faye knew the child. She must think Kali had found a place to hide.

Just on the other side of the parking lot, a narrow stone-paved path took a winding route to the church cemetery. That's where McDaniel would go if he were looking to hide, and that's why he'd gone there immediately. The graveyard was appropriately spooky, rows and rows of leaning headstones and crumbling crypts and silence. He'd looked behind all the headstones and in all the crypts. He'd even peered down into Frida's open grave. There had been no little girl there, and there were no tracks to say that there ever had been.

He'd continued down the only other path serving the graveyard, but that walk had been just as fruitless. An opening in the trees at its other end had lured him on, but it had turned out to be nothing but the same road that passed by the church, so he'd turned back to find more promising places to search.

So Faye thought the child was hiding, and he knew that she hadn't run to the graveyard to hide. That left the acres and acres of woods backing up to the church. Everybody but him had seized on those woodlands immediately and had begun to search them. Even Faye was sure that this was the answer, and maybe she knew what she was taking about. After all, she was the one who said she'd seen the girl's love for the great outdoors.

She had stood outside the church's door for an uncomfortably long moment, studying the ground. Then she'd begun an organized search of the church's small yard, fanning out from her starting place inch by inch, just as she must organize her work as an archaeologist. Rather than risk stomping on whatever it was she was looking for, he sat on the church doorstep and watched her progress. It occurred to him that her approach was as instinctive and thorough as the work of the police dogs who would soon arrive.

She worked slowly, choosing where she put her foot before she took each step, but she got results. On a spot of sand miraculously missed by the trampling feet of searchers, she found a single footprint, child-sized, with a millimeter-deep impression at the heel. McDaniel's own daughter had worn black patent-leather Mary Janes, so he had smiled when he saw Kali in hers. There were no other little girls Kali's age at the funeral. He knew deep down that this footprint belonged to the missing child.

The footprint was too close to home for him. It made him imagine his own daughter cowering in the woods or in a very old cemetery or in the trunk of a car. The footprint was dangerous. It threatened to knock him off balance and steal the clear thinking he needed if he hoped to find this child.

Kali had left the print very close to the church building, so it told them little about where she might be. It served no function other than to remind him that the girl was real. Faye didn't even look at him as she resumed tracking the girl, following the direction of the single footstep and walking steadily away from him. He rose and followed.

He heard voices and looked far ahead, into the trees. Armand was out there again, talking to Jeremiah, but Kali was not with them, so he was not interested. Where was the little girl in the patent-leather shoes?

Faye was moving more swiftly than she had been before she saw the footprint, but her pace was still deliberate. McDaniel's frustration was a physical thing. His stomach hurt. His head hurt. His heart hurt. He simply followed her and held back the urge to tell her to hurry.

When they reached the creek, she paused at the edge, standing on a patch of grass and examining the sandy clay of the creekbed. He barely heard her murmur, "Yes," but he knew what the single soft syllable meant, and he leaned over to see what she'd found.

It was only a partial print from Kali's mid-foot, surrounded by mud tramped by all the people searching for her. Again, he saw the shallow depression made by her low heel. Its sharp edge cut across the footprint, separating the heel from the print of the Mary Jane's midsole. It wasn't much, just a few square inches of information, but it gave them a direction.

"She was headed upstream," Faye said, heading left. He followed her.

# Chapter Thirty-eight

Faye, with McDaniel close behind, found Kali in a hollow that the creek had carved into the riverbank, cowering in water up to her waist, surrounded by rushes. Faye was astonished by how well the girl had hidden herself. Any number of people had walked past without seeing this child who didn't want to be found.

From the reflexive way McDaniel reached out both arms to seize her, Faye knew that he had spent time with children he cherished. She realized that she knew nothing of his off-duty existence, and she supposed that it hadn't occurred to her that he might have a life outside of his work. This did not make her feel good about herself.

Kali fought him, slapping at the hands reaching out for her until Faye knelt in the cool water and reached out her own arms. She would never forget the steely power of the girl's hands grasping her. Kali clutched Faye's neck and wrapped both wet legs around her waist, staying that way for the long walk between her creekside hiding place and her frantic Uncle Laneer.

After that, Faye withdrew to the stone bench behind the church, where McDaniel brought her a blanket, a cup of coffee, and his thanks. He settled beside her, maybe because he felt like taking a break and maybe because watching dripping-wet and overstressed citizens for signs of shock was part of his job description.

From Faye's perch on the stone bench, she could keep her distance from all the hoopla in the church parking lot, while still having a good vantage point for viewing the goings-on. This gave Laneer and Sylvia plenty of privacy for showering Kali with kisses while delivering the obligatory "What were you thinking?" lecture, but it didn't keep Faye from seeing their every move.

Cars were rolling out of the parking lot now, moving slowly to miss the remaining searchers, who were still milling around as if they couldn't believe that the crisis was past. Mayfield, Linton, and Richard waited in a clump, shuffling their feet now and then, but standing still. Their pants' hems were muddy, their ties were gone or loosely knotted, their white dress shirts were sweat-stained, and they were all holding their suit coats draped over one arm.

Jeremiah was leaning into the passenger door of his car, carefully draping his suit coat over the passenger seat headrest. Nearby, Walt was doing the same thing. The two of them joined Mayfield, Linton, and Richard for a conversation that looked, from Faye's distance, pretty cordial for one involving a group of men who differed so widely in age and life history. Judging by body language, she thought they all looked happy that Kali had been found.

Faye's phone buzzed. She pulled it out of her pocket to take a look. Then she looked again.

Her surprise must have shown, because McDaniel's faced tensed. "What?"

"I asked Phyllis Windom to run some stats on unsolved murders of black women under thirty within a five-hour drive of Memphis. Here, look." She handed him her phone.

"Five hours is a long way to drive. That'll take you to Chattanooga. Jackson, Mississippi. Up into Illinois. Further."

"This is my point. There are apparently a lot of people to kill within a day's drive of Memphis, and we can't be sure the police departments in all those cities are communicating with each other."

He was still processing the big chunk of America that lay within easy reach of where he sat. "God. Five hours will take you to St. Louis. And think of how many states. Tennessee, Mississippi, Louisiana, Arkansas, Kentucky, Missouri, Alabama, Illinois. Maybe Indiana. But St. Louis beats them all when it comes to killings."

"Murder isn't all that common and Windom needs enough data to work with. Thus, St. Louis."

He looked to the northwest as if he could see St. Louis and its arched stainless-steel gateway. "What other instructions did you give your numbers-cruncher?"

"First, I asked her to filter out women who were definitely shot or knifed or basically just killed any other way besides being beaten to death. Bodies with no known cause of death? I told her to keep them in the data set. I also asked her to remove victims who were raped."

"Wind all this back a minute, Faye. You're putting a lot of stock in some flowers found in a few graves. It's a big jump from a bunch of flowers to a rampaging serial killer. The odds are still hugely in favor of Frida being killed by an angry boyfriend. Like maybe one of those guys—"

He waved in the general direction of the cluster of men chatting several yards away. Linton saw him and pointedly turned his back.

"—or maybe a thief, or a rapist who didn't have time to get what he wanted. In the grand scheme of things, people who just keep killing for no good reason are rare. Extremely rare, compared to all the regular old shitheads I deal with on a daily basis."

She shifted herself on the bench, trying to find a cool spot of concrete and trying to think of a way to explain her logic to him. "You don't have to agree with me. The citizens of Memphis pay you to follow your best ideas. It's probably the most economical use of your time to go with the usual scenario. Do the people of Memphis want you to waste your time playing long shots?"

"Probably not."

"Me? I'm just the woman you asked to be your go-between with a community that doesn't like police officers much. Nobody's paying me, so I can chase all the long shots I like. If I don't break the law or get in your way, you can't make me stop. Besides, do you really want me to?"

"Not particularly, but you can't get insulted if I spend my own time chasing leads I believe in."

"Shall I stop telling you about what Phyllis Windom did for me?" She waggled the phone at him. "I have news...."

"Go ahead. Give me your news that I didn't ask for."

"Fine. When I talked to Windom about how to massage the data, I told her to ignore bodies that were dumped, because I was only interested in victims who were buried."

"That's going to cut your numbers. It's hard work to bury somebody, and a lot of killers don't take the trouble. And also, there's bound to be victims who get buried and we never find them. That's why you bury people—to put them out of sight."

"Isn't cutting the numbers a good thing? We want to

cut them down to one, right? One killer. And then we want to nail him." Faye dragged a finger over her screen, scrolling through Windom's massive text. "You're right, though. It sure did cut the numbers. It cut them enough to make me think that we were headed in the right direction. I also asked her to slice the data by month, based on the victim's estimated date of death."

"Now you're dreaming. You're not always going to get that date, not if she's been buried awhile."

"Agreed. But Phyllis Windom is a guru of big data, especially partial data. She's good at filling in the gaps."

"If you say so."

"I also asked her to go back twenty years, hoping that would give her enough data to do statistics."

"Twenty years?" He laughed, and stretched his long legs out in front of him, crossed at the ankle. He looked like he wished very much that the concrete bench had a back. Faye certainly did. "Damn, woman. You don't ask for much."

"I wanted to get back to a time before this killer was active. And also, when you're dealing with a guru of big data, you've gotta give her big data to work with."

"You certainly did that."

Faye tapped Windom's attachment and took a look at her data. There were so many numbers. It was as if they were metastasizing on her phone's screen, right in front of her eyes. Faye squinted at the screen, then gave up and pulled her reading glasses out of her purse.

"After that, I asked her to hand-prune the data."

"Do what?"

"I asked her to highlight entries that looked promising, then look at the notes and use her own judgment about keeping each one."

"Is that cool? Scientific method, double blind, and all that jazz."

"We're not writing a dissertation. Instinct and dumb luck work sometimes, you know."

McDaniel laughed so hard that she thought maybe he was having a breakdown. The man had been through a lot. He stopped just as she gave him an uncomfortable "You okay?"

"So," she continued after he pulled himself together, "hand-pruning the data. I told her that if anything in the police notes made it sound like it wasn't our killer, because... oh, I don't know...the victim had been dismembered and buried without her pelvis, then she should throw it out."

"No pelvis? You still haven't convinced me that we're dealing with a serial killer, but you have a helluva imagination."

"Maybe so, but Windom works cheap. And by cheap, I mean free. Shouldn't we at least let her look?"

He took a long slow breath through his nose and blew it out through pursed lips. Then he handed her phone back to her. "Why don't you just tell me what you think this chart says?"

"My mind has been focused on July ever since Syvlia told me that two of the other women she knew about had also been found in July. The coincidence of three women found in the same month made me ask myself, 'Why July?'"

"July is one of the months when murder peaks, that's why. Also August and December."

"You knew that, but I didn't, so I kept asking Windom questions. And thinking."

"You do a lot of that."

Faye wasn't sure how to take that, so she just said,

"Yeah." Then she tapped on the phone screen and held it up to his face. "Here's a graph of all the murders that Windom thought were worth keeping in her data set. She sees a pattern that stretches back six years. You can see peaks in the data in July, August, and December, just like you'd expect. See here? And here and here? But do you see another one? Look, she's put in a baseline charting what you'd expect to see in those months."

He took the phone again and said, "Are you talking about March? That's not much of a peak."

"No, it's not, but Phyllis Windom says it's enough different from the baseline to be statistically significant."

"I'm almost following you. What happens in March?"

"Spring Break."

# Chapter Thirty-nine

*He'd almost gotten there first. He would have managed it, if he had chosen to go upstream instead of down when faced with the sweet-sounding babble of an untrammeled creek. It had been a coin flip and he had lost.*

*Now he needed to decide how to play his end game.*

*The girl was close by, so close, but she was flanked by Laneer and Sylvia, and he couldn't imagine how long it would be before they would willingly let her out of their sight.*

*If he couldn't silence her, then he must go far away and stay gone, because she had seen him at his work. But if the next hour went well, and if he found a way to neutralize Dr. Faye Longchamp-Mantooth, there was a chance that he could stay right where he was, living out his days in a place where he knew how to do his killing and how to hide it.*

*There was a comfort in his mundane, everyday existence. The fear of leaving it was profound. It drove him. He had a sense that his job, his house, and his lumbering old car constrained the beast in him. Without those things, he might disappear into the beast completely, never withdrawing into the everyday. His murderousness would no longer be cyclical. It would be ongoing. Normality would no longer be an option and, without that refuge, he would undoubtedly be caught, jailed, executed. Frida's death would stand as his last act of passion, and he was not ready to be done with passion.*

*He said his good-byes to the men around him. As he did so, he painstakingly began to sow confusion.*

# Chapter Forty

"Spring Break?"

McDaniel was shaking his head. "Are you saying that these women were killed while they were on vacation? Is Corinth, Mississippi, a hot spot I don't know about?"

"No, but the killer could be on a school schedule."

"A teacher. Are you talking about Walt Walker?"

"Yes, maybe. Or a student. Or, I suppose, somebody who just happens to kill during school vacations."

She watched him mentally sort through his suspects. Unless he was keeping some of them to himself, all the people on it were with them now. Several of them lived their lives by the academic calendar.

Faye's suspect list ranged wider than McDaniel's, taking into its grasp people she didn't know who lived in Birmingham, St. Louis, Nashville, and beyond, but it also encompassed people right here in Memphis. Her suspects included everyone McDaniel had put on his short list because they knew Frida personally.

Mayfield. Linton. Walt. Richard. Armand. Reverend Atkinson. Even Jeremiah, who seemed earnest about helping the men and women who worked for him, fit the profile.

Kali had described a big man, and they were all big. Walt was a teacher, and Richard and Jeremiah were students, so they had school vacations off, generally speaking. Walt volunteered at the playground, but she didn't have the impression that he was there every day. Jeremiah took contract work like the job they were doing for Faye, but as far as she knew, he hadn't had any clients since the university ended its spring semester. Richard was working now, but she had no knowledge of any other jobs that would have kept him busy during school breaks. Armand worked for himself. She had no idea what schedule Reverend Atkinson kept, nor Mayfield and Linton.

It made Faye antsy to realize that she could throw a rock and hit several people whom she and McDaniel both thought were capable of murder. But had all of them been in the Memphis area for that long? Jeremiah had lived in Memphis all his life. He and Armand seemed to go way back. Richard had said that he'd visited his grandmother in the summers. Linton was definitely newer to town than the rest of them. She didn't know about Walt Walker, but he seemed established in the community.

McDaniel's thoughts were tracking closely with hers.

"Students," he mused. "Your data went back twenty years. That's a long time to be a student. It's even a long time to be a teacher. How old is Walt Walker?"

"Old enough to have been a teacher for twenty years. Maybe twenty-five years. But that's beside the point. Look at Windom's data again. We're not talking about twenty years. The elevated murder rate in March only goes back six years." She could see him doing math in his head so she did the same math out loud. "That means that those killings started happening when Richard was about fifteen. Fifteen? Really? Do we keep him on the suspect list?"

"Yes." On this point, McDaniel tone was crisp and sure. "He's the youngest man we know about who has a long history of being around Frida. He could have met her that long ago when he was visiting his grandparents. And he's been on a school schedule for the entire six years. If we're going to take your serial killer theory seriously, we have to keep Richard on the suspect list."

Faye was dubious. "Most serial killers start in their twenties, so fifteen would be unusual. In their teens, they're usually still dismembering stray cats, but I guess the data are all over the map."

"What about Mayfield and Linton? Are they off your suspect list because they're not in school? They're not off mine."

She shook her head. "I might have let Linton off the hook if somebody told me he hadn't been in town that long, but he has. Sylvia said so. The six-year window may actually point to him, since that's around the time he left the Navy and moved here. As for the school schedule pattern, we don't know enough about Mayfield's and Linton's employment histories. Maybe one of them was unemployed at the times when the killer would have had to drive for hours to do one of the killings. Or maybe one of them works an odd shift schedule that matches the killer's pattern. Just because the database has uncovered data points that look like the killer is constrained by the school year doesn't mean it's the right answer. Either of them could even have been working at an after-school program during those years."

"They're in their late twenties, so they're certainly old enough."

"Jeremiah and Armand are also pushing thirty," she agreed. "They're all easily old enough to have committed a six-year string of killings."

"Richard and Jeremiah both work for you. It doesn't bother you to cast blame on your employees?"

"I met them on Friday. I like them, but I know nothing about them."

• • ● • •

Joe thanked the convenience store cashier, who had reassured him that he was on the right path.

"People been asking for directions all day, looking for the funeral of the girl that got killed. GPS signals are iffy out here. Can't nobody believe that people drive all the way out here to go to church, but they do. It's a real pretty place. I think that's why they come. Sad thing about that poor girl."

Joe had agreed with him and bought a pack of gum to be polite, then he'd headed back out to his car. The cashier had said he was nearly there.

When his phone rang, he was pulling out of the parking lot, past the pumps and the empty metal shell where the pay phone used to be. He answered and his daughter's voice said, "Dad?"

Her tone of voice was off, and it made him want to push the accelerator to the floor. Everything about today said that he needed to get to his wife. Or maybe back to his daughter. Or maybe even to his son in Florida. Joe was a sheepdog at heart. He didn't like it when his herd was strung all over creation.

"Dad, turn on the radio. Ninety-eight point nine."

"What's wrong? Is it about your mother?"

"Maybe. They're saying that there's a little girl missing. She's the daughter of a woman who was murdered last week. Dad, that has to be the woman Mom dug up. Her name was Frida, right?"

Joe grunted yes.

"They say that the little girl went missing in the woods behind the church where her mother was being buried. That's where Mom is, right? And it's where you're going?"

He gave another affirmative grunt.

"They're saying that witnesses watched the little girl run away and then, poof. She was gone. Dad, that doesn't make any sense. Something's wrong. Somebody grabbed that child. And Mom's out there in the middle of it."

"I'm almost there."

"Great. Just charming. Then both my parents will be in the middle of it. I should have stayed in foster care. It was way more stable than this."

Joe gunned the engine and scratched out of the parking lot. "We're stable enough. And your mother's not going to be in the middle of this for long. Not if I have anything to say about it."

McDaniel wasn't often impressed, but Faye Longchamp-Mantooth had impressed him. He had followed her line of reasoning as she described her work with Phyllis Windom, albeit just barely. If the archaeologist and the retired big data guru had accomplished the things Faye claimed they had over the course of an afternoon, some police department should put them on the payroll. Or maybe even the FBI should hire them.

Speaking of the FBI, he was going to have to call them, now that Faye had given him a reasonable basis to suspect that Frida's killer was working across state boundaries. That should be a fun conversation.

*So what physical evidence do you have that these murders are all related, Detective?*

And his answer could only be, *None? I guess? Unless you count a few flowers so dried-up and dead that they look pretty much like dirt. But I think you should send somebody down here to check it out anyway.*

*You've got witnesses? A solid suspect?*

*Nope. And nope.*

*Then what in the hell have you been doing for the last few days? I guess we'll send somebody down there to clean up your mess.*

Charming. Just charming.

Laneer was perched on the bumper of his car, using his handkerchief to clean the mud off Kali's face when Walt approached.

"Mr. Walker. Can I help you?"

"I'm sorry to bother you, but Linton said that the detective wants to talk to Kali about what she saw on the day when her mama got killed. I told him I'd come over here and get her because…you know…" All three of them knew that the thing he didn't say was "I came over here to get Kali for Linton, because he knows how much you two don't like him."

Laneer pocketed his handkerchief and leaned forward to hoist himself off the car bumper. His first effort failed, so he tried again.

"Keep your seat," Walt said, stretching a palm out to both Laneer and Sylvia to indicate that they should both stay where they were. "Nobody should suffer what you two just did. I saw you two running around, doing your best to find this child. I'll walk her over there."

"You're a good man," Sylvia said, "taking care of little Kali the way you do."

Walt reached out his hand, and Kali took it.

• • ● • •

Faye was shifting her weight on the bench. McDaniel thought she looked like a woman who wanted to take action but wasn't sure what action to take. Suddenly, she sat up ramrod straight and looked at him. "Phyllis Windom seems uncommonly good with incomplete data."

McDaniel didn't seem to know how to respond to that, so he watched over her shoulder while she turned her entire attention to writing a text to Windom.

> We can't track all the suspects for all of the past six years, but we know something about where some of them were in school. Or teaching it. I'll send you what I can find. See if you can eliminate anybody based on school schedules. Thanks!

Faye pressed "Send," then went to work on a text giving Windom the websites of Jeremiah's college, Richard's community college, and Walt's school system. She couldn't find a thing to help Windom track the comings and goings of Mayfield, Linton, or Armand, but this information would be a start.

"If this works," McDaniel said, "you're building the prosecution's case for them. You know that?"

"It's not my first priority, no, but I'm happy to help put this murderer away."

She looked for the gaggle of suspects gathered in the parking lot, but they'd each gone their own way. "Did you see where those guys all went?"

McDaniel nodded to his right. "Armand's over there by his car. Don't see the rest of them."

"While Phyllis Windom is working her magic, I kinda want to keep my eye on the lot of them."

"Not sure how it will help, but I'm with you."

McDaniel stood and headed right. Faye went left, and they stepped into the parking lot, which had emptied quickly after Kali was found. She fought the urge to check her phone every few steps to see whether Phyllis Windom had worked a miracle.

# Chapter Forty-one

Faye found Linton as he exited the church. He said he had been in the bathroom, and maybe he had. Jeremiah was sitting in his car, enjoying the air conditioning. From a distance, she could see McDaniel speaking to Mayfield, who was tugging nervously at the knot of his tie. Armand was standing at the rear of his car, looking for something in his trunk. Where was Walt Walker?

She stopped to speak to Sylvia and Laneer, who were sitting together in the front seat of Laneer's car. Both were dozing, eyes closed and heads lolling. They'd had a hard day. No, they'd had a hard week, actually, and the years ahead didn't look easy. Even with the help of a loving candy lady, Laneer was well past the age when he could have expected to be responsible for a girl who was growing up.

He jerked awake when Faye's shadow fell on his face, and she was sorry to disturb him. She went ahead and asked her question anyway. "Have either of you seen Walt Walker?"

Before they could answer, she checked the back seat and said, "And where's Kali?"

"She went with Walt," the old man said. "He said the detective needed to talk to her."

"No, he didn't," Sylvia said, completely awake and Sylvia-like in her drive for accuracy. "He said that Linton said that the detective needed to talk to her. That ain't the same thing."

Faye scanned the parking lot looking for McDaniel and Sylvia saw her.

"We told him."

"You told—"

"The detective was just here a minute ago, and we told him that Linton told Mr. Walker to take Kali to him, but they must have just missed him."

Faye's mouth didn't want to work, but she managed to say, "I'm sure they did."

She looked around her for Linton, but she didn't see him. She didn't see Walt Walker, either. She did spot McDaniel speaking to Armand and Richard. There was no child at his side.

McDaniel's patience was visibly frayed. Maybe past frayed. Maybe it was, like Faye's, ripped apart at the seams.

"Tell me one more time," she heard him say. "Who said what?" Then he stood silently and listened to the two men tell confusing, contradictory stories.

"Mayfield told us that Mr. Walker said that Kali needed to talk to you," said Armand. "He said that she must know something about who killed Frida, and she needed to tell you everything right now."

"Linton said he'd go find her," Richard said.

"No, he didn't. It was Mr. Walker that said he'd go find her. Linton wanted to go, but Mr. Walker didn't trust him to do it."

"He didn't say that." Richard had taken a step back from Armand, as if to get a better look at him or to get out of his reach.

"He didn't say it, but he thought it. Nobody that trusts Linton lives to be happy about it."

"What about your friend Jeremiah?" Richard said, standing still, alert, hands at the ready. "He agreed that Mr. Walker should be the one to go get the girl."

Armand bristled. "Because only a fool trusts Linton. Everybody knows that. What've you got against Jeremiah?"

Faye saw that McDaniel's own hands were ready, if this disagreement escalated to something physical, but she was glad that he was holding back. She needed to hear the story these men were telling, and so did McDaniel.

Why the confusion? Maybe it was a coincidence that neither of these intelligent men could remember the details of a conversation they'd just had. Maybe one or both of them was lying or trying to confuse the detective, but Faye thought something else was at play. She thought that someone had set out to deliberately confuse them.

Laneer and Sylvia had not seemed confused. They had been very clear that Walker had come to fetch Kali, so Faye considered their recollections to be fact. Now Walker was nowhere to be seen. They were also very clear that Walker had said that Linton sent him. Now Linton was nowhere to be seen, either.

It made no sense for Walker and Linton to be working together, so one of them had the girl and was using the other one for cover.

Faye looked around her one more time.

No Walt Walker.

No Linton.

And no Kali.

# Chapter Forty-two

Faye was pretending that she was Joe. She had success-fully tracked Kali once, so she was trying to do it again, but she didn't have Joe's magic eyes. Nevertheless, she was scouring the ground between Laneer's car and the church for footprints, while keeping an eye on where all the key players were. Linton and Walt were nowhere to be found.

Neither was Kali. Faye doubted that Kali had run away again. Walt was the last person seen with her and he would have sounded an alarm if she'd gotten away from him. Faye's gut said that somebody had the child, and Walt Walker was the obvious suspect.

But what about Linton? Why was he missing? Did he take Kali from Walker, perhaps to stake a claim as her stepfather? But again, Walt had sounded no alarm. Was Walt missing because he was trying to get Linton to give Kali back to Laneer? Or, worse, was he missing because he was trying to keep Linton from killing again?

McDaniel had been questioning witnesses and his face said that those witnesses had been no help at all. He hustled across the parking to see what Faye knew. "Linton?"

"I saw him coming out of the church a few minutes ago," she said, gesturing at the door behind her. "I don't see him anywhere now."

"I'll search the church. You just showed me what you can do as a tracker. Until my officers get here with their dogs, you're all I've got. Find that girl."

He threw the church's side door open, the same one where Kali had fled her mother's funeral. Reverend Atkinson was standing on the other side, and McDaniel almost mowed him down as he hurried inside the church.

Reverend Atkinson joined Faye where she stood searching the ground for new footprints. His face was as distraught as hers.

"Did you find her? I've been inside praying for Sister Frida and hoping that maybe one of you forgot to come in and tell me that the little girl was safe. Then I got to the point that I couldn't wait any longer. I know I'm doing Kali more good by praying for her, but I just have got to know something."

His eyes raked over Faye's frantic face, and he said, "Ah. I see. You don't have any good news for me." Looking up at the darkening sky, he said, "It's getting too late to lay Sister Frida to rest today. Maybe it's providential. We'll have to delay the burial."

Faye asked, "What do you mean?"

The minister's eyes swept the church, the garden, the parking lot, the creek, the trees. "When I think of what happened to Sister Frida, I want to pray. I need to pray, or I'll be seized with the kind of anger that doesn't help a soul. It will do me good to pray over her all night tonight, and maybe it will do her good, too. Maybe it will bring her peace. She surely deserves it."

Faye agreed with that thought, as far as it went. Frida certainly deserved peace, but Faye thought that Frida deserved something more; Frida deserved justice.

She looked around her, puzzled. "It hadn't occurred to

me to ask where Frida would be buried. I don't see a cemetery. Will you be taking her back into town?"

"We have our own graveyard. It's just through those trees a bit. We think that the people who built this place wanted to give the dead some extra quiet, so they can rest peacefully in God's own arms. Every prayer I say between now and then will be for sweet Kali to be standing there with us tomorrow to see her mother laid to rest."

Faye looked in the direction where the minister was pointing, and she saw a narrow opening in the trees. She was already walking before he'd finished speaking.

# Chapter Forty-three

*He had the girl now. He had the flowers. Providence had provided a grave.*

*Providence had not provided a shovel, but he could make do. He could step away from his unsatisfying plan to drown her and use a weapon that was almost as good as a shovel.*

*Ted Bundy had used a stout log for his final rampage, but there were no stout logs at hand. The thin brittle sticks littering the ground in this woodland were no help at all.*

*In his trunk, though, was a lug wrench that was as sturdy a weapon as a shovel. It waited for him in the car he had parked at the other end of this shady lane.*

*He walked down the dirt path, suppressing the urge to whistle. Joy was rising, and his step was light because he was one step closer to restoring order. At rock bottom, this was always his motivation, when he was sane.*

*When he wasn't sane, he became disorder personified. Then, when he came back to himself, he was compelled to return to his orderly life. It might not look like much to others, but it was his life, and he loved it.*

*It had been so easy to convince Kali to come with him to look at her mother's resting place. Now she waited, gagged with her own belt and bound with his tie and her white satin hair ribbon. She waited in a dark, silent crypt, and outside it was an open grave surrounded by all the flowers he could possibly need.*

# Chapter Forty-four

Faye stood at the spot where two people had stepped from the open ground of the churchyard onto a stone-paved path that led into the trees and, according to Reverent Atkinson, toward a church graveyard. She reached down and almost touched the shallow depressions in the soil. Side by side, a man's footprints paralleled a little girl's.

Her finger hovered over one of the prints, shaped like a small foot wearing small shoes.

She knew where to find Kali now. He had taken her to the cemetery at the end of this path, where her mother would soon be buried.

Of course he had. This killer had shown his fascination with burial and its trappings, time and again. Here was a graveyard, close at hand. Where else would he go?

She reached for her phone and texted McDaniel.

He took her to the graveyard. Come quick.

Then she stepped onto the stone path. She would have liked to have waited for McDaniel, but this was a hunt where seconds counted.

She found herself counting her steps—one, two, three,

four—and the meditative act of counting freed her brain of the fear long enough for a moment of insight. Every time he killed, the murderer transported a shovel and, perhaps, a body. This was not something a man could do on foot. Frida's killer must own a car.

Her thoughts turned immediately to Jeremiah's tank-like ride and to Walt Walker's barge of a car. Their trunks were ample for any purpose. Armand seemed plenty prosperous enough to be a car owner. On the other hand, if Richard owned a car, it wasn't in Memphis.

What about Linton and Mayfield? She remembered seeing Mayfield on foot as he passed Kali's house. The parking lot at the convenience store had been empty both times she shopped there, so Linton and Mayfield had walked to work. Everything argued against either of them owning a car. When McDaniel caught up with her, and surely he'd be doing that any second, she would tell him to focus on Walt, Jeremiah, and Armand.

She wished for a weapon. On any ordinary day, she would have had one.

Faye always carried a pocketknife in the cargo pockets of her work pants and, oh, how she wished she were wearing them today. Conversely, she wished she were really and truly dressed up, with a wicked pair of stilettos to wield, but no. She was wearing a plain dress and flat shoes, and she didn't even have on a belt or a pair of pantyhose that might serve as a garrote.

She did, however, have a purse. It was made to carry with a dress while going to church, so it wasn't much more than a large leather drawstring pouch on a long shoulder strap, but it was heavy. Joe rarely picked up her purse without asking, "Did you pack your anvil?"

Today, she wished she actually had packed an anvil.

Her overstuffed wallet, sunglasses case, and keyring were heavy, when it came to carrying them around all day on her bum shoulder. When used as a weapon against a very dangerous man? Not so much.

She squatted and searched the ground around her. There weren't many rocks bigger than pebbles, but she grabbed them by the fistful and dumped them into her purse. Hefting it a time or two, she knew that a few pebbles weren't enough to stop a killer for good. Her plan, such as it was, could only be to immobilize Walt...Linton... whoever, and to do it before they landed a hit. In hand-to-hand combat, she would lose. Not being suicidal, she hoped it didn't get that far.

Her strangely loaded purse wasn't much of a weapon, but she didn't have any other ideas. Not unless praying for miracles counted.

• ● ● ● •

When McDaniel got Faye's text, he turned and ran. He left the sanctuary where he was crawling under every pew, looking for Linton, Kali, or even just a clue. He ran past Reverend Atkinson, who barely looked up from his prayers for Frida. He ran past Frida herself, lying waxen and beautiful, wearing a daffodil-yellow dress and resting under a blanket of pink carnations. He just ran.

Heads turned as he ran past. He tried to let their faces register as he sprinted past. Without turning his head to look, those faces were distorted in his peripheral vision. Maybe he recognized them. Maybe he didn't.

Richard.

Ayesha.

Armand.

No Linton.

Jeremiah? Did he see Jeremiah? Mayfield? Walt? He was moving too fast to be sure.

The stone path to the graveyard was straight ahead of him but he didn't take it. Somewhere to the left of the path he saw something moving in the woods, and it was wearing a white shirt.

Faye and Kali were both wearing black. He ran headlong after the white shirt.

Joe had found the church and he had found the problem. There was obviously a problem, because people were milling aimlessly around the church parking lot, and some of them were crying. As far as Joe was concerned, there was a second problem, because Faye's car was in the parking lot, but she wasn't.

He had tried the direct approach first, by accosting random strangers and asking if they'd seen Dr. Faye Longchamp-Mantooth. The first four strangers said they didn't know her. The fifth one, though, said she worked for Faye, but didn't know where she was at the moment. This was progress, he guessed.

"I know the little girl was missing," he said. "Kali is her name, right? Did somebody find her?"

"Yes," she said, and Joe was much relieved, until she said, "but then she went missing again. Nobody seems to know what's happening."

"What about the detective? I think his name is McDaniel."

The young woman's eyes had darted around the parking lot for a long moment until she said, "Oh, there he is!"

Then she had pointed at a medium-sized man, sandy-haired, running like he was being chased by wolves.

Behind the detective, a van labeled "K-9 Unit" was pulling into the parking lot, but Joe saw no benefit in talking to people who couldn't possibly know where his wife was. McDaniel was the one who could help him find Faye.

When faced with the detective in charge of the case, moving like a man whose panic switch had been tripped, Joe knew what he had to do. He set out to chase McDaniel. And to catch him.

When Faye reached the graveyard, nobody was there. Worse than that, she saw no sign of Kali's footprints. Once she reached the end of the stone path, she saw the prints of a big man wearing dress shoes everywhere she looked, but the smaller prints were gone.

Faye knew Kali. Presuming the child was alive and able, she was fighting. Faye heard nothing.

Was he carrying her? Faye studied the man's prints. Joe would have known by the depth of his footprints, but she didn't have Joe's skill.

She walked through the nearest gate and paused to look around. Kali's kidnapper had left tracks all through the area near her, weaving in and out of the headstones and crisscrossing his own trail time and again. Then he had walked out the only gate other than the one that Faye had just entered. His trail continued on, disappearing into the shadows of overhanging trees. She wasn't sure whether to follow it, because she didn't know if he was carrying Kali or if he'd hidden her somewhere.

Faye had been so sure that she would find Kali here. The killer's obsessions pointed to this burial ground.

Under other circumstances, she would have enjoyed exploring the lovely old cemetery. It was bright and alive with rose-of-sharon bushes, and climbing roses clambered over the graves and the fence surrounding it.

She might have stood there for an hour, weighing her chances, if she hadn't heard a faint sound, thin, hoarse, desperate.

She crept cautiously past row after row of small headstones. Only a few things in the graveyard were taller than she was, and they were the mausoleums that stood at its center. If the killer came back, he would see her before she had time to hide. As she crept forward, she prayed that McDaniel was on his way.

The sound came again, tenuous enough to be blown away by a breeze, but it was real. Clutching her only weapon, a purse loaded with a few ounces of pebbles, Faye stepped forward. As she did, she left the gate open behind her, in case she needed to get out fast.

There were simple headstones all around her now, more with each step, some so old that the lettering had worn off their faces. Chubby-cheeked stone cherubs marked the graves of infants. Archangels, hand-carved wings outstretched, decorated the mausoleums ahead of her.

She passed a small tent made of somber gray canvas, with a few folding chairs waiting beneath it, next to a big pile of soil. Beyond, a deep rectangular hole yawned. The darkness at its bottom terrified Faye, but she knew that she had to go there. What if he had put Kali in her own mother's open grave?

Fighting memories of Frida in her first grave, mortally injured but alive, Faye walked to the edge of the open pit and looked down. No one was there, and she was profoundly relieved, but Kali was still missing.

Then she heard the faint sound again.

Faye held her breath and listened, really and truly listened. And there it was. Another sound, not a voice this time. Something firm was striking the ground, and it was coming from her right.

It could have been the sound of a killer letting the blade of a heavy shovel drop a few inches to the ground, but it wasn't. Or she believed that it wasn't. This sound was coming from the same direction as the quiet little whimper, and she thought it was the sound of a determined little girl throwing herself to the ground, again and again, trying to get herself free.

Faye looked at her feet, hoping to find footprints that told her which direction to go. They were there, but she wished by all that was holy that they led somewhere else, anywhere else.

The sound led her straight to the biggest crypt at the center of the graveyard. At its door, she saw the footprints of a large man wearing dress shoes, who had entered the crypt, then come out and walked away.

# Chapter Forty-five

McDaniel moved through the trees as silently as he could manage. The man in the white shirt was alone, which he supposed was a good thing. He didn't know where Kali was, or Faye either, but he knew that neither of them was being held by this man.

The dress code for a funeral was frustrating him. Every single man who might have grabbed Kali was wearing dark pants and a light shirt. To find out who this man-in-a-white-shirt was, he would need to move closer. So he did.

The man was running hard, like someone with a destination. He could see something McDaniel couldn't see.

Kali? Faye? Both? McDaniel had no idea. But as his quarry moved his head back and forth, scanning as he ran, he gave himself away. A stray glint of light reflecting from his shaved head revealed him to be Linton, who was running with the efficiency and power of a man with military training.

Joe could see Detective McDaniel and, ahead of the detective, he could see the person the detective was chasing, a big man with a shaved head. Like everyone else but Joe, he was wearing dress clothes. He didn't seem to know that McDaniel was after him, because he wasn't so much running away from the detective as he was sprinting across McDaniel's path from left to right.

The ground beneath Joe's feet was slick with pine straw and leaves, but he maneuvered over similar terrain every day of his life. His surefooted lope gave him a distinct advantage over the two men in front of him, who were navigating through brushy undergrowth in stiff, slick-bottomed dress shoes.

Joe was gaining on them when he realized there was yet another person in front of the bald man. This man, also in black dress pants and a white shirt, didn't seem to know that he was being pursued, because he was sauntering at a normal pace and swinging something heavy and metallic. The bald man was almost on him before he turned to defend himself, but he did a good job of it. The bald man went down.

His victory was short-lived, because Detective McDaniel was on the two of them in two steps. Without hesitation, the victor drew his arm back again, and Joe could see that it was holding a lug wrench, as deadly as it was ordinary.

Joe would never forget the power of his next blow. It made him realize that he had never seen anyone strike another human being with no holds barred. In every other fight he'd ever witnessed, both people wanted to win but, at their core, neither wanted the other person dead.

This man truly did not care whether McDaniel lived or died.

The lug wrench landed dead in the middle of the detective's chest, then the man wielding it turned and ran like someone who knew for damn sure that his opponent wasn't going to be bouncing back any time soon.

Joe was still several steps back, but he was fast. He could have caught the fugitive, if he'd been willing to coldly step over McDaniel's prone body and be on his way. He couldn't do it.

Joe knelt beside the detective. McDaniel was unresponsive.

Joe grabbed his wrist, looking for a pulse, but he didn't find one. He shook the man hard.

"Detective McDaniel. Can you hear me?"

Nothing.

Joe knew that a heart, when stopped by a blow like the one McDaniel had just taken, could be a hard thing to restart. An external defibrillator was the tactic of choice, and even a defibrillator failed more than it succeeded. Not far away, less than a minute if he ran, was the K-9 unit he had seen coming into the church parking lot. Surely, they were equipped with lifesaving devices that could restart a heart.

Joe hefted the man off the ground, draped him awkwardly over one shoulder, and hauled ass for the church. Running while carrying a full-grown man was unspeakably hard. Knowing that he was probably running away from Faye was worse, but he didn't know for sure that she was in imminent danger, and the man on his back was three minutes from death. Getting help for McDaniel was the right thing to do.

The logic in his decision was unassailable, as was the mercy, but running full-tilt away from his wife when she could be in danger was sheer agony.

Faye followed the tiny sound to the biggest crypt in the graveyard. Its bronze door hung just a millimeter ajar.

Guarding the door was a marble statue, time-worn, of a seated woman draped in a shroud with lilies cascading out of her lap. As Faye reached for the door handle, she felt guilty for disturbing the statue's rest.

The door was heavy, and Faye would have worried that it wouldn't open if the drag marks beneath it didn't prove that somebody had just opened it. The door ground over individual grains of sand as she dragged it open, so slowly, hoping that the hinges didn't let out a rusty scream. Instead, she heard only a low metallic groan.

When Faye had the door open a foot, maybe, she slid into the crypt. The narrow opening only let in a little light, just enough for Faye to see that this crypt wasn't just for looks. She braced herself for bones and the decayed scraps of shrouds. Buttons, perhaps, if the dead had worn clothes beneath those shrouds.

A pile of objects occupied a corner of the small chamber, and the light reflecting on them revealed the human bones she had dreaded—skulls, femurs, ribs and more. The bones were so old that the crypt didn't smell of death. It smelled of dust and age and eternity. They put her in mind of the goddess Kali, who adorned herself with garlands of skulls. If there were ever to be a time for Kali-the-goddess to watch over her namesake, that time was now.

Faye saw only darkness, but there was something besides bones hidden in this place. Her eyes caught motion, and they saw dark hair, dark dress, dark skin, dark shoes. Kali.

Faye was fumbling for her phone and its flashlight function, and she dropped it when she heard the familiar sound of something firm hitting the ground. The girl, bound hand and foot, was thrashing like a fish desperate for water.

Faye's eyes were adjusting to the dim light admitted by the barely open door. Finally, she could see the child. Kali was covered with a century of dust and decay, but she was alive.

Dropping her purse, Faye threw herself onto her bandaged knees and began struggling with the man's tie binding Kali's ankles. The child made frustrated, wordless noises through the gag until Faye put a finger to her own lips. Then she unfastened the sparkly black belt wrapped around Kali's mouth and thought of murder. The person who had done this to a child did not deserve to walk among human beings.

Kali knew this as well as she did. Her whisper was faint, but Faye could hear every word.

"Shut the door, Faye. Shut the door and hold it closed."

"Shh. It'll be okay. I'm here now. Be quiet while I get you untied, so that nobody hears us until we're ready to run."

The knots binding the little girl's hands required so much of Faye's attention that she never would have seen the text on her phone's screen if it hadn't been face-up where she had dropped it. Hoping it was McDaniel, announcing that he had failed to meet her because he'd been busy arresting the killer, she looked at the incoming text. It was not from McDaniel. It was from Phyllis Windom.

I checked vacation schedules for the schools you mentioned. There's no match between the killings and any of the colleges and universities you mentioned. But Walt Walker's elementary school? Bingo. I think he may be your man. Good work, Faye.

Faye worked to free Kali's hands, but her hair ribbon was tied tight around them and the man's tie binding her feet was tighter.

Kali's voice was so faint that it hardly even qualified as a whisper. "He's out there, Faye. Mr. Walker. He lied to Uncle Laneer. Brought me here. Picked me up and carried me. Tied me up." She was trembling so hard that Faye had to support her with both hands. "Faye. He's coming back."

So she and Phyllis Windom had found the right algorithm. It was Walt Walker who had spent his school vacations preying on women. It was Walt who had packed a shovel into the trunk of his car and used it to beat Frida to death. It was Walt who had buried her alive. It was Walt who had driven to Alabama and Arkansas and Mississippi to do the same thing to other doomed women.

And it was Walt who had done this to Kali. But Faye had known this already, because she recognized the pale green tie she held in her hands.

● ● ● ● ●

Faye wouldn't have thought that a silk tie would have been so hard to unknot, but Walt had bound Kali's feet so tightly that the tie was cutting hard into her skin. She didn't have the luxury of slicing through the silk, not when her pocketknife and everything else useful that she owned were safe in her hotel room.

As her eyes adapted to the darkness, she began to see things that she wished had remained invisible. A pile of long bones filled the crypt's far corner. Nearer by—close enough to reach, actually—she saw a pile of skulls, maybe seven of them.

All of the bones were stacked so neatly. Was it someone's job to do housekeeping in mausoleums, cleaning out old bones and making way for new ones? She didn't want to know.

The ceiling was low and Faye couldn't stand the thought of brushing it with her hair. She didn't much like the idea of kneeling on a floor littered with human bones, either, so she stooped over Kali until she was able to free her. Taking the girl's ankles in her hands, one at a time, she rubbed the circulation back into them.

"Do you think you can run? If you can't, I'll carry you, but we can go faster if you run."

"I can run. I can run right now, so let's go. He said he was coming back."

Faye had one hand flat on the heavy door, ready to run, when she heard the raspy creak of another set of old hinges. She hadn't closed the gate to the pathway leading to the church. If someone was entering the fenced graveyard, the sound of an opening gate could only come from the other one, where she had seen the prints of a pair of men's dress shoes leading away from the graveyard.

"He's coming back, Faye. Just like he said he would."

Faye had no doubt that Walt was armed. In her mind, he was carrying a shovel like the one that killed Frida.

She and Kali had no weapons. They were cornered. They didn't have his years of experience in killing. They only had one factor in their favor.

He didn't know that there were two of them.

Joe left McDaniel with people who could help him, then was immediately back in the woods, tracking his own steps. He could get himself back to the point where the detective had been injured. From there, he could track McDaniel's attacker. Maybe the man's trail would get Joe to Faye.

• • ● • •

Faye picked up Kali and put her behind the door where she would be hidden when Walt opened it. She took the spot opposite Kali, by the door's latch, with her back to the wall.

She needed to disable Walt in the split-second that his sun-dazzled eyes spent searching the mausoleum's floor for the little girl he'd left hogtied. She wished she believed that she could take him out with a purse full of pebbles, but she didn't.

It would take him only seconds to walk from the gate to where they waited. As those seconds ticked down, Faye had only one idea for improving her makeshift weapon and she needed to do it fast.

She reached down and grasped something smooth, cool, and heavier than it looked. Trying not to think about what she was doing, she flipped the skull over and poured the pebbles into the cavity where someone's brain had been, then she slid it into her purse and knotted the drawstring.

As she drew the drawstring through her fingers slowly, she assessed its length and judged where to hold it for the best possible swing. Then she waited without even trying to hide, ready to strike fast. There would be no second chance.

Kneeling face-to-face with Kali, she whispered, "Promise me one thing?"

The little girl was too scared to speak.

"When you see a chance, run. Don't wait for me. Just go. Do you hear me?"

Kali never said a thing. She didn't have time.

# Chapter Forty-six

*He saw no one. No one was coming to stop him. If his luck held for five more minutes, the time to stop him would have passed.*

*Bloodlust was crowding out logic, and he knew it. Linton and the detective had both seen him, and he doubted that he'd managed to kill them with a single blow each. Logic said that he should run to his car and drive away, but the bloodlust was saying, "Wait just a moment longer. The girl is waiting. When she's dead, then you can run."*

*He knew that McDaniel would have called for dogs by now. If Laneer had an article of Kali's clothing for them to smell, his level of jeopardy was about to skyrocket.*

*But none of that mattered, because he was Death now, with the lug wrench swinging as easily as a shovel in his hand. He would remain Death until Kali was silent and still.*

*He pressed his palms to the crypt's moldering door and pushed. The door pushed back with the weight of its years, but it yielded.*

# Chapter Forty-seven

Running. Linton was back on his feet and he was running. He was running to save the girl who had been his daughter since she was five years old.

She was still his daughter. Even if he and her mother had ever divorced, she would still have been his daughter, because you don't divorce children. But they weren't divorced. Frida was his wife until the day she died, and Kali would be his daughter until the day he died. That's the way being a father worked. He wasn't perfect but he wanted to be better, and he was her father.

He could see Walt Walker's white shirt and dark pants moving among the old headstones, and he was gaining on him. Linton was younger, he was stronger, and, this time he would make sure that the bastard never hurt another soul.

To do that, he needed to get to Walt before he got to Kali.

The door opened, grinding against its uneven doorsill. Its ponderous size, its age, the execrable condition of its hinges—all of these things slowed it down and this skewed the situation ever-so-slightly in Faye's favor.

It was hard to wait, but she was only going to have one swing. After that, she was just a small woman trapped by a physically powerful man in a chamber with no exit.

His face cleared the plane of the door and, as she'd expected, it was turned slightly downward toward the spot where he had left Kali. Then he took one more step forward, and his head fully cleared the door.

During the instant that he stood confused by the empty floor, she stretched her arm out as much as she dared in the small space, giving herself the maximum possible lever arm to swing her pathetic weapon.

Holding her purse with both hands, she stepped into her swing for power, hinging her shoulders toward Walt Walker. The pebble-and-skull-weighted weapon struck him full in the face.

Running. He was running.

Joe found the spot where McDaniel's heart had been stopped by a lug wrench. He stood there, looking for tracks and listening. Far ahead of him, he heard the sound of footfalls, so he lunged in that direction, stretched his long legs out, and ran hard.

Within minutes, he caught sight of the bald man, who was also running his heart out, but there was no sign of the man who had assaulted Detective McDaniel. Trusting that the bald man knew where he was going, Joe ran, giving over every ounce of his strength to the legs that carried him and to the pumping arms that carried his gait.

The blood spurting out of Walt Walker's nose suggested that Faye and her pathetic weapon had broken it. His cheekbone was split open. Faye could see that she'd done damage, significant damage, but it wasn't enough. He was still conscious. He was still vertical. His hands were still operational, ready to grab, crush, and break anything they could reach.

More to the point, one of those hands still held a lug wrench that would be just as deadly as any shovel he had ever swung.

He shook his head to clear it, flinging out droplets of blood. Then he turned his eyes to Faye.

She swung her weapon again, knowing that it wouldn't be enough this time, either. The impact made him totter, but he stayed on his feet, as she had known he would.

She took a single step back. This wouldn't save her, but it might give Kali an opening to dart out the door. Another step back put the mausoleum's cold wall on Faye's spine, and still he came for her.

One of his big feet moved toward her, then the other began to move, but stopped short. He tipped his head to look at her as if he, like Faye, could not understand why he hadn't already struck her a killing blow. Then he dropped face-first to the floor, scattering the piles of bones.

Faye backed toward the door, wondering why Kali hadn't run. Had she been hurt by Walt Walker's falling body? Faye knew she hadn't heard the child cry out.

Then there was a flash of green near the floor as Kali yanked Walt's tie from beneath his shin.

"I knew he'd be harder to trip than you were." She waved the tie. "This helped a lot."

Faye had no confidence that Walker would be down for long. She thought seriously about beating him into submission, and perhaps to death, with his own lug wrench, but she wasn't confident that she had the strength to do it before he grabbed it back and used it on her.

Only one option made sense. She snatched Kali off her feet and ran. She ran out the open crypt door, past rows of old headstones, out the open iron gate, and straight into Joe's open arms. Behind him stood five officers, guns drawn, and a police dog. Beside him stood Linton.

"Drop your weapon," said the officer who seemed to be in charge, and that was when Faye turned around and saw Walker loping up behind her. He was bleeding and he was limping, but the lug wrench was in his hand and he was advancing fast.

"I said drop your weapon."

Walker's eyes were like gray river stones embedded in cold clay. If he could hear and understand the officer, Faye saw no evidence of it. He was limping from Kali's attack on his leg and he was bleeding from Faye's attacks on his face, but he was still coming.

Faye didn't want Kali to see a man shot. She clamped her hands over the little girl's eyes and waited for a painfully loud sound and the smell of gunpowder.

Instead, she saw the police dog leap the distance between him and the advancing murderer. Just as he was trained, he took Walker to the ground, where the man lay groaning but alive for the police officers to take into custody.

Faye knew she should be glad that he was alive, but when she thought about the things he'd done, she wasn't so sure. As the police converged, the vengeful part of her hoped that they tased him, at the very least.

A heavy hand fell on her shoulder, and Linton said, "Thank you. So much. Thank you for saving my girl."

He gently but insistently took Kali from Faye, set her on the ground, and knelt to wrap both big arms around the child.

"I'm sorry—so, so sorry. I can't stand to see you hurt or scared. I never meant to hurt your mama and I'm so sorry I did. We all paid a big price for what I did. Maybe could you let me be your daddy again?"

Kali didn't answer Linton but she didn't struggle in his embrace. She just laid her forehead on his broad shoulder and cried.

# Chapter Forty-eight

It took a while for Joe to ditch Faye, but he managed it. She probably thought it was weird that he wanted to ditch her, now that they were reunited after spending most of the summer apart, but he was a man on a mission. Something needed to be said, and he planned to say it.

He'd thought about this conversation all summer, while he was at home on Joyeuse Island with the kids and she was here in Memphis working. He was thinking of it now, as he stood in the reception area of the police department, waiting to be shown back to Detective McDaniel's office.

"I came to say thank you," he said as he settled himself into McDaniel's guest chair.

"For what? Phyllis Windom did more from her wheelchair in Schenectady than I did. She and your wife had identified Walt Walker as the killer before I was willing to even consider their serial killer scenario."

"I already thanked Phyllis Windom. And Faye. I'm here to thank you."

"But for what?" McDaniel asked again. "You're the one who saved *my* life. I hope I thanked you properly at the time. I think I did, but stopping a man's heart messes with his brain, too. I lost my car keys in my own house three times this morning."

"You thanked me, but there was no need. I was glad to do it."

"Nevertheless, I owe you. And I owe your wife. Without the two of you, Kali Stone might be dead and there might still be a serial killer on the loose."

"That's the other reason I came to say thank you. For him."

"Huh," McDaniel said, taking off his reading glasses and laying them on the desk. "For putting him away? Like I said, your wife had more to do with that than I did."

"The way I see it, it took the both of you, but yeah. I want to thank you personally for that. But I also want to say thank you to the Memphis police who left him alive to pay the price for the things he did."

"There's no way he can pay that price. Even if he gets the death penalty, he'll only die once."

"Yeah, but the people who had him at gunpoint that day? They left him alive to face the death penalty, and they take their cues from you. Nobody would have blinked if those people had shot a serial killer who was charging them with a deadly weapon. Maybe, while he's sitting in jail and waiting for justice, he'll tell us about the all the other women he killed. Maybe their families will have some peace. Please tell those officers thank you for me."

"It will be my pleasure."

"I know it eased Faye's mind that they didn't kill him."

At this, McDaniel's mouth actually dropped open. "After she saw what he did to Frida? After he kidnapped that adorable little girl she loves so much? After she fought him off in a freakin' grave? There's no part of her that wants him dead?"

"I'm pretty sure every part of her wants him dead. It's just that watching those officers do everything they could do to keep him alive restored her faith in the law, at least somewhat. You watch the news, so you know that black men don't always come out alive in situations like that."

"I do, and it breaks my heart."

"I can tell that about you, and that's why I came here today. You do know that you scared her about to death that first day?"

"Huh?" McDaniel said again.

"She said you were short with her. Asked her a bunch of questions over and over. Faye really believed you suspected her of attacking the woman she'd just saved, just because she wasn't white."

McDaniel closed his eyes and blew out a long breath. "That breaks my heart, too, but I do watch the news. I understand why she felt that way, but I'm not like that. Most people in this city don't look like me. If I can't set that aside and do my job, then I need to go home."

At that, Joe leaned forward and rested his elbows on his long thighs. "Don't go home. The world needs people like you."

McDaniel laughed.

"I wasn't joking."

"I know. I'm just laughing because your wife thought I was acting like a doofus because I don't know how to talk to black people. Want to know the real reason I bungled the job of questioning her?"

"Sure thing."

"I don't know how to talk to pretty women."

# Chapter Forty-nine

Faye hated good-byes, and she was very good at avoiding them.

No, that wasn't true. She successfully said good-bye all the time. On most warm mornings, she said good-bye to Joe when he hopped in his john boat to go fishing. Some-day soon, she would say good-bye to Amande at the door of a dormitory far from home. Many years from now, she would say it to Michael when he left for college. She man-aged partings like these by telling herself that she would see them again.

Jeremiah was a different story. As she wrapped her arms around him, she thanked him for being such a help to her all summer. She told him that he was the reason their project had been such a success, because he had found the wonderful young people who had coalesced into a truly remarkable group of colleagues.

"You changed their lives, you know," she whispered in his ear, so that none of the young people standing around them would hear. Then she made the rounds, shaking hands and hugging, as appropriate for each one's person-ality.

"Good-bye," she said, time and again. "Good-bye," and

she knew that she was saying the kind of good-bye that was final.

Oh, she might see Ayesha again, or Richard or Stephanie or Davion or Yvonna or Jeremiah. One or more of them might make a career in archaeology, and then she might see them at conferences. It wasn't out of the realm of possibility that they might work together again someday.

She would certainly be reaching out to them through e-mail and social media, taking an interest in their lives and doing what she could for them professionally. If Jeremiah and their workers took nothing else away from their summer in Memphis, they now had someone who would write them enthusiastic references for any job they ever wanted. That was no small thing. But their days of working shoulder to shoulder, laughing over lunch, and kicking back in the evenings were over, and this meant that Faye had to say good-bye. So she did, and she wiped some tears, and she moved on to some even harder good-byes.

There was a big part of Faye that still wanted to swoop in and rescue Kali, just as she had rescued Amande, but there was a difference between the two girls. Amande had truly had nobody to take care of her, and this wasn't true of Kali.

Faye knew this. Standing in Laneer's living room and watching him with Kali underscored it for her.

The old man sat on his piano bench beside the little girl, helping her pick out chord progressions and melodies. Kali's face glowed and her body swayed with the music. Now and then, she even laughed.

Sylvia was in the kitchen, cooking up a meal that smelled nothing like potato chips and ice cream. Every few minutes, her voice boomed through the open kitchen door, announcing that Kali's playing was "Beautiful! Just beautiful!"

Linton had stopped by with a bag of fruit purchased at the convenience store and a new pair of sneakers for Kali. Faye sensed that his status was still precarious. Laneer was going to want to see a lot more good behavior before he even let Kali spend the night at Linton's house, which used to be Kali's house, but Linton was trying.

If Laneer didn't have enough years left to see Kali all the way to adulthood, Faye could see that Linton wanted very much to be the one to do it. Only time would tell how her relationship with her stepfather would play out, but Linton was aiming for redemption and maybe he would find it.

This was Kali's home now. It was full of music, and it was full of family. Faye needed to leave her here with them. She needed to say good-bye.

Linton was fond of saying, "You don't divorce children," and Faye agreed. She took it a step further. She did not say good-bye to children, at least not forever.

She had plans to invite Kali to Joyeuse Island for summer visits, and she couldn't wait to see what the little girl who loved the Mississippi River thought about the Gulf of Mexico. She'd already given Kali an I'm-going-away present, an inexpensive and indestructible cell phone. Putting the child on her cell plan was Faye's way of keeping her close, and she was already being rewarded for it with texts Kali was sending her from right across the room.

Her phone buzzed again, and she tapped the screen to see what the child had to say.

**Listen 2 this 1. Ur gonna like it**

Laneer laughed as Kali elbowed him away from the keyboard so that she could use both hands. A familiar bass line rocked the old upright piano.

The funky "Bomp-bugga-bomp-a-bomp" of the theme from *Shaft* made Faye laugh, too. The broad smile on Kali's face made her certain that, at least for now, it was okay to say good-bye.

# Notes for the Incurably Curious

Because my books deal with history and, sometimes, with people and places that actually existed, I often hear from readers asking whether a particular anecdote or character was real. These notes give me a chance to share the answers to some of those questions. In *Undercurrents*, none of the characters were based on real individuals, but I did make a trip to Memphis in an effort to get the city and its local flavor right.

There really is a large state park within the city limits of Memphis. T.O. Fuller State Park is an 1,138-acre park within fifteen miles of downtown. The park provides extensive recreational facilities as well as natural areas. It was the first state park open for African-Americans east of the Mississippi River and, like my fictional Sweetgum State Park, many of its facilities were built by the Civilian Conservation Corps. It was named for Dr. Thomas O. Fuller, a prominent African-American man who lived in Memphis and dedicated much of his life to promoting the African-American community.

The Civilian Conservation Corps did employ segregated crews, just as I described in *Undercurrents*.

The unnamed museum in *Undercurrents*, along with its prehistoric mound complex and hands-on archaeological laboratory, is based on the C.H. Nash Museum at the Prehistoric Chucalissa Archaeological Site. The museum's mound complex was discovered during construction of T.O. Fuller State Park. The park, the museum, and the mound complex are all excellent reasons to visit south Memphis. Just don't expect to find Faye there.

I often change the names of state parks and museums in my books in this way, because I don't want to suggest that the real places are prone to murder and mayhem, but I made an exception for Tom Lee Park. I felt that Lee's heroism in saving thirty-one survivors of a capsized steamboat deserved commemoration.

I also could not resist letting Faye and Kali enjoy the very real Peabody Hotel and its iconic ducks. While researching *Undercurrents*, I made it a point to dine at The Peabody myself, so that I could properly portray their visit. I can still taste the amazing bread pudding, which I ate for you, dear reader. All for you...

To see more Poisoned Pen Press titles:

Visit our website:
poisonedpenpress.com
Request a digital catalog:
info@poisonedpenpress.com